W9-CBV-888

#1

E-mail

From: Max Zirinsky, Courage Bay police chief

To: Dan Egan, Courage Bay fire chief

Dan, we've got a problem.

Good news is, I think I've got the solution.

Seems communication between the police department and the fire department is at an all-time low. Turns out that for the past year, your arson investigator Sam Prophet and my bomb squad specialist Nora Keyes have both been dealing with cases that involve a possible serial bomber. Perp's MO involves packing explosives into a cell phone and then dialing the intended victim. Prophet's named him the Trigger.

I nearly exploded myself when I found out that we've been conducting separate investigations for the same guy. Bad enough our little city's been dealing with a serial killer—the Avenger. Now we've got the Trigger to contend with.

So here's my proposal. When it comes to their cases, Investigator Prophet and Sergeant Keyes are both as territorial and adversarial as two pit bulls. But they're also the best in their respective fields, bar none. I propose we combine their talents and put them on the case together. They'll fight the idea at first, kicking and screaming, but you know as well as I do that they're pros. With the two of them working together, the Trigger doesn't stand a chance.

About the Author

CODE**RED**

Although she's lived in Texas, Kentucky, Tennessee and Massachusetts, **Jacqueline Diamond** now resides in Brea, California, with her husband, two teenagers and two formerly stray cats. She's the author of more than fifty books for Harlequin and nearly twenty other novels, including mysteries and fantasy. She writes for Harlequin's Intrigue and American Romance lines.

CODE RED

JACQUELINE DIAMOND

THE TRIGGER

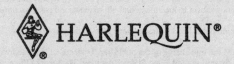

HARLEQUIN®

TORONTO • NEW YORK • LONDON
AMSTERDAM • PARIS • SYDNEY • HAMBURG
STOCKHOLM • ATHENS • TOKYO • MILAN • MADRID
PRAGUE • WARSAW • BUDAPEST • AUCKLAND

If you purchased this book without a cover you should be aware that this book is stolen property. It was reported as "unsold and destroyed" to the publisher, and neither the author nor the publisher has received any payment for this "stripped book."

HARLEQUIN BOOKS
225 Duncan Mill Road, Don Mills,
Ontario, Canada M3B 3K9

ISBN 0-373-61294-X

THE TRIGGER

Copyright © 2004 by Harlequin Books S.A.

Jacqueline Diamond is acknowledged as the author of this work

All rights reserved. Except for use in any review, the reproduction or utilization of this work in whole or in part in any form by any electronic, mechanical or other means, now known or hereafter invented, including xerography, photocopying and recording, or in any information storage or retrieval system, is forbidden without the written permission of the publisher, Harlequin Enterprises Limited, 225 Duncan Mill Road, Don Mills, Ontario, Canada M3B 3K9.

All characters in this book have no existence outside the imagination of the author and have no relation whatsoever to anyone bearing the same name or names. They are not even distantly inspired by any individual known or unknown to the author, and all incidents are pure invention.

This edition published by arrangement with Harlequin Books S.A.

® and TM are trademarks of the publisher. Trademarks indicated with ® are registered in the United States Patent and Trademark Office, the Canadian Trade Marks Office and in other countries.

www.eHarlequin.com

Printed in U.S.A.

Dear Reader,

During my six years as a reporter at a newspaper, I sometimes began my day at a police station. After reading the log, I consulted the watch commander, the traffic sergeant and the detective lieutenant.

Later, while working for the Associated Press in Los Angeles, I wrote about events ranging from plane crashes to trials. I've also researched police and fire operations in books and online for my Harlequin Intrigues and for several hardcover mysteries written as Jackie Hyman.

One member of my longtime critique group is a sheriff's investigator, Gary Bale, who's been incredibly helpful. He even understands that sometimes, for dramatic purposes, I have to take a few liberties with my characters' actions (but not the kind that would make him throw a book across the room!).

Writing for this series gave me a sense of coming home. I'm delighted to have been a part of CODE RED.

You can e-mail me at jdiamondfriends@aol.com or write me at P.O. Box 1315, Brea, CA 92822. You can catch up on my latest books at www.eHarlequin.com or at www.jacquelinediamond.com.

Thanks for reading!

Best,

Jacqueline Diamond

The author wishes to thank Gary Bale
for his expert help and keen insight.

CHAPTER ONE

THE CALL CAME as Sergeant Nora Keyes ate a sandwich in her office upstairs at the Courage Bay police station. It was the kind of sandwich nutritionists frowned on, overflowing with bacon and mayonnaise, a sandwich that didn't worry about whether a long life lay ahead, that wasn't afraid to take risks. It suited her perfectly.

Unfortunately, she didn't get to finish it.

The call came from Detective Grant Corbin. "We've got a weird one out here at the Sleepyhead."

The Sleepyhead Motel, adjacent to Courage Bay's municipal airport, was a homespun establishment that featured separate cabins scattered among the trees. Because of its privacy, it had a reputation as the lover's lane of motels in this California coastal city of 85,000.

"How weird?" Nora had seen plenty of oddball cases in her eight years on police forces, beginning with the LAPD and moving north to Courage Bay after being hired as Bomb Squad Specialist. "Should I activate the squad?" The other members were drawn from the ranks of regular police officers and swung into action as needed.

"No, the fire department did a Render Safe. The place is clean." Standard procedure in a bombing required making sure no unexploded devices put investigators at risk.

Someone else had performed a Render Safe? "Wait a minute. That's my job," Nora said.

"Sam Prophet handled it."

At the mention of the fire department's arson investigator, she had to swallow the impulse to argue jurisdiction. In all fairness, Nora had to admit that Sam's training overlapped her own, including Police Academy training as well as courses in his specialty area. He also packed a gun. Still, it irked her to think that the arrogant man had involved himself with a case that was, apparently, about to become her responsibility.

She and Sam did their best to avoid each other, and not merely because of interdepartmental rivalry. They just plain didn't get along.

Soon after she'd arrived in Courage Bay four years ago, they'd been paired at a training seminar to solve a fictional bomb-related arson case. Although Nora appreciated the need to be thorough and methodical, she'd quickly grasped which way the clues were pointing and, aided by an intuitive leap, reached the right conclusion.

By contrast, Sam had insisted on continuing to gather as much information as possible and reanalyzing all known facts, looking for variant patterns that could prove her wrong. When Nora irritably pointed out that their suspect might be absconding to Canada while they poked along, he'd accused her of taking a Wild West attitude.

During the ensuing argument, she'd flung out the term "macho" and he'd thrown in the word "slapdash." Although they'd managed to tone it down before they created an embarrassing incident, they'd given each other a wide berth since then.

"What kind of case is it, exactly?" Maybe, Nora thought, she could leave this one in Sam's hands and avoid a conflict.

"We've got a twofer—a small fire in front of a cabin and a moderate blast that detonated inside the same cabin at about the same time," Grant said. "There's one unconscious victim with head wounds, ID'd as Carl Garcola, age forty-seven, a local resident."

A fire and a separate blast at the same time—that definitely qualified as weird, Nora thought. Because of their respective areas of expertise, no wonder both she and Sam had been called in.

Unusual incidents no longer surprised her. When she'd moved here from L.A. four years ago, she'd feared the city might prove too boring for her daredevil nature, but she knew now that Courage Bay never had a dull moment. The pace had accelerated during the past year with a rash of bombings, fires and homicides.

The city's emergency personnel served a large outlying area and had developed expertise in coping with the area's disasters, natural and otherwise. Even so, investigators—including Nora—had been working overtime to try, so far unsuccessfully, to solve these recent attacks.

Another thought occurred to her. "This guy Garcola. With all the murders we've had, he could still be in danger. Someone might not want him to wake up."

"I'm sending an officer to escort the ambulance to the hospital and stay by his bedside," Grant said. "Both for his protection and in case he comes out of it and starts talking."

"Any witnesses?"

"Not to the actual explosion," Grant said. "We need you to go through the cabin. How fast can you get here?"

"I'm on it right now." Nora's brain raced ahead. Bombs left a signature along with multiple clues, but careless tromping around could muddy the trail. "I probably don't need to say this, but please don't disturb anything. That goes for Mr. Prophet, too. I'd appreciate it if he'd stay out of there."

While performing the Render Safe, Sam must have already gone inside without notifying her. No matter how high an opinion the arson investigator might hold of himself, Nora trusted her own knowledge and judgment more.

"Don't worry," came the response. "All we've done so far is the basics." That meant starting a crime log, setting up a perimeter, taking pictures and diagramming the crime scene. "I'll make sure nothing's tampered with."

"I'll be there as fast as I can," Nora promised.

"In your car, that'll be no time." Everyone knew she drove the speediest coupe this side of a racetrack.

"I'll floor it," she promised. Knowing that Sam was poking around *her* bombing site provided a good reason to put the pedal to the metal.

Nora hadn't always been this assertive. Years ago, she'd allowed her fiancé to talk her out of enlisting in the Navy and into joining the LAPD, where he was already employed. She'd thrown herself into her new career, envisioning a marriage that was a true partnership, until she actually started working with Len and got wise to what a control freak he was.

It had taken over a year to give up on the relationship, and a few more years to realize that one police department wasn't big enough for the two of them. Since then, she'd learned that it paid to stick up for herself right off the bat.

Nora took one more bite out of her sandwich before tossing it into the trash. Then she seized her purse and headed out.

THE AMBULANCE AND PARAMEDICS WERE pulling away from the crime scene when a red sports car whipped into the parking lot of the Sleepyhead Motel. The car's polished surface gleamed in the June sunshine as an officer running crowd control waved the driver through. Among the dozen or so watchers, someone let out a wolf whistle.

Sam Prophet recognized the car even before he saw the person behind the wheel. Heck, everybody at fire headquarters knew who owned that speedster. You couldn't miss Nora

Keyes zooming around town in her convertible, mahogany hair streaming in the breeze and designer sunglasses making her look like a movie star. It was just like Nora to drive her own vehicle instead of using a larger, safer, department-provided one the way Sam did.

Plenty of guys considered her hot stuff. The way he'd heard it, a couple of cops had nearly come to blows over her last year and it had taken a firehouse hose to break them up. The woman spelled trouble, not that Sam needed to worry. Nora Keys was the last woman in Courage Bay he'd ever want to go out with.

Or work a case with. He considered her competent, but he didn't trust her with a complicated situation like this one. The woman not only acted on impulse but also had a fiery temper.

Unfortunately, it didn't look as if he had much choice. Well, they'd get along fine as long as she recognized that she'd stepped onto *his* turf.

So far, today's incident bore the hallmarks of a serial arsonist Sam had been investigating since last August, although he refused to jump to conclusions. This might be the work of the same perpetrator, but he wouldn't know until he'd done more research. Hours and perhaps days or weeks of detailed work lay ahead, work that he hoped would finally enable him to put a name to the faceless person who had already killed at least one victim.

The sports car halted between a patrol cruiser and a fire truck. Several uniformed men from both departments turned to stare as a slim, feminine figure slid from the interior.

For someone who'd paid her dues on two police forces, Nora sure didn't walk like a cop. Or dress like one, either. Grudgingly, Sam conceded that her suit and powder-blue blouse had a businesslike air, but those long, silky legs and pumps made a man's instincts take a quick right turn toward the bedroom. And he suspected Nora knew it.

Grimly, Sam straightened his six-foot-one-inch frame and squared his shoulders. If he were going to head to the bedroom, it wouldn't be with this firebrand.

She must have noticed his frown, because her stride broke for a fraction of a second, and he saw her eyes narrow. Good. She wasn't any more eager to tangle with him than he was with her.

Despite her aversion, Nora marched toward him. At least she had the sense to use the narrow taped trail Sam had laid out to minimize contamination.

"Have you been inside?" she demanded without preamble. "I mean, aside from the Render Safe?"

What did she think he'd been doing for the past half hour, listening to the radio? "I took pictures and diagrammed the place." Even though he was duplicating the work of the police officer in charge, Sam liked to keep his own records.

She gritted her jaw as if holding back an angry torrent of words. Sam braced himself for an argument over territory, but she apparently thought the better of it, because her next question was on another topic. "Any change in the victim?"

"Still out cold," he said. "It's a miracle he survived."

Hands on hips, Nora surveyed the charred ground and broken glass in front of the rustic cabin. "I guess the main issue is whether the fire outside is related to the explosion inside."

"Is that the main issue?" Sam replied tautly. "I'd have said it was, Who did this and why?"

"Cute," she snapped, not at all abashed by his attempt to put matters into perspective. "We're talking jurisdiction here."

In Sam's opinion, this was clearly a matter for an arson investigator. Besides, he'd arrived first and had already started work. "You want to fight over turf?"

"No," Nora said. "I want you to concede that this is my case."

"Not likely!"

Grant Corbin ambled over. "You two are a real piece of

work. You make the Hatfields and the McCoys look like good buddies. Why don't you just work together?"

"Too many cooks spoil the broth," Sam answered stiffly.

"Whatever happened to 'Two heads are better than one'?" The detective grinned, taking obvious delight in baiting them.

Sam tried not to bite, but he couldn't help it. "That assumes the two heads are equally competent."

"Or that one of them isn't actually a horse's behind masquerading as a head," Nora snapped. Before he could respond, she addressed Grant. "What have you got so far?"

Deciding to let the insult go unanswered, Sam settled back to listen. Although he'd already been over this territory, reviewing facts for a second or third time could yield new insights.

Grant flipped open his notebook. "According to the manager, Mr. Garcola checked into the motel about 11:30 a.m. The witness glimpsed a woman in the passenger seat but he can't give me a description. And no, she didn't sign the register."

"She wasn't hurt in the blast?" Nora asked.

"We don't know because we haven't found her," the detective said.

She made a note. "Okay. Then what happened?"

"At about five minutes past twelve, the manager smelled smoke and heard a woman screaming. He came out to see flames blocking the unit's front door and a woman running toward the street."

"Was he able to describe her?"

The detective gave the particulars: medium height, short blond hair, T-shirt and jeans. "Another guest reported seeing a woman running through the field behind the motel at about the same time. This one had long dark hair and wore a dress."

"Mr. Garcola sounds like a real swinger," Sam said dryly.

"The manager's sure there weren't two women in the car when Garcola arrived?" Nora asked.

"Not unless one of them was hiding," the detective said. "Like I told you, it's a weird one."

"What about the manager?" Nora asked. "Is there any reason to think he's got a hand in this?"

"Not really. He's fuming about the damage to his cabin. He says the workmen just got finished with repairs from the earthquake." The area had suffered a shaker four months earlier.

In the parking lot, the forensics team pulled up. As soon as they came over, Grant filled them in and then began making assignments.

"I can take the inside," Nora told him. "I want to examine the blast pattern before anyone messes it up."

It went against the grain for Sam to submit meekly, and he resented the implication that he might damage evidence. On the other hand, plenty of work remained to be done outside. Although he'd already bagged the badly burned, gasoline-soaked rag he'd found by the door, the entire area had to be searched for footprints and other evidence.

Besides, Grant controlled the crime scene. And the detective was nodding his assent to Nora's suggestion.

"Let's get to it," he said. Reluctantly, Sam complied.

Nora headed for her car, presumably to fetch her equipment. And, no doubt, to throw some practical clothes over that pretty-girl outfit.

Sam hoped they could hand in their findings to Grant and let him coordinate the crime probe. Eventually, someone higher up would decide whose bailiwick this case fell into, and there'd be no further need to interact with Ms. Keyes.

From now on, he considered her the invisible woman. Or at least, he thought he did, until Grant said, "You'd better stop staring at her butt before she turns around."

"I wasn't staring," Sam replied indignantly. "I was thinking."

"Yeah, but the problem is, we all know what you were

thinking about," the detective said, and went to greet the forensics team.

Sam refrained from making a sharp retort. He considered it beneath his dignity. Besides, he couldn't think of one.

THE BLAST PATTERN. The amount of damage. The fragments of a cell phone found in the debris.

As the hours went by, Nora became more and more convinced she knew at least part of what had happened, because it reminded her of two previous cases she'd worked. Nothing explained the fire outside the doorway, but she had a theory about that, too.

Sam would probably accuse her of jumping the gun. It *was* a matter of intuition, but in Nora's experience, intuition had a way of turning out to be right.

By late afternoon, her rumbling stomach reminded her of the unfinished sandwich. Nor was that the limit of her physical discomfort, she realized.

The air-conditioning had been turned off to prevent currents from disturbing the evidence, and beneath her coveralls, she could feel herself sweating. The flat-soled spare shoes she'd retrieved from her trunk chafed her stocking-clad feet, and her hair might never recover from being stuffed into a protective cap to keep it from sullying the scene.

Still, she'd made progress. That was what counted.

Emerging into the bright summer day, Nora squinted. About to go to the car for her sunglasses, she noticed Sam approaching.

He had a well-coordinated way of moving as he strode along the path, she conceded silently. Although she'd never been impressed by his dark-blond hair or tanned skin, up close she saw that his gray eyes took on smoky depths. They made her wonder if, beneath his rock-solid exterior, the arson investigator might actually possess a personality.

A trick of the light, no doubt.

It must have been the heat that made her pull off the ugly cap and shake out her hair. There was nothing she could do about the rest of her getup, though. Not that she cared what she looked like around him.

"You done already?"

His question gave Nora the impression he believed she'd rushed the job. Well, what else had she expected from him?

"I'm taking a break," she said. "I thought I'd see if the motel manager sells snacks."

At close range, Sam smelled of smoke and sun-warmed skin, reminding her pleasantly of her father and brothers, who ran a demolition firm in L.A. She'd helped them out in high school and college and at one time had set her sights on joining the Navy in the hope of becoming a SEAL, although personal plans had sidetracked her.

So what if his scent tickled her endorphins? Nora wondered, bringing herself sharply back to reality. So did the smell of the leather seats in her car.

Sam glanced toward the main building. "Watch out for the potato chips. They're stale."

"Thanks." The tip was a small courtesy but a useful one.

Before she could decide whether to take a chance on the stale snacks or head to a nearby drive-through, Grant joined them. "To update you, the nursing supervisor says Mr. Garcola's in stable condition but still comatose. He must have been across the room when the bomb detonated, because aside from some second-degree burns and abrasions, his biggest problem appears to have been hitting his head when he fell."

"There haven't been any women seeking treatment for burns?" Nora asked.

Grant shook his head. "No, but we got some more information about Mr. Garcola. According to his wife, he planned to fly his plane to San Francisco this afternoon on business.

She had no idea why he might have been at the motel. I didn't mention the two women."

"Any idea what Mrs. Garcola looks like?" Nora asked. "I'm betting she's the short-haired blonde."

"Now that's impressive." Sam didn't try to hide his sarcasm. "Unless you know more about this case than you've let on, you must have gotten psychic vibrations from the crime scene."

"Grant?" she persisted.

A bit sheepishly, he said, "Actually, the detective who interviewed Mrs. Garcola at the hospital said she fit the description of the first woman, except for the clothes. But she had time to change."

"Lucky guess," Sam muttered.

Nora might have let the comment pass, but a couple of other cops had drifted over to listen and her pride refused to knuckle under. "Yes, it was a guess, but a logical one. Given the scenario, I'm guessing Mrs. Garcola followed her husband and his mistress to their rendezvous. It wouldn't surprise me if she lit the fire to scare the heck out of them."

"What about the explosion?" Grant asked.

Nora and Sam both answered at the same time.

"Probably a cell phone," she said.

"I'm betting it's a cell phone," Sam said.

They both stopped in surprise. Nora regarded Sam with suspicion. He must have actually been reading her reports. How else could he know about the two prior incidents involving plastic explosives hidden in cell phones and detonated by dialing the number from a remote location?

She'd deliberately kept the details from the press. And although, ideally, fire and police officials should keep close tabs on each other's work, in reality, coordination between the departments often fell by the boards.

One of the firemen, Huff Robertson, glanced uneasily at his pocket. "Is there a problem with phones exploding?"

"Not by accident," Nora said. "I've had two cases since last fall in which people were killed by bombs planted in their battery packs."

"You're kidding!" Sam's face colored. "I'm looking into three arsons set off by cell phones, including a fatality."

"You had a fatality? Why haven't I heard about it?" she demanded.

"Maybe you don't read my reports."

"It doesn't sound like you read mine, either!" It upset Nora that the same bomber might have claimed another victim without her realizing it. The fact that Sam hadn't put two and two together either provided little consolation for such a huge oversight.

Grant whistled. "I'd say the left hand doesn't know what the right hand is doing."

"You got that right," Sam muttered.

Despite the competitive attitude between the two departments, every training course Nora had taken stressed the importance of teamwork. She and Sam had let their personal antagonism get in the way of doing the job, a fact that, in retrospect, she deeply regretted.

Well, she couldn't change the past. The important point now was that one perpetrator might be responsible for five attacks. Make that six as of today. She and Sam needed to go over the clues and see what the cases had in common.

"Isn't it kind of hard to plant a bomb in a cell phone?" Huff asked.

"Not really." Sam took one from his pocket, turned it over and slid out the flat, rectangular battery pack. "All you need to make a bomb are three things: an explosive, a blasting cap to set it off and a power source for ignition. You've got a battery right here, and everything else can fit inside."

"You've seen plastic explosives before," added Nora. She could make that statement with certainty because she ran bomb-training exercises for both departments. "You know how lightweight they are."

Plastic explosives such as Semtex, which resembled children's Play-Doh, packed a wallop. A pound of it could bring down an average-size house, and a few ounces could easily kill a person. It was malleable enough to fit, along with a blasting cap and battery, inside a pack of cigarettes. Or, obviously, a battery pack.

"Yeah, but wouldn't you have to actually get your hands on somebody's cell phone, rig it and return it?" Huff asked. "That could be tricky."

"There are several ways you could do it," Nora said. She'd already made up a list of possibilities, which included slipping an additional cell phone into someone's purse or pocket or substituting one phone for another. Most people didn't examine the devices closely enough to notice the difference.

"Hold on." Sam indicated the other personnel drifting over to listen. "I think it's best if we keep the details to ourselves."

Nora shrugged. To her, it made more sense to fully inform the other officers and firefighters so they'd know what to be on the lookout for. However, she and Sam had enough issues to sort out without arguing over nonessentials. "Fine. Obviously, we need to compare notes and figure out which of us takes over from here."

"I've been working on this since last August," Sam declared, staking his claim. "How about you?"

"I learned about the first *bombing*—" she emphasized the word "—in October."

"It would appear I have first claim," he announced.

Nora couldn't believe his gall. "The use of explosives clearly makes this my territory."

"If you two don't quit, I'm going to send out for a referee's whistle." Grant glanced at his watch. "It's getting close to dinnertime. Here's my suggestion. The two of you go grab a burger, sit down and hash this out. If all else fails, flip a coin. The loser hands over his or her notes and bows out gracefully."

"Sounds reasonable to me," Sam said.

"I'm sure we can both be objective." Unworried, Nora tossed back her hair. Obviously, a serial bomber was a matter for the bomb squad specialist. The fact that fires had resulted came in a distant second.

"Your car or mine?" Sam asked.

She glanced at the tan government-issue sedan he drove. Boring. Plus, she recalled hearing that he had a penchant for rescuing stray cats. Much as she liked animals, they shed like crazy in warm weather, which meant she'd be picking hairs off her suit for the rest of the day.

"Mine," she said.

"You sure? It's kind of cozy, don't you think?" Something about the way Sam cocked his head and gazed down at her gave the impression he was trying to intimidate her.

Nora drew herself up to her full five foot seven. "I can handle it. Can you?"

A lazy grin spread across his face. "Hey, no problem."

She went to clean up in the motel manager's bathroom and waited with what patience she could muster as Sam did the same. Not until they were in the car and her hand bumped his thigh for the third time while she was changing gears did Nora realize exactly what he'd meant by cozy.

She wished she weren't so tinglingly aware of the hard muscles in his legs. Like most firefighters, he kept in superb shape.

Eager to get this over with, Nora nodded toward a chain restaurant by the road. "How about that?"

"They stopped carrying grilled chicken on their menu a few years ago, and everything else is loaded with fat," Sam said. "I know you've got a reputation for making doughnut runs, but I prefer healthy food."

"And so you should, at your age. When I start pushing forty, I'll cut down on the fat, too."

He chuckled. "Now, that might hurt my feelings, except that I'm thirty-five and I happen to know for a fact you're only three years younger."

"Been scoping out my vitals?" She shot past her favorite chili dog stand. No point in even asking.

"Some of the guys were wondering and one of them nosed around," he said. "You're a hot topic when things get dull at the firehouse."

She ignored the barb. Besides, she couldn't concentrate on comebacks as she cornered sharply and he swayed against her. The man had broad shoulders; she'd give him that. "If you want chicken, we'd better head for the Bar and Grill."

"That's downtown." The Courage Bay Bar and Grill, located near the central police and fire station, was a favorite hangout for emergency workers, and the menu provided a change from fast food.

"You got a better idea?" Nora asked.

"No. Actually, I'm enjoying the ride."

He'd said that to annoy her, she knew. Sam Prophet didn't enjoy her company any more than she did his. "If we eat in the bar, we can get quick service."

"You in a hurry?" He had to be kidding. The man was more of a workaholic than she.

"Not at all," she replied sweetly. "Maybe we should eat on the rooftop patio. If we stretch things out until dark, we could listen to music, maybe dance a few slow ones. What do you say?"

Sam retreated like a turtle pulling its head back to safety. "The bar's fine."

A few minutes later, they reached the restaurant, an atmospheric site occupying an old brick movie theater that dated to 1914. As she tucked her car into a parking space along Jefferson Avenue, Nora hoped she'd been right about the quick service.

They could hit the highlights of their cases while they ate. After that, it must be obvious even to someone as stubborn as Sam Prophet that she was the best-qualified person to handle this case. Deciding who took it from here was going to be a no-brainer.

CHAPTER TWO

SAM DIDN'T KNOW WHY he'd taken such pleasure in needling Nora during the drive. She brought out the worst in him, he supposed.

Although she'd once accused him of being macho, that wasn't the case. He respected women colleagues and, in general, had no doubts about their expertise.

Still, he had to admit, the protective side of him hated the thought of a woman putting herself in danger, but Nora had the right to make that choice. Everyone who worked in emergency services took risks.

Nobody knew that better than he did. During his early years as a firefighter, Sam had watched his father die in a blaze. Learning that it had been set for the insurance money had inspired him to become an arson investigator.

He glanced at Nora as they strolled into the dim interior of the restaurant. Despite her feminine appearance and swingy, rich mahogany hair, she moved with an almost aggressive confidence. But surely even she had to admit that this case belonged to him.

He'd worked three of the previous five incidents, more than she had, and there'd been a fire set outside the doorway of the cabin. Unless the other two cases differed significantly, it seemed obvious that the bombs were being used primarily as incendiary devices.

As always when he came in here, Sam's throat squeezed

at the sight of the sign reading Lest We Forget Their Selfless Acts of Courage. It hung above a wall of photos of emergency personnel who'd died in action.

Peter Goodman, the paramedic son of the restaurant's owners, had perished while treating victims of a chemical spill ten years ago. Ben Prophet was up there, too, smiling from atop his fire truck, just the way his son remembered him.

A hostess hurried toward them with menus. "Where would you folks like to sit?" At only a few minutes past five, the place was sparsely populated, so they had plenty of tables to choose from.

"We'd like a table in the bar," Nora said. "Away from the traffic area, please."

"Sure thing." She led them past the long, U-shaped bar, where a couple of men sat nursing drinks. To Sam, the place still carried the faint, aging scent of cigarette smoke, although it had been illegal to smoke in a California restaurant or bar for years.

The men turned to watch Nora pass. So did a couple of guys quaffing beers at a table.

She stood out, Sam conceded silently. The hostess was a pretty young woman, and objectively speaking, he supposed she might be considered as good-looking as Nora. But she lacked the intensity, the intelligence, the physical awareness. Oomph, his father would have called it.

Sam called it trouble.

At the table, the hostess handed them menus. "Can I get you folks anything to drink?"

Since they were on duty, he requested a soft drink and Nora asked for iced tea. "Are you going to order an appetizer?" she asked him after the hostess left. "I might get the potato skins."

"Don't you know those are dripping with fat?" he queried, mostly to see what kind of reaction he'd get.

"I hope they deep-fry them in lard," she shot back. "Then brush them with shortening and douse them in salt, with maybe a spritz of butter on top."

"Sounds delicious," he said blandly. "But I think I'll pass."

A waitress stopped by. After they ordered sandwiches— hot pastrami for her, roast turkey for him—Nora rested her elbows on the table. "Let's get to the point. Tell me about your cases."

Sam would rather have heard about hers first, so he could marshal his arguments in advance. However, she'd beaten him to the punch, so he conceded the point with good grace.

Obviously neither of them needed notes, he mused as he started. They'd both been working their cases hard.

The first incident had begun last August when a fire erupted at an old warehouse on the south side of town, he explained. The next day, he and Fire Chief Dan Egan had been investigating on-site when a second blaze occurred. Although Sam had suffered burns and a compound fracture to his leg, he had long since healed. Dan, however, was still undergoing treatment for the contact burn to his side.

Nora rested her chin on her palm and listened intently. In spite of his innate resistance, her attention sparkled through Sam like a glass of champagne.

"I remember that," she said. "I started to look into the matter myself but the department pulled me off."

"That's probably because the FBI didn't want you stumbling into the middle of their investigation," he explained. "I'm sure you read some of the details in the newspaper."

She nodded. "Yes, I did."

As it turned out, the warehouse was being used to store smuggled Freon, an illegal refrigerant damaging to the ozone layer but needed by individuals and businesses to keep their existing air conditioners and refrigerators running. Banned by the Environmental Protection Agency, it sold briskly on the black market—briskly enough to be worth a lot of money. However, the warehouse had also leased space to other businesses, one of which had apparently been the target of the initial blowup.

"The tricky part is that although the smugglers set the second blaze to cover their tracks, the first fire appears to have been a coincidence." The fire department hadn't released that information to the newspaper to avoid interfering with an ongoing investigation. "Someone had jammed a cell phone loaded with Semtex beneath a support beam."

"You mean the bomber was trying to bring down the warehouse?" she asked.

"I don't think so. The charge was too small. It only damaged the immediate area."

He broke off as the waitress brought their platters. Sam's turkey sandwich bristled with sprouts, tomato slices and other healthy trimmings. Nora's hot pastrami oozed spicy mustard and dripped wonderful-smelling juices. Resolutely, Sam averted his gaze to keep his envy from showing.

Nora polished off a few bites before continuing. "Okay, let me get this straight," she said. "That case involved an explosive device, right?"

"Resulting in a fire," Sam returned stubbornly. "It was arson." He refused to yield the point. He'd put too much work into this case to hand it over.

She didn't press the point, at least not immediately. "You said this wasn't connected to the Freon operation, so what was the target?"

Sam had a ready answer. "Several companies sustained damage, but Finder Electronics incurred the biggest loss."

"To what kind of product?"

"Computer chips."

More of that fabulous sandwich disappeared into her delicate mouth. Sam tried to focus on his turkey. Oh, the heck with it, he decided, and pretended he was eating pastrami, too. Surprisingly, the turkey tasted better that way.

"Why would a company store computer chips in a common warehouse where someone could steal them?" Nora said.

"They'd gone out of date. The company wasn't ready to dispose of them yet—somebody mentioned research value. But the fire pretty much wiped them out."

"What about the second case? When did that happen?"

He had to think for a moment. "December."

She frowned. "I had one in October."

"Let's discuss that one next, then." Taken in chronological order, the bombings might make more sense.

"No, I want you to finish," she said. "You seem so certain your cases aren't related to mine."

"I never said that." At least, Sam didn't think he had.

"Tell me about it anyway," Nora urged him. "The next incident."

How had she managed to get her way about skipping over her case? Prepared to argue, he dismissed it as a waste of time.

"There was an explosion in a truck loaded with crates," Sam said. "Burned most of the contents. After I traced the cause to another planted cell phone, I started calling my arsonist The Trigger."

Nora slammed one fist onto the table. Dishes rattled and iced tea sloshed in her glass. "You named the guy? You actually got that far along and you never informed me?"

"I couldn't put it in my reports," Sam pointed out. Nicknames like that weren't part of official business.

She glared at him. Did she have to take this so personally? he wondered, uncomfortably aware that nearby diners were regarding them curiously.

"Okay, so you didn't make it a point to notify the police department about this Trigger," she growled. "As if we could read every report the fire department issues! Let's move on. You said there were crates in the truck. What did you find in them?"

Struggling to keep an even tone, he said, "Auto parts. The truck was making a delivery to an automotive shop at the Fortune Mall. The auto parts were property of a company called Esmee Engines, which claimed it had no idea who might want to damage its equipment."

"Could the attacks be random?" Nora asked.

Not in Sam's opinion. "Someone went to a lot of trouble to hit specific targets."

"You see? It's a bomber, not a firebug." Nora fingercombed a hank of hair back from her face. "If the attacks had been random, I might have agreed with you, at least in a couple of the cases. But this Trigger isn't just out for thrills and there's no apparent insurance motive."

"Nevertheless, the result was a series of fires, and that's arson." Sam intended to stick to his principles. Capitulation to Nora Keyes had become unthinkable.

"Oh, come on! This guy's too clever to be an arsonist," she contended.

"I've never considered that either one had a lock on intelligence." Sam couldn't imagine where she dug this stuff up. Besides, he resented the implication that arsonists lacked brains, since that implied they must be easier to catch.

"Arsonists go for the money or the excitement, and they're usually pretty crude," Nora insisted. "Bombers are smarter and they show it. In fact, sometimes they overcomplicate things just to prove they can do it."

That didn't sound very bright to him. "What makes you think the Trigger's such a genius?"

"Look at the way he bought himself distance from his blasts—activating cell phones by calling them, which means he could be miles away," Nora pointed out. "And he covered up his trail so well that he struck repeatedly—maybe six times—before we got wise."

"Mainly because we're disorganized," Sam forced himself to admit.

Her mouth worked as if she wanted to dispute the point. But she couldn't. "You have a point."

"Thank you."

"I gather your third case was the fatality," Nora said. "That must have been nasty."

"Isn't it always?" Although they came with the job, deaths still disturbed Sam. For weeks or months after working a fatality, he suffered sleep disturbances and anxiety, a common reaction among rescue personnel. On TV shows, the characters bounced from one tragedy to another with barely a reaction to the mayhem they witnessed, but stress posed a serious hazard for real cops, firefighters and paramedics.

"What happened?"

"It occurred in March," he said. "Subsequent to the aftershock." February's quake had been followed by numerous tremors, including one sizable enough to cause damage.

"You don't have to remind me," Nora said. "It knocked me against a chair. I got a bruise on my thigh."

The mention of her thigh tempted Sam to glance in that direction, unlikely as it was that he could see her lap across the table. Besides, he didn't want to think about her body parts. It was hard enough just sitting across the table from her, inhaling her light fragrance, feeling the hum of her restless body transmitted through the furniture.

Until this moment, he hadn't acknowledged to himself that she affected him. Honesty forced him to admit—silently—that he'd been powerfully aware of Nora as a woman since she whirled into the motel this afternoon in her speedster.

He attributed his lapse to a lack of female companionship.

Sam's mother kept urging him to find a girlfriend. So did his sister, although she hadn't entirely forgiven him for breaking up with a friend of hers six months earlier.

He didn't want a new girlfriend. He still didn't know what had gone wrong with the last one, except that the closer they got, the more uncomfortable he'd felt.

Sam forced himself to concentrate on the subject. "As you may recall, the jolt collapsed a convenience store and set off a fire in a basement."

"How could I forget? Two women died in separate incidents," Nora recalled.

The deaths had stirred a scandal about the fact that the fire department was spread so thin during the quake's aftermath that the rescue crews couldn't respond quickly enough. Finally the city council had approved the necessary increase in funding, although any celebration had been tempered by the knowledge that nothing could bring back the dead women. Two men related to the victims had taken hostages at City Hall in protest over the women's deaths, and before the crisis was resolved, two more people had died.

Sam finished his sandwich before continuing. "Here's the catch. The quake only killed one of the women, the one in the convenience store."

"I think I'm starting to get the picture," Nora said. "But why would your serial bomber plant an explosive in a woman's basement?"

"To kill her. Besides, he didn't plant it in the basement. She carried it there in her pocket."

Nora nibbled at a dill pickle before asking, "Why? Who was she?"

"A forty-seven-year-old divorcée named Patty Reese. No kids and no known enemies."

"Ex-husband?" Nora hazarded.

"He'd long ago remarried and moved away. They parted

by mutual agreement and nothing indicates he bore any grudges," Sam said.

"What was she doing in the basement?"

"She grew orchids. All she had down there were personal effects and gardening equipment. And flowers." The brutality of the murder had shaken Sam as much as anything he could recall.

Nora didn't speak for a moment. Finally she asked, "Did you find any connection to the other cases, besides the device?"

"Not so far," he said.

"Any connection to Finder Electronics or Esmee Engines?"

The woman was more thorough than he'd given her credit for, Sam realized. Although he'd covered all these points himself, it helped to have someone else sift through them afresh. Maybe it *could* be useful to have another viewpoint.

For the span of one meal, anyway.

"She worked as a products manager at Speedman Company," he said. "Three companies, three blasts, same apparent perpetrator."

Nora tapped her fingers on the table. When the waitress came by to ask about dessert, they both shook their heads. Apparently even the ravenous Ms. Keyes had her limits.

Sam found himself eager to learn how her cases meshed with his. "You mentioned two fatalities."

"Both my victims were men who answered calls while in their cars," she said. "One died in October, the other in February."

Sam regarded the dates he'd jotted in his notebook. "That spaces the attacks pretty evenly over the past year."

"There's more," Nora said. "One of my guys—Julius Straus—worked for Finder Electronics. The other one was a lab technician at Esmee Engines."

They stared across the table at each other. Sam couldn't deny the obvious even if he'd wanted to. "That would be one heck of a coincidence if the cases aren't related."

"Yes, but *how* are they related?" Nora appeared to be speaking more to herself than to him. "If we'd put this together earlier, we'd be a lot further along."

"Let's not waste time on might-have-beens." Reaching across the table, Sam plucked a fallen strip of pastrami from her plate and popped it into his mouth. Delicious.

"I wonder where Carl Garcola works. I'll check with Grant." Nora took out her phone and then paused. For a moment, Sam didn't understand why she wasn't dialing, and then it hit him.

"Spooked?" he asked.

Her wary expression answered the question for her. "It's silly," she said. "Nobody's handled this phone but me."

"That's probably what those other people thought."

She examined the back of the cell, presumably for any sign of residue or tampering. "Well, if someone were clever enough to have planted a bomb, he'd have dialed my number while we were both in the car. He could have wiped out two investigators before we got a chance to put our heads together."

"A charming way of looking at it." Despite his determination to eat healthy, Sam couldn't resist downing one of the French fries piled on his plate, and then another one. Oh, heck, if he was staring death in the face, he might as well eat the whole batch. So he did.

Nora dialed. They both tensed, and then smiled at their attack of nerves.

"Grant?" she said into the phone. "It's Nora. Do you happen to know who Carl Garcola works for? Thanks. Yes, it does. Sam and I think our cases are related. I'll fill you in later." She clicked off.

"Well?"

"Esmee Engines," she said.

Sam let out a long breath. "Well, well, well."

Nora dropped the phone in her purse. "You see my point? We're talking about a killer, not an arsonist."

Did she have to be so stubborn? "You're like a dog with a bone," Sam snapped. "I've been following this guy a lot longer than you have. I'm the one who gave him his name."

"Big deal. 'The Trigger.' It sounds like somebody's horse," she scoffed.

"You got a better suggestion?"

"I leave naming things to the public information office," she told him. "It's kind of a sideshow, wouldn't you say?"

"Spare me the gratuitous insults." Sam had been rather proud of the moniker until now. "You're acting rude and childish."

"And you're not?"

He had to admit, he hated the way he behaved around her. That made him even angrier. "Why don't you get off my back?"

Nora's eyes flashed. "Look, Sam, it's obvious we rub each other the wrong way. You're a pain in the butt, and so am I."

"Nice of you to acknowledge it."

"Nevertheless, this is obviously a bomber, not an arsonist. It's my case." She folded her arms and regarded him through narrowed eyes. "We're not going to be able to share it. Why don't you bow out gracefully?"

Most of the time, Sam considered himself a reasonable man. Logical, even methodical. He got the job done and he didn't worry about who took the credit.

And he liked women, both as friends and as colleagues. Although he couldn't seem to make a relationship work, he attributed that to his long and often irregular hours.

But no way would he meekly hand over his cases to the bullheaded Nora Keyes. Despite the tension between them, they were going to have to hammer out some way of conferring that didn't involve too much personal contact.

"Today's incident involves a fire—a *separate* fire," he added for emphasis.

"Fine. You can probe that little flare-up to your heart's content," Nora said. "What did it do, scorch a whole square foot of dirt? Probably someone threw away a cigarette."

"It was a gasoline-soaked rag, for your information, but that's typical of your approach—slapdash." He knew he shouldn't say this, but he couldn't help it. Correction: He didn't want to help it. "You're dismissing the situation without knowing all the facts."

"Sam Prophet, you know why I should take over these cases?" Nora demanded. "It isn't just because these bombings go far beyond arson, although that ought to be clear to anyone. But the real problem is, you'd slow me down. I've got to hand it to you, you're a good investigator, but you're a plodder and people are dying. For all we know, this guy's got a whole list of victims, and if we don't catch him fast, they're all going to end up in body bags."

Sam felt steam pouring out of his ears. "What you call plodding, some people call paying attention to detail," he snapped. "You're well-trained and you have ability, but you jump to conclusions." Although Nora started to interrupt, he plowed ahead. "Sometimes, I grant you, that can be useful. Other times it can lead you astray. I've seen investigators miss crucial details because they already had their minds made up. That isn't going to happen on my watch."

"It may startle you to learn that a person can be intuitive and systematic at the same time," she informed him tartly. "Sticking to the clues without trying to see where they lead is like wandering around in a forest staring at the ground. You miss the big picture."

"I'm not stupid, Sergeant."

"And I'm not sloppy, Investigator."

They'd both risen from their seats and braced themselves against the table to confront each other. Sam didn't realize how odd this must look until he heard the rasp of someone clearing his throat and turned to see who it was.

Chief of Police Max Zirinsky regarded them warily from a few feet away. Recalled to himself, Sam eased into his seat. Nora straightened and flexed her shoulders, as if she'd stood up to stretch.

"Looks like you two need someone to put out the fire," the chief said.

"Just a little jurisdictional dispute." Sam intended to save further details for his own boss, Fire Chief Dan Egan.

To her credit, Nora didn't try to make a case for herself. Instead, she said briskly, "Investigator Prophet and I discovered we've been working on related cases. It's possible that one serial bomber, whom he's dubbed the Trigger, is responsible for a total of six attacks, including the one today out at the Sleepyhead. So far, there've been three fatalities and one serious injury."

Zirinsky's startled gaze swept over them both. "How long has this been going on?"

"The first case occurred in August," Sam admitted.

"You mean the two of you have been working similar cases and nobody figured out the perp might be the same guy?"

"That's right, sir," Nora said.

Sam wondered if the police chief was about to register an explosion of his own, although that went counter to his impression of Zirinsky as a levelheaded guy who respected his officers. Sure enough, he responded, "It looks like Chief Egan and I need to work harder at communicating. I'm going to discuss this with him and we'll decide how to proceed."

"Very good, sir," Nora said.

Sam merely nodded. He wondered what criteria the chiefs would use in deciding which of them should take the lead. He hoped they picked him, but supposed he'd have to accept whatever they ruled.

The chief had more on his mind, as it turned out. "Do you think there might be a connection to any of our other murders?" he asked.

"Which ones?" Sam asked. Sad to say, even a medium-size city like Courage Bay had its share of homicides, but most were attributable to domestic disputes, personal feuds and robberies.

"We've had a couple of fatal shootings, a strangling and several other suspicious deaths that remain unsolved," Max said. "Since the victims had all previously been accused of serious crimes but got off for one reason or other, we have to consider that it might be the work of a vigilante. I call them the Avenger cases."

"Off the top of my head, I don't see any connection to the Trigger, but it's worth checking out," Nora said.

"Agreed." The chief regarded them with strained humor. "In the meantime, try to keep a lid on your personal animosity, okay?"

"We'll do our best, sir," she said.

After the chief left, Sam glanced down at his plate. He'd cleaned it, consuming far more than he'd intended. Nora, on the other hand, had left quite a bit of her meal.

"Don't worry, it won't go to waste," she told him. "I'll take it home for a bedtime snack."

He had a mental flash of her in a semitransparent nightgown, curled on a bed, sliding a French fry between those full, sexy lips. And quashed the thought fast.

The waitress, accustomed to emergency personnel, provided separate checks. Sam grabbed his. "I'll meet you by the cashier." He saw no point in hanging around and risking another argument. If he hadn't been foolish enough to ride here in her car, he'd have left.

"Suits me." Nora asked the waitress for a take-out box, then settled down to wait.

Feeling unaccountably grumpy, Sam strolled across the room. A group of off-duty firefighters lounging at the bar gave him knowing grins.

"Man, I never saw a chick get to you like that," teased firehouse mechanic Bud Patchett. "What gives?"

"Turns out a few of our cases overlap," he said. "We had a little disagreement about who's in charge."

Bud quirked an eyebrow. "Well, if I were you, I'd stay on her good side. That's a sweet little car she drives. I wouldn't mind working under that hood."

"Nobody's going to work under anybody's hood," Sam muttered, surprised at the flicker of distaste he felt at the idea of Bud or anyone else putting the moves on Nora.

"Hey, man, just making conversation." The mechanic downed a swallow of beer. "Lighten up."

"Sorry." He broke off as Nora, take-out box in hand, approached.

They drove back to the crime scene in silence. That seemed like a good start to Sam.

CHAPTER THREE

SHORTLY AFTER EIGHT O'CLOCK, as the June twilight faded, Nora let herself into her apartment about half a mile south of the police station. Her parents had been urging her to invest in a house, but with this kind of work schedule, how could she find the time?

Besides, Nora couldn't possibly run a place of her own when, in four years, she hadn't even managed to decorate a rental decently. The no-frills furniture she'd hurriedly bought at an outlet store would probably still be here twenty years from now, she reflected glumly.

She'd made a haphazard attempt at brightening the place with a multipronged, multicolored lamp that cried out for a high-tech décor, and then hadn't been able to resist the traditional seascape that dominated one wall. Despite a bookcase full of reference volumes, the coffee table overflowed with paperbacks, many of which had bookmarks semipermanently inserted in the pages.

Well, so what? Nora liked a casual environment. Sam, on the other hand, probably lived in a place straight out of an architectural magazine.

She could still see his face just before they'd parted. There'd been a black smear on one temple where he'd accidentally brushed his face while working outside. They'd both filled Grant in on their latest findings, then avoided making eye contact as they left the Sleepyhead. With luck, that would be the last time they had to scrutinize the same crime scene.

Still, Sam's steady manner, devoid of the anger he'd shown at dinner, had had a calming effect on Nora. She regretted now that she'd hurled the word *plodding* at him. He really did a good job, although not, she reminded herself, any better than she did. If only his personality weren't so unbending!

She felt dusty and drained, and the minutiae of the investigation—shards of glass, blood spatter, debris fragments, the blast pattern—filled her mind. She needed a dip in the complex's spa to wash it all away, Sam's memory as well as the dirt that had sifted through her protective clothing

After sticking her leftover pastrami sandwich in the refrigerator, Nora changed into a swimsuit. She chose a retro 1940s-style one-piece with white polka dots against navy fabric.

What did Sam Prophet look like in swim trunks? she wondered as she slid her feet into thong sandals. All hard muscles, judging from what she'd seen of him with clothes on. She wondered if he had scars on his back to match the marks he'd accumulated on his arms, and whether his deep tan went all the way down to…well, to…

Now, why was she trying to picture Sam in the buff?

Her brothers used to comment that Nora got bored with guys who threw themselves at her. Maybe that explained why she couldn't stop thinking about the most contrary man she'd ever met.

The way he'd blown up at her over dinner had been downright embarrassing. And it had to be *her* boss who'd observed them! She didn't care what kind of impression he made in swim trunks or how far down his tan descended. Sam didn't interest her on a personal level.

Annoyingly, however, he dogged her thoughts all the way out to the spa. She kept imagining clever ripostes she might have made and arguments that would have put him in his place, until the sight of steam rising into the cool of evening finally restored her to the present.

A young couple sat on the underwater bench, leaning together with eyes half-closed, lost in each other. The only other occupant was Elaine Warner, a fifth-grade teacher who lived a couple of doors down and with whom Nora had gone to the movies a few times. A cute brunette with short, curly hair, she qualified as an ideal neighbor: friendly but never nosy.

The two women greeted each other as Nora lowered herself into the heated pool. Jets swirled the water noisily around them, precluding conversation.

Blissfully, Nora sank back and escaped from the worries of the day. Her mind drifted to fragments from recent TV shows, snatches of gossip at the PD, Sam planted in front of the motel cabin glowering at her... She had no idea how much time passed before the couple left and Elaine switched off the power.

"I hope you don't mind," she said. "I thought it might be nice to have silence under the stars. Much as I love kids, the noise level in the classroom gets to me once in a while. Sometimes I like to just sit and listen to the night."

"I'd like that, too." Nora let the stillness seep through her. Leaning her head back, she gazed up into the darkening sky.

From nearby came the rumble of a passing car. A small plane buzzed overhead. The mellow music of a Yanni album drifted from an apartment window, and somewhere a cat yowled for attention or, maybe, love.

Elaine broke the silence. "I guess I wouldn't mind some adult conversation," she said ruefully. "That is, if you're in the mood."

"Sure." Nora could only take so much silence before she, too, got restless. "Just as long as we don't discuss police business. I've had enough of that for one day!"

"That must be tough," her neighbor sympathized. "I'm sorry I complained about the kids. I'm sure my problems pale compared to what you go through."

"Oh, I don't know about that, but it can be exhausting." Arms draped over the lip of the pool, Nora let her hips and legs float. "I have to admit I like solving mysteries for fun and profit. But speaking of Prophet reminds me of a guy I had to work with by that name. Dealing with him was the toughest part of the day."

"Sam Prophet?" Elaine asked. "I thought he worked in the fire department. Isn't he an arson investigator?"

Nora hadn't expected the name to ring a bell. "Yes, but our specialties overlap. Arson is a crime, after all." Unable to restrain her curiosity, she added, "How do you know him?"

Elaine's nose crinkled. "It's a long story. Let's just say he gets on my nerves, too."

Nora knew she ought to let it go. If Sam rubbed other people the wrong way, what difference did it make to her?

On the other hand, she might have to interact with the guy again and it would help if she gained some insight. She decided to take a chance. "I don't want to pry, but he drove me crazy today and I'm afraid the same thing will happen again. Is there anything you can tell me about him that might help?"

Elaine only hesitated for a moment. "I'm not sure it will do any good, but I'll tell you my experience," she said. "A year ago, I couldn't mention his name without wanting to throw things, but I got over it."

"You mean there's hope?"

"Excuse me?"

"Maybe in a year I won't want to throw things when I hear his name, either," Nora joked.

Her neighbor laughed. "I suppose I might as well tell you the whole miserable tale. At least you'll be forewarned."

"Forewarned about what?" Nora sat up, bringing her full attention to bear.

"About a year ago, I made the mistake of falling for the guy." Elaine grimaced. "His sister introduced us—she teaches first grade at my school—and I was thrilled when he asked me out. Well, he *is* good-looking, as you probably couldn't help noticing."

"I suppose so, in a purely objective sense." The image of Sam dating this attractive young woman made Nora uncomfortable, although she certainly didn't assume the man to be a hermit. "What happened?"

"Over the next few months, we started getting serious. At least, it seemed serious to me. We went out every weekend." Elaine sighed. "He acted so kind and gentle, so understanding—I was crazy about the guy."

Nora couldn't picture Sam deserving that description. "Kind and gentle? He practically bit my head off tonight at dinner." To forestall the implication that they'd been on a date, she added, "We were discussing a case and, well, let's just say tempers flared."

"Sam has a temper?" Elaine seemed genuinely surprised.

"A temper? That's an understatement. He jumped to his feet and shouted at me across the table." Honesty made Nora add, "Of course, I did the same thing to him. I'm sorry. Please finish your story."

"That's interesting. I never saw that side of him." Her neighbor considered for a moment before picking up the thread. "I felt like things were developing between us, so I invited him to drive to San Luis Obispo with me for the Fourth of July. It's a special event and I wanted my family to get to know him."

"It sounds like you were paying him a compliment." Nora hadn't introduced a man to her family since breaking off her engagement.

"Exactly," Elaine said. "I'd praised him to everyone and they were eager to meet him. But he obviously didn't feel the same way."

"What did he say?"

"It wasn't so much his words as the way he reacted," she

explained. "When I invited him, his forehead puckered and I could feel him pulling away. He said he might have to work on the Fourth of July and that he'd get back to me. Something seemed wrong. I knew it wasn't simply about his job."

A pang of conscience pricked Nora as it occurred to her that perhaps she shouldn't be listening to such intimate details about Sam's past. She didn't worry too much about it, though. After all, she'd gotten the distinct impression he'd been discussing *her* with Bud Patchett at the bar earlier.

"I didn't hear from him for a couple of days," Elaine continued. "Then one night he dropped by. He had the courtesy to do it in person, I'll give him that."

"Do what in person?"

"Dump me." She made a wry face. "He decided we'd gone too far too fast. Oh, he made some noises about remaining friends, but he wanted out. I felt as if I'd been sucker punched. I couldn't even answer him. Finally he left, and I never heard from him again."

"That was cruel." For all her negative impressions of Sam, Nora had never heard that he had a reputation as a hit-and-run artist.

"You're not kidding. I still don't understand what happened." Exasperation laced her words. "For weeks I worried about what I might have done wrong or whether he'd heard some gossip about me. Mary—that's his sister—tried to find out, but he just mumbled some generalities to her, too."

"Do you think he was just leading you on?" Nora asked.

"Angry as I got, I never believed that," Elaine said. "Sam's not a jerk. In some ways, I still like and respect him. Maybe he got scared of making himself too vulnerable. Who knows?"

She turned as the metal gate to the spa area scraped open, admitting a woman and three young children hauling water toys. "Looks like we're getting company. I think I'll head inside."

Nora was in no mood to be surrounded by a lot of splashing, either. "Thanks for leveling with me."

"It's the least I can do," the teacher said. "I figure knowledge is power."

"I appreciate it." As the youngsters clambered in around them, the two women separated amiably.

Strolling back to her apartment with a towel slung over one shoulder, Nora wondered what on earth had been going through Sam's mind. The man was in his mid-thirties, more than old enough to get serious, and he must have liked Elaine to go out with her for so long. Why had he ducked and headed for cover?

Len, the L.A. police sergeant she'd nearly married, had been the opposite: eager to commit. They'd met when he came to address one of her criminal justice classes at California State University, Los Angeles. Nora had enjoyed his quick mind and no-nonsense way of looking at the world, and hadn't minded that he was nearly ten years older than she.

He'd talked her out of her plan to enlist with the hope of becoming a Navy SEAL and encouraged her instead to apply to the police department after graduation. When she did, however, she made an unpleasant discovery. Len hadn't expected her to make it through the police academy and succeed as an officer.

His plan had been to pretend to care about her career and then, when she failed, to steer her into a less demanding field so she could focus her energy on stroking his ego. Apparently he'd been attracted more by her youthful admiration and naiveté than by her abilities and courage.

After she joined the force, it seemed the harder she worked, the more critical he became. For a while, she'd believed the problem must rest with her, and had redoubled her efforts to please him. It had been her family, seeing her uncharacteristic self-doubt and increasing stress level, who'd asked the pointed questions that helped set her straight.

She didn't know which experience had been worse, hers or Elaine's. Elaine's, probably, Nora decided, because at least she'd benefited in one respect: Len had steered her away from a military career that she'd later determined wouldn't have suited her independent nature.

Elaine, on the other hand, had lost her heart to a guy who didn't deserve it. Or who, at the very least, was incapable of making her happy.

Independence was the key, Nora thought as she slipped into her apartment. She liked running her own show. Maybe someday she'd find the perfect guy, but she didn't intend to hold her breath.

Humming, she went to change, and realized she'd developed an appetite. Thank goodness she had the leftover pastrami sandwich for a snack. Cooking had never been Nora's favorite activity, and besides, she couldn't wait to start reviewing her notes from today.

MAX ZIRINSKY KNOCKED on the open door of Nora's office and entered without waiting for a reply. The police chief's wary expression immediately alerted her that she might not like what he intended to say.

Don't tell me you're giving the case to Sam! She bit down on the response. Running the police department was Max's job, not hers.

"How's it going this morning?" he asked.

Nora indicated the stacks of files on her desk. "I just got my hands on the records from the other murders you mentioned, the ones attributed to the Avenger. I haven't had time to review them yet."

Although murders not involving explosives lay outside her purview as bomb squad specialist, Max's mention of them had stirred Nora's curiosity. Besides, if the same person did prove to be both the Avenger and the Trigger, her familiarity with the bomb-related cases might help her spot similarities.

"Well, don't worry about those just yet."

"Really?" This seemed like a bad sign.

"Dan Egan and I decided on how we want these Trigger cases handled." Max leaned against the edge of her desk. A tall man with black air and green eyes, he remained strikingly handsome in his midforties, although Nora had never felt any sparks between them. One of these days he was going to make a terrific match for someone else, though.

Feigning nonchalance, she widened her eyes to indicate interest while bracing herself. Of course one of the detectives, probably Grant, would take the lead, with Sam to assist him, she reflected unhappily.

"I know this is going to be difficult," the police chief went on, "but we've decided we want you and Sam Prophet to work together on this."

"Together?" Hearing her voice shoot up an octave, Nora strained to bring it under control. In the most professional manner she could muster, she amended, "I'm sure we can both advise the supervising detective as needed."

"That isn't what I meant," Max said. "You're both experienced investigators in your own right, and time is of the essence. We're putting the two of you in charge, jointly."

"You mean you're making Sam and me a team?" She hadn't imagined anything as devastating as this.

Inquiries into serial murders involved weeks or months of intensive work, with ten-to-twelve-hour days often spilling over into weekends. They required coordination, communication and a level of closeness that Nora didn't even want to think about.

"Is that a problem?" the chief asked.

As a self-respecting police sergeant, she could only give one response. "Of course not, sir."

"Good." Max nodded at the case files. "Sam's probably on his way over here right now. I'd like you to review those together. It should help you start thinking of yourselves as a team."

"Absolutely." The word came out barely audible, because most of the air had just disappeared from Nora's lungs.

"Whatever support you two require, don't hesitate to ask." Max watched her sternly. Despite his genuine concern for his officers, he held them to high standards. "I don't need to tell you that this investigation has top priority."

"Yes, sir." She refocused her thoughts on the stakes. Three people were dead, one lay in a coma, and there'd been two additional bombings, with possibly more to come. Her petty feud with Sam Prophet paled by comparison.

The chief handed her another file. "Here's the latest from forensics. I've directed that all further material be forwarded to your office."

"Thank you."

After he left, Nora sat clutching the file and staring at the wall. She couldn't believe Max had ordered her and Sam to form a team, not after their public argument yesterday.

Yet, grudgingly, she conceded that the pairing made sense from a management standpoint. The two of them had complementary characteristics, with her bursts of insight and his exhaustive attention to detail.

Moreover, they'd both accumulated a certain expertise in the Trigger's operating methods, and their training prepared them to track him better than anyone else in either department. In a situation likely to attract a high profile, the city needed to employ its best talents.

A groan echoed from the walls of her small office, startling her. Nora glanced around before she realized that the groan had come from her own throat.

The Trigger presented the greatest challenge of her career. And she was going to have to battle every step of the way with a man who, she had to admit, attracted her more than he should, and irritated her at the same time.

Well, when the going got tough, the tough went to the ladies' room. Nora reached for her purse to do just that.

A large frame blocked her doorway. Although Sam Prophet stood no taller than Max Zirinsky, his presence had enough impact to dwarf the space around him. That might have been because of the thunderous expression he wore.

"This wasn't my idea," he said, "in case you were wondering."

"I never for one moment suspected that," Nora assured him. "And believe me, I didn't suggest it."

"We could make an official request for them to choose one or the other." Sam's glower dared her to agree.

"So you can keep the Trigger for yourself?" she demanded.

They regarded each other assessingly. When it came right down to it, she reflected, they had no choice. They were professionals with a single goal: to get to the bottom of a series of crimes, hopefully before anyone else got hurt.

"Is that what you really think?" Sam asked quietly. "That I'm in this for my own ego?"

In truth, she didn't. "I think we'll get more done together than separately," Nora said. "Certainly more than either of us would alone. We're going to have to grit our teeth and bear this."

"Agreed." Without further ado, he stepped forward and shifted aside some of her paperwork to make room on the desk for his own stack of files. "Here's the paperwork from my cases."

"I've got mine and the other homicides Max mentioned. They don't appear to be related to the Trigger, but you never know." Nora surveyed the cluttered surface, her gaze coming to rest on the folder Max had handed her containing the latest findings on the Sleepyhead bombing. "I suggest we get cracking on yesterday's case before the trail grows cold. We can review the other material later."

"I disagree," Sam said. "Let's not go off half-cocked."

Terrific. They'd been partners all of five minutes. "Well, that didn't take long." She tried to make a joke by adding, "Our first fight...of the day."

He gave no hint of a smile. "We can't solve these cases until we find the connections between them. There's a mountain of material to get through. The key to the solution may be right in front of us, but we'll never find out if we don't take the time to search."

The man was going to mire them in minutiae. Exactly what she'd been afraid of! Even with the two women who'd fled yesterday's scene still to be identified and interviewed, he wanted to spend hours poking through past reports.

Calling him a knucklehead wasn't going to help. She'd promised Max to work with this guy, so she'd do her best.

They were still standing, Nora noted. She eased into her chair. "Have a seat, Investigator."

Sam lowered himself stiffly. "As I said, I don't believe in going off half-cocked. Let's take this one step at a time."

"This isn't a static case, Sam." Nora rested her elbows on two uneven piles of documents. "It's developing and we've got to keep pace with it. We can't let the trail grow cold while we look for links. A man may be dying and there are witnesses who could vanish."

"I believe Grant already interviewed the witnesses." Sam's impatience bristled despite his attempt at a level tone. "Our job is to see the big picture."

"Yes, but there are vital pieces missing." Nora had read Grant's preliminary report first thing this morning, which, she reminded herself, Sam probably hadn't. "He talked to people at the scene but he didn't finish. Apparently the victim's wife was so distraught at the hospital last night that she became nearly incoherent."

"That's understandable, considering her husband's in a coma and he got hurt while having an affair," Sam said.

"Frankly, I'm not convinced he did the right thing letting her go home and sleep it off. She appears to have been one of the people who fled the scene." Although Nora sympathized with a betrayed wife, the woman remained the prime suspect, at least for setting the exterior fire.

Still, Mrs. Garcola had been cooperative, even waiving her right to an attorney. Besides, the detectives must have been exhausted last night. In such a complex case, not all avenues could be pursued at once.

"Anyway, we need to talk to her," she concluded. "Pronto."

Sam weighed the matter. "Maybe we should split up."

"I like to have another officer with me during an interview," Nora countered. While one interviewer focused on the witness, the other often picked up subtle clues from the environment or from body language.

"I meant that I could conduct the interview and you could plow through the background," he clarified.

"Great idea!" Nora snapped. "Since you think I'm so hasty, it should be the other way around. Besides, Max and Dan obviously consider two heads better than one."

Sam folded his arms. "This is crazy. We argue about everything."

On that issue, she agreed. Still, they needed to come to terms. "There are worse things than arguing. At least this way we consider all the angles."

An unwilling grin tugged at the corners of his mouth. "You have a point."

His response virtually amounted to waving a white flag.

Maybe they could reach a truce after all, Nora thought with her first ray of hope.

"Would you like some coffee?" Hospitality might further break the ice. And caffeine ought to take the edge off his grumpiness.

He held out for a few seconds before conceding, "I'd love some."

She was on the right track. "Black?"

"You bet."

Nora poured them each a cup from the pot stationed on top of her file cabinet. "Well, what do you say?"

Sam sipped his brew. "Not bad."

"Fresh-ground," she said. "But I didn't mean the coffee."

He cast a resigned glance at the piles of paperwork. "It does make sense to talk to the wife this morning. I had the impression Grant had already taken care of it. By the way, I looked into Sam Garcola's condition—it's unchanged."

"I know. The officer on the scene gives me regular updates." Ironically, Nora added, "Gee, maybe we ought to stop by his room. The sound of us arguing might wake him up."

"The way we were hollering last night at the restaurant, I suspect we could wake the dead." This time the grin reached beyond a mere quirk of the lips, all the way to his eyes.

Good heavens, the man had a sense of humor. If she'd known that a cup of coffee had such a salutary effect, Nora reflected, she'd have personally delivered it to him at the door.

She placed a call to Mrs. Garcola, who reluctantly agreed to talk to them before leaving for the hospital. After hanging up, Nora said, "She sounds nervous. I wonder if she's just concerned for her husband or if there's something more."

"Let's not second-guess her." Sam got to his feet.

"Are we just interviewing her or interrogating?" Nora considered the woman a suspect but, she supposed, she had to respect her partner or they'd never make it as a team.

"At this point, I consider her a friendly witness," he answered.

"Okay." That was as much of a concession as Nora intended to make, she mused as she headed for the door.

Moving past Sam, she wondered why she'd never noticed how sexy a suit and open-collared shirt could look on a man. She liked the way he wore his hair, too, a bit long on top with a hint of sideburns.

If only he didn't dispute every word that came out of her mouth, they might actually get along, she thought, and scooted out the door.

CHAPTER FOUR

THE GARCOLAS LIVED in a canyon inland from the coast. Sam was glad Nora hadn't argued about taking his larger vehicle, so he didn't have to feel her hip rubbing against his the whole way over.

He wasn't immune to pleasurable responses. Heck, half the members of the fire department would have loved to trade places with him yesterday, but Sam didn't go for easy thrills. Well, okay, so maybe he didn't mind easy thrills, but he prided himself on his professional detachment.

As he drove, they discussed possible motives. One thing they agreed on: So far, the Trigger's targets appeared too narrowly chosen to indicate terrorism or thrill seeking.

"There's always the possibility of financial gain," Sam suggested as they wound between hills bright with greenery from the spring rains. In a month or so, if the weather followed its usual dry summer course, shades of brown would predominate. "I don't see any one person or company receiving all the insurance payoffs, but someone could be trying to damage a competitor's business."

"Except that there's three different companies involved," she pointed out.

He wasn't ready to dismiss this line of thought. "They're all in technological fields."

"Electronics, engines and race cars. That's a pretty big

range." Her scoffing tone put his back up, until Sam reminded himself that he believed in skepticism.

"Even so, they might have been putting some kind of bid together, a project they could work on jointly," he said. "A competitor could be aiming to discourage them."

"By attacking low-level employees and blowing up out-dated chips?" Nora said. "I don't buy it."

"Any other suggestions?"

"We can't overlook jealousy, at least when it comes to the Garcolas." Nora stretched her shoulders. Didn't the woman realize that when she moved that way, it tightened the fabric over her breasts?

Sam trained his eyes on the road and his mind on business. "I suppose it's possible this attack was an anomaly. Unrelated to the others."

"Mrs. Garcola might have set the fire. Still, that leaves the cell phone. It's hard to believe a jealous wife would acquire that much expertise or run that much risk just to get back at her cheating husband." Nora appeared to be dismissing her own suggestion.

"If we set aside jealousy, that still leaves spite or revenge." Those seemed the most likely motives to Sam. "Either of them could apply to all the Trigger attacks."

For once, Nora went along with him. "It's a strong possibility. But spite or revenge over what?"

"If we knew the answer to that question, we'd be halfway to catching our perp," Sam said.

"I was asking rhetorically."

"I was answering rhetorically," he muttered.

"An ex-employee?" Nora speculated. "But surely the same person wouldn't have worked for all three companies. I guess we'll have to see what we find out."

"When all else fails, look for the evidence."

"I just love sarcasm," she retorted. "It's so productive."

He decided against arguing. "Sorry. You're right."

She didn't answer, but gave an appreciative nod.

They pulled into a driveway that wound downhill before curving in front of a 1960s ranch-style house. Sam observed a weathered swing set in back. According to Grant's account, the Garcolas had one daughter, currently attending UC Santa Barbara just up the coast.

He saw nothing out of the ordinary—no indications of excessive, unexplained wealth that might indicate criminal activity, for example. In fact, the place could use work, although the neglect wasn't severe. Leaves filled the gutters and the paint had chipped around the door and windows. He guessed that Carl Garcola put in a lot of overtime on the job—or, perhaps, making hanky-panky with his girlfriend.

The woman who answered their ring stood a few inches shorter than Nora, with short blond hair as in the witness's description. Despite her makeup and freshly brushed hair, there was a tightness to the eyes that indicated she'd been crying.

"Come in." Fran Garcola ushered them into a living room filled with handicrafts, from the crocheted comforter tossed across the back of the couch to an Indian-style rug on the wooden floors.

"Did you make these yourself?" Nora asked. When Fran nodded, Nora said, "You're very talented!"

"I belong to several local crafts organizations." The woman sat on the sofa and twisted her hands. "I helped organize a sidewalk art sale last November."

"I'm impressed."

Fran smiled a little at the compliment. She stopped twisting her hands.

Sam wished he had the same gift for small talk. He preferred to cut to the chase. That worked fine with men but didn't inspire women to share confidences, he'd discovered.

After setting up her tape recorder, Nora helped the woman

review the events of the previous day. She'd been shopping at the supermarket when the fire and explosion occurred, Fran said in a strained voice, although she admitted she'd lost her grocery receipt. When Nora suggested one of the checkers might remember her, she blinked a few times before nodding.

"Did you know your husband was having an affair?" Sam interposed bluntly.

Their subject hugged herself protectively. "I had my suspicions but I didn't want to believe it. I mean, he flew his own plane. Sometimes he'd go away on company business and I had no way of knowing what he got up to."

"They say a spouse always knows these things," he commented.

She stiffened. "Well, I didn't!"

Nora redirected the witness smoothly. "You said he flies his own plane. What does he do on these trips?"

"Esmee Engines builds and tests race car engines," Fran explained. "Carl attends trade shows to see what the competitors are doing. He's also a toy car hobbyist, so he goes to those conventions, too. He claims I'd just be in the way, so I don't go along."

"Does he own his plane?" Sam asked. When she nodded, he said, "May we have your permission to search it?"

Since they couldn't yet link this bombing definitively to the others, they needed to rule out the possibility of the victim's involvement in industrial espionage or smuggling, which might provide a motive for someone to try to kill him. And if Carl *had* been using his personal plane for illicit purposes, he could have stored incriminating evidence on board.

"Carl would have a fit!" protested his wife.

"I'd rather not have to obtain a search warrant," Nora said.

Sam knew they didn't have enough evidence for one, but he admired the way Nora phrased the warning.

"It would be helpful if you gave us permission," she added.

"You won't damage it?"

"I can't promise no mess, but we'll be careful," Nora assured the woman. To Sam's relief, Fran nodded.

He and Nora exchanged glances. They'd made progress, but the question of what had really happened yesterday remained unanswered.

Much as he wanted to take over the questioning, Sam had to admit that Fran obviously responded better to a woman. So he gave his partner a subtle nod and held his peace.

"Mrs. Garcola, let's return to what happened yesterday," Nora said. "A woman matching your description was seen running toward the street. Another witness saw a second woman with long dark hair fleeing through a field at the back. Can you identify either of these women?"

"No." The word snapped out vehemently. "I can't."

"We could put you in a lineup for the witnesses," Sam warned.

"I'm not a criminal! My husband is lying in the hospital, possibly dying. I should be there right now! And you want to put me in some stupid lineup?" Fran got to her feet. "This interview is over."

Sam stood, also, uneasily aware that his threat had precipitated this blowup. He'd been trying to shake her up, not make her angry.

Nora remained seated. "I'm going to level with you, Mrs. Garcola."

What was she doing? Only the presence of a third party prevented Sam from demanding that Nora explain herself.

"We've got two possibly unrelated crimes," Nora went on. "There was a fire in front of the cabin that burned itself out, leaving only a black mark on the pavement. We also have a bomb that subsequently detonated inside the cabin, causing your husband's injuries."

"The—the fire didn't cause the explosion?"

"Not as far as we can tell." Nora ignored Sam's attempts to catch her eye. She must know he didn't like revealing this much to a witness. "In all honesty, Mrs. Garcola, the fire may have saved the second woman from harm by causing her to flee."

"Really?" She appeared to be wavering.

"The fire isn't the real problem," Nora continued. "You see, this bomb may be related to other cases we're investigating. If it is, your cooperation might save lives."

Sam wasn't thrilled that she'd just provided Fran with a cover story she could use to mount a defense if, in fact, she really had tried to kill her husband. He'd known Nora was impulsive, but if she'd just blown the case, this nonsense about working as a team ended right now.

NORA DIDN'T MISS the warning signs emanating from Sam's bristling figure. Heck, a person five counties over couldn't have missed his displeasure at her tactics.

But she knew Fran was lying and she had a good idea why. The woman must be guilt-ridden at the possibility that she'd nearly killed her husband, not to mention petrified about going to prison.

What was the use of forcing her into a lineup? She'd demand a lawyer and their ability to get to the bottom of this would hit a roadblock. Better to persuade her to talk voluntarily, even if that meant taking a calculated risk by disclosing confidential information.

Ideally, Nora should have discussed the tactic with her partner ahead of time. Still, if he hadn't threatened the woman and nearly gotten them kicked out, it might not have been necessary.

"You can't repeat what I've just told you to anyone," Nora added. "If word gets out, it could help whoever's behind these attacks. And that's the person who tried to kill Carl."

"I won't say a word." Fran dropped back onto the couch. "I never meant to hurt anyone."

Sam stopped fidgeting. Nora hoped that meant he'd decided to give her credit for having some sense.

"I'm sure you didn't," she said in her most sympathetic tone.

A tear slid down the woman's cheek. "I suspected Carl was having an affair with his secretary. Her name's Bethany Peters and she's got long dark hair, like you described."

Nora took notes, although the tape recorder ought to be capturing this. Better to get something down twice than risk missing it.

"How did you know they were at the motel?" she asked.

"Carl called yesterday to say he was flying to San Francisco and he'd be back later that night," she said. "The motel's right by the airfield. I'd heard that pilots use it to make assignations. I just—I couldn't stand it anymore. I told myself that I wanted to prove his innocence, so I drove over there, hoping I wouldn't see his car in front of a cabin. But I did."

"Do you always carry gasoline and rags in your car?" Sam asked.

From the way Fran's face tightened, Nora feared she might clam up again. However, finally, she answered. "Sometimes I forget to fill the tank, so I keep a couple of gallons in a container in the trunk. The rags are for cleaning the windshield."

"When you approached the cabin, did you see or hear anything unusual?" Nora probed.

Fran shook her head. "No."

"Can you think of anyone who might want to harm your husband?" Sam put in.

Another negative response.

"What about his cell phone?" Nora asked. "Who had access to it other than him and you?"

"He carries it in his jacket, but he probably takes it off at work, so anyone at Esmee could have gotten to it," Fran said.

"Does he ever leave it in the car?"

"I suppose he might."

"Does he keep his vehicle locked?" Sam asked.

"Usually, unless he's only going to be gone for a few minutes."

Now they were getting somewhere. Even Sam seemed satisfied, so Nora let him continue with the questioning.

"Might he have left it in his car at work?"

"It's possible," Fran said.

After a few more questions failed to elicit any additional information, Nora thanked the witness. "You've been a big help," she said. "There's one more thing. I'd like to run a few names by you and see if any of them ring a bell."

"Okay."

She read off the list of the Trigger's victims. Only one netted a nod: Lance Corker, a lab technician at Esmee.

"My husband supervised him," Fran said. "I think he performed some kind of tests on engine parts. A parking garage collapsed on top of him during the earthquake. Carl got terribly upset when he heard."

Initially, the death had been attributed to the quake. But Nora's investigation, in conjunction with the coroner, had placed Corker's death a day earlier and attributed it to a cell phone exploding in his car. That, however, remained confidential information. "We're looking into it."

The woman regarded them fearfully. "I've told you everything I know. I've admitted setting the fire. What happens now?"

"If our investigation bears out your story, it should work in your favor." Sam's gentleness surprised Nora.

Fran blinked back tears. "Does that mean I won't go to prison?"

"We can't make promises," Nora said, "but you do have a clean record." She had run a background check earlier. "It's up to the district attorney whether he decides to file charges."

"The worst thing I ever got was a speeding ticket." Another tear broke free. "I'm sorry."

"Thanks for your cooperation. If you think of anything else, please give us a call." She handed over her business card. "And I hope your husband recovers quickly."

"So do I," Fran said. "I'm angry about what he did, but I never meant to hurt him. If he's truly sorry, maybe…well, we'll see. I'm going to the hospital in a little while, like I said. I hope he wakes up."

"If he does, maybe we can find out who did this and save someone else's life," Nora responded. Before they left, Nora obtained Fran's written consent for them to search the airplane.

Outside, she made a point of not meeting Sam's gaze until they were both in the car. "Well?" she said as they pulled out of the driveway. "Are you going to read me the riot act?"

"That was a dicey tactic." The noncommittal tone masked his true reaction.

"It paid off," she said stubbornly.

"I grant you that." When his gray eyes swept over Nora, she saw a reluctant approval in them. "You're quite a risk-taker."

"Taking chances gives me an adrenaline rush," she admitted. "Don't worry, I'm not foolhardy. I grew up in a family of demolition experts. They impressed on me early that having courage doesn't mean acting stupid. Anyway, you must be something of a daredevil too."

"Why do you say that?" He steered around some broken pavement left from February's earthquake.

"You're a firefighter. That's not a job that appeals to desk jockeys."

"My dad was a firefighter. It's a family tradition." Sam slanted her a grin that warmed his face. "Besides, I like getting physical. Lifting heavy objects, throwing equipment around, spraying a zillion gallons of water all over the neighborhood. That's fun stuff."

"You don't get a chance to do much of that as an arson investigator," she pointed out.

"I've mellowed with age."

That statement invited a crack. "You coulda fooled me."

"Maybe I have."

Nora could have sworn she saw a twinkle in his eye. Most likely it was sunlight or insanity.

Yet apparently he had an easygoing side, after all. Elaine had been surprised to learn about Sam's temper, and although he'd come on too strong for her taste with Fran, when he smiled, he looked quite…human.

He'd said he liked getting physical. Nora had to acknowledge that he projected a powerful physical presence, from the subtle male scent that permeated his car to the calm confidence with which he handled the wheel.

He might have appealed to her when she was younger, when she'd sometimes fantasized about curling inside a man's arms and letting him help shoulder her burdens for a while. If she were the type of woman who had a weakness for strong, take-charge men, she'd be susceptible.

But Len had cured her of that weakness. Besides, look what had happened to Elaine. When she'd tried to lean on Sam, he'd folded.

Nora snapped back to the present as they turned off the road that ran toward town. "Where are we going?"

"Esmee Engines," Sam told her. "I figure that's the obvious next step. You want to call ahead?"

Her brain sifted quickly through possible scenarios. "No. Let's not give Bethany Peters a chance to get her guard up."

"Another thing," he said. "We ought to make sure the plane's secured. If Carl Garcola *was* using it for illicit activities, someone might decide to destroy the evidence."

"Agreed." She placed a call to Grant Corbin. When she explained what they'd learned and that they had Mrs. Garcola's permission, he offered to take the forensics team and conduct the search himself.

"Max explained about you and Sam heading the investigation, but you can't handle everything yourself," the detective pointed out. "If we have a serial bomber on our hands, we need to hit this one hard."

"Go for it," Nora said. "Thanks, Grant."

"He's right," Sam commented after she repeated the conversation. "There are advantages to making a team effort."

"Does that apply to you and me, too?"

"I suppose we got further with Mrs. Garcola together than either of us would have separately." He switched onto Washington Avenue.

"True." Mischievously, she added, "Don't tell me you're going to propose we make this arrangement permanent!"

"You like that idea?"

"I might slit my throat."

"We can't have that." Abruptly, he sobered. "About this secretary. We should take her down to the police station for interrogation."

Nora shifted mental gears to keep up with him. "Bad idea. It'll freak her out. At best, she turns hostile. At worst, she'll call a lawyer and the trail goes cold while he plays legal games."

"She's either our key witness or a suspect," Sam insisted. "She must have been in the room with the victim, she fled the scene, and she's made no attempt to offer testimony. I'd say she was pretty hostile already."

"Maybe she's just scared," Nora countered. "Look at it from her perspective. She's having an affair with her boss, which might get her fired, depending on the company's policies. Then a bomb goes off and he's nearly killed. She's way over her head. I think if we reassure her, she might open up."

"I disagree." His fingers tapped the steering wheel. "She might be protecting someone. Say, a jealous boyfriend that she figures is behind it."

"All the more reason to handle her with kid gloves," Nora

said. "Remember how Fran Garcola reacted when she realized she hadn't caused her husband's injuries? She was so relieved, she spilled everything."

Sam considered for a moment. "We'll give it a try," he said finally. "But frankly, I think she needs to be scared."

Nora supposed he had a point, but decided to go with her instincts. Still, she could see that this team approach had advantages. It was Sam who'd thought of securing the airplane immediately. Although that would have occurred to Nora as soon as she read over her notes, it might have been too late to prevent damage.

Okay, so two heads might sometimes be better than one. But two tempers were definitely more combustible.

They found Esmee Engines in a light-industrial area, identified by a small sign in front. In the middle of a large parking lot sprawled a low white building nearly identical to the offices of practically every other high-tech company in the area.

"Fran said they make race-car engines," she noted as they got out. "I wonder where they keep the sports cars."

"I doubt they test them here." A pucker formed between his eyebrows. "Come to think of it, there's a test track over at the Speedman Company, a couple of miles south. Maybe they use that."

"Didn't you say one of your victims worked for Speedman?"

He gave a slow nod. "That's right."

Excitement quickened Nora's step at the possible link among the cases. Computer chips...automotive engines...a test track. Either a grudge or professional sabotage loomed large as possibilities.

Maybe she and Sam would find the key faster than she'd anticipated. If they did, they might put this thing together before anyone else got hurt.

But first they had to bypass Bethany Peters' defenses. And Nora had a feeling that wasn't going to be easy.

CHAPTER FIVE

NORA LOOKED AS IF she were enjoying the thrill of the chase, Sam thought as they entered the gray-carpeted lobby and showed the security guard their badges. While the man placed a phone call to announce their arrival, Sam wished her presence didn't keep making him lose focus.

Although discussing matters with Nora had been productive, he preferred the clarity of solitude, not to mention the absence of a sensuously rounded figure and glowingly alive face. Men didn't function at their best when a woman aroused their hormones. At least, he didn't.

At last a middle-aged Hispanic man emerged from an interior hallway. "I'm Ramon Nunez, president of Esmee Engines." He shook hands as they introduced themselves. "We're very upset about Carl's injuries. What can I do to help?"

"We'd like to talk to his secretary," Nora said. "We thought she might have some insights."

"Of course." Nunez escorted them along a corridor. "Any idea who might have done this?"

"That's what we're trying to find out." They entered a plush conference room. "Mr. Nunez, is there anyone who might hold a grudge against Carl personally or against your company?"

"Against Esmee?" the president asked in surprise. "There are always a few disgruntled former employees, I suppose, but no one I'm aware of. As for Carl, he never mentioned any problems."

"The company hasn't received any threats?" Nora asked. He shook his head.

"What about lawsuits?"

"Not currently," Nunez said. "I've only been working here about a year, though, so I could check with our lawyers."

"I'd appreciate it," Nora told him.

Checking out lawsuits was only one of many possible avenues, Sam reflected. You never knew which one might turn out to be useful.

"I'll send Mrs. Peters in," Nunez added. "Please make yourselves comfortable."

After he left, Nora said, "I noticed he called her *Mrs.* Peters. That means there's a potentially jealous husband lurking around."

"She could be widowed or divorced."

"I'd say it's unlikely," Nora countered. "If she had a private place, why would they use a motel?"

Trumped again, Sam reflected grouchily. "Unless there are nosy neighbors," he added to be contrary. "Or a roommate."

While he set up the tape recorder, Nora wandered around the room, inspecting the fax machine and other business-related equipment. Her restless movements kept her slim figure and wind-tossed mahogany hair in the forefront of Sam's awareness.

The woman's vibrant energy made him wonder, unwillingly, how she would feel pressed against him. Images of Nora had troubled him since the first time they met, four years ago, but until now they'd had the decency to appear only on rare occasions. Riding in her car yesterday had stirred up longings that were wreaking havoc with his resistance.

Well, he could hardly demand that Chief Egan break up the team because he found Nora too sexy. He had to get past this temporary resurgence of adolescent lust, and the best way to do that was to work as hard as possible, Sam reflected.

A moment later, the door opened to admit a woman who matched the description of the second escapee, except that today she wore her dark hair in a twist. Tall and athletic, Bethany Peters appeared to be in her late thirties, younger than Fran Garcola. She wore a long-sleeved blouse and slacks a bit heavy for the summer weather.

She fidgeted as she studied them. "Am I—is there some kind of problem? I haven't done anything wrong. I mean, anything criminal."

"Why don't you tell us what happened?" Sam suggested.

Bethany edged onto a chair. "Carl and I—well, we didn't mean to get involved." She averted her eyes. "It started a couple of months ago. We'd been flirting for a while, but neither of us meant anything by it. At least I didn't think so."

The story that unfolded had a familiar ring. Boss and secretary, both married, stayed after hours one night, ate dinner together and, afterward, yielded to their urges. Then came a series of lunchtime trysts and excuses to work late.

Yesterday, they'd decided to meet before Carl took off for a work-related conference in San Francisco. "I parked down the street from the motel so no one would see our cars together," Bethany said.

"Do you think someone might have followed you?" Although Fran had claimed she'd cruised the motel lot on a whim, Sam had to consider the possibility that she'd been stalking the pair.

"Carl was paranoid about that kind of thing," Bethany said. "I'm pretty sure no one saw us."

"Did you notice whether he wore his jacket when you left Esmee?" Nora asked. "Or did he leave it in the car?"

"I'm not sure."

"His wife says he usually kept his cell phone in the pocket," Sam put in. "It's important to know if someone else might have had access to it."

The secretary frowned. "I don't remember about the coat, but he did make some comment as we left the office about hoping he hadn't missed any calls."

Bethany seemed less intimidated by him than Fran, Sam noted. Perhaps she was more accustomed to dealing with men, or maybe he'd absorbed some of Nora's less confrontational approach. "Did he always lock his car?" he asked.

"As far as I know," came the response.

"Is anyone around here good at breaking into cars?" Nora put in.

Bethany managed a weak smile. "Are you kidding? This place is full of tech types. Anytime someone leaves his keys inside, he doesn't have to bother calling the auto club."

So much for that line of questioning, Sam reflected. In this environment, clearly they weren't going to identify a suspect by his lock-jimmying skills.

Nora steered the witness back to her narrative. "Tell me about you and Carl at the motel. What happened after you got inside?"

Color stained Bethany's cheeks as she described how they began to undress. Apparently they hadn't progressed far when the smell of gasoline and smoke reached them.

"I'm terrified of fire," she said. "When I realized I couldn't get out the door, I panicked. Carl opened the window and boosted me through it. The cabin blew up before I even had time to turn around to help him."

She'd fled across the field in fear before she realized Carl must still be inside. Hearing sirens, she'd decided to leave rather than return to find out what had happened. "I knew he'd be taken care of and I didn't want to get in trouble."

"You weren't hurt?" Sam asked.

"I got a lot of glass cuts." She indicated her long sleeves and pants. "Fortunately none of them on my face."

"Then what did you do?"

"I called in sick for the afternoon. But people had their suspicions about Carl and me and they know he got injured. I've been getting funny looks all morning."

Sam prepared himself to ask the next, delicate question when Nora beat him to it. Indicating the woman's wedding ring, she said, "Any chance your husband did this?"

"Andy? No, of course not!" She looked genuinely horrified.

"Jealousy can spur people to do strange things," Nora prompted.

"No, he wouldn't. Besides, he couldn't. Andy's in Houston on business."

"You're certain?" Sam asked.

"Well, yes." Bethany hugged herself protectively. "Does he have to find out about Carl and me?"

"We'll need to confirm his whereabouts," Nora told her. "And Courage Bay is a small town in some ways. It would be better if you broke the news to him yourself before he hears it elsewhere."

"In fact, we need you to call him right now," Sam said. "If you'll give me the phone number, I'll place the call myself." He wanted to monitor what Bethany told her husband. If he *had* been the bomber, or if the two turned out to be conspirators, it could reveal a lot. "Did you say his name was Andy?"

"Andrew." Uneasily, the secretary produced a phone number for a hotel in Houston. Going through the switchboard, Sam asked for Andrew Peters. After hearing the man's voice, he handed over the phone.

Listening on an extension, he heard Bethany explain that she'd escaped from a small explosion yesterday. Then, painfully, she admitted what she'd been doing at the motel.

Sam didn't enjoy eavesdropping on such a personal conversation. He took no voyeuristic interest in other people's messy lives. But investigations into murders and attempted murders often got messy.

Andrew Peters sounded genuinely shocked and upset. His mood didn't improve when Sam spoke up, identified himself as an arson investigator and began asking questions about Andrew's whereabouts on the previous day. Obviously taken aback to realize he might be considered a suspect, the man provided details and the names of witnesses. Since he'd been in business meetings all day, that wasn't difficult.

When Bethany got a chance to resume speaking, she begged her husband's forgiveness. Sam felt a twinge of sympathy for what lay ahead of her, but not too much. It had been her choice to break her marriage vows.

After she promised to meet her husband's plane the next day, Bethany hung up.

Nora handed the secretary a box of tissues. "Thank you. I know that was difficult but it did help."

"Just a few more questions," Sam said.

"Is that really necessary?" the woman choked out.

Unfortunately, it was. "We understand Mr. Garcola flew his own plane," he said. "Have you seen anything to indicate he might have been involved in illicit activities—say, smuggling or industrial espionage?"

Bethany paled. "Oh, my gosh, I hope not. I don't know anything about it. I love working at this company. If he was mixed up in something like that, it could cost me my job."

"Do you know if anyone held a grudge against Carl?" Nora put in.

"Maybe his wife—I mean, if she suspected he was cheating," the secretary said. "Other than that, no, although it's a little scary."

"What do you mean?" Sam prompted.

"All these people dying," Bethany said. "And now Carl getting hurt."

"All what people?" Did she see a connection among the bombing attacks specifically, or was she referring to the number of deaths that had occurred citywide? Sam wondered. "Please explain yourself, Mrs. Peters. We're dealing with homicides here."

Instead of answering, Bethany pushed back from the table. "I'm not going to say any more. Like I told you, I love working at this company. I just went through a horrible experience with my husband right in front of you. Aren't you satisfied?"

"We're trying to find out who did this," Nora said.

"Well, find out from somebody else," the woman replied. "I had no idea Carl might be mixed up with anything illegal or that this was something more than a jealous wife giving him a hard time. I should have gotten a lawyer in the first place."

With that, the secretary ran out of the room.

NORA BELIEVED they might have wandered around the corridors of Esmee Engines for hours seeking Ramon Nunez's office if she hadn't stopped to ask directions from a workman in blue overalls. Although Sam had insisted they didn't need help, he seemed relieved.

Did the man always have to be so stubborn? And he'd certainly botched the situation with Bethany. Still, Nora conceded that he'd gotten caught up with the seriousness of the case and forgotten the sensibilities of his audience. She didn't want to judge him too harshly.

Besides, she appreciated the calm, masterful way he faced down the president's personal assistant. After trying to stall them, the woman yielded to his insistence and reluctantly buzzed her boss, then ushered them into his expansive quarters.

Nunez rose to greet them. "Is there a problem, officers?"

"You tell me." Sam's belligerent tone seemed perfectly on the mark this time. "Mrs. Peters let slip something about 'all these people' getting hurt before she clamped the lid down. What's that about?"

During the pause that followed, Nora hoped the president

didn't also plan to call a lawyer. It came as a relief when he gave an apologetic shrug. "I assure you, I did answer your questions truthfully."

"But not completely," she said.

"I suppose not." Ramon's jaw worked as he obviously wrestled with his conscience. Finally, he said, "You know the corporate mentality. We're supposed to avoid negative publicity if we can."

"Talk to us," Sam demanded.

Remaining on his feet, Nunez leaned against the desk. "I didn't expect this kind of development when I got transferred here a little over a year ago."

"From where?" Nora asked.

"Wonderworld headquarters in Atlanta. That's our parent company."

"Wonderworld?" She hadn't paid much attention when she'd seen the name in the business section of the local paper. There'd been no mention of it in any of her case files.

"It's the multinational corporation that owns Esmee Engines and a couple of other subsidiaries around here," he explained.

She guessed what they were before he spoke again. As for Sam, he mouthed the names along with Nunez: Finder Electronics and the Speedman Company.

"We aren't covering anything up, I assure you." The president spread his hands placatingly. "I knew there were inquiries about Lance Corker's death, but as far as any criminal conspiracy being involved, you people played your cards close to your chest. I read about Patty Reese and Julius Straus in the newspaper, that's all. As far as I knew until today, these were unrelated, accidental deaths."

"Until today?" Sam repeated.

The president indicated a copy of the morning newspaper on his desk. "Carl getting critically injured in an explosion—well, that's too much of a coincidence. Then when you two showed up, I figured this must be serious. I put in a call to headquarters but I haven't heard back yet."

"Lucky for us," Nora muttered.

"Listen, Mr. Nunez, the best thing you can do for your company right now is to cooperate." Sam's resonant tone gave his words emphasis. "We have no reason to suspect any wrongdoing by Wonderworld or its subsidiaries, but obstruction of justice would be a serious charge."

"Not to mention that whoever's doing this may not be finished," Nora put in. "We don't want to see anyone else killed."

"Agreed." The president regarded them cautiously. "What can I do to help?"

"Can you find out about any projects that might have linked these individuals?"

"It might take a day or so," Nunez said.

Sam handed him a business card, and Nora added hers. "We'd also like to know about lawsuits that involved the victims, or anything they shared in common."

"I'll get right on it," Nunez promised. "Headquarters can fire me if they want to, but the safety of my workers comes first. Besides, if someone's targeting Wonderworld employees, I could be in their sights."

"Good point." Sam shook hands with the man, and Nora followed suit.

Afterward, they requested to see Carl Garcola's office. Nunez allowed them free rein except to the password-protected computer, because it had access to confidential company data. As a precaution, they collected a boxful of papers, although Nora saw nothing that aroused her suspicion.

When they were on the road, she said, "I feel like we're finally making progress. But I'm not convinced Nunez won't buckle if Wonderworld puts the screws to him."

"Maybe he'll change his mind back again if *we* push hard enough. I don't think he'd be too happy about spending a few nights in jail." Sam's phone rang. He pulled over and took out the instrument. "Prophet here."

As he proceeded with a cryptic conversation, Nora wondered if she would ever again take the safety of cell phones for granted. Each time she heard one ring, she got a jolt of adrenaline.

"How's the hamster doing?" Sam said into the phone.

The hamster? What kind of conversation was this, anyway?

His next line didn't track at all, as far as she could tell. "Personally, I'm crazy about overcooked spaghetti, but I'm not sure about my partner." He cleared his throat. "That's a long story...I'm not sure...I'll call you back."

Nora didn't say a word. Hamsters and overcooked spaghetti. That made an odd combination.

Sam flipped the phone shut. "That was my sister, Mary Orly. She teaches first grade and the kids had a near-tragedy this morning." His joking tone took the edge off the words.

"Involving a hamster?" she inquired.

"Right." Sheepishly, he went on. "Mr. Hamm escaped from his cage, gnawed through an electrical cord and gave himself a shock. He seems to be recovering but the kids are upset."

She couldn't restrain her curiosity. "What was the part about spaghetti?"

"She asked if I'd come over and talk about fire safety, electrical cords, that kind of thing. I've told her I'd be happy to address her class anytime I'm not tied up, and under the circumstances, she thinks having a guest speaker from the fire department should reassure them. She offered to treat me to lunch in the school cafeteria."

Nora checked her watch. Almost time to eat. "I don't mind if we stop by, but isn't that the public information officer's job?"

"Mary said a firefighter came out last month while her class was on a field trip," Sam told her. "Since this is the last week of school, they don't have time to schedule a return visit."

"Then let's get over there."

Sam called his sister back and then related the conversation to Nora. Not only had Mary offered to buy them both lunch, she'd promised to throw in ice cream bars. That definitely made it a go, in Nora's opinion.

Mariposa Elementary School lay in an aging residential area where Spanish-style stucco dwellings rubbed shoulders with 1920s bungalows. At the school, Sam removed a small suitcase from his trunk and carried it into the administration building, where he and Nora signed themselves in at the front desk.

Once approved, they exited through the back into an outdoor mall flanked by freestanding wings that housed classrooms. It had been ages since Nora visited an elementary school, since explosives experts didn't go around performing demonstrations for kids.

The sound of childish voices drifting from the playground brought a rush of memories from her own school days. She'd been a tomboy, scrappy and quick to stand up for herself. That hadn't always made her popular but it had made her strong.

"Do you visit here often?" she asked Sam.

"I come for special events to support my nephew." A cluster of diminutive figures hurried past them, overshadowed by his tall frame. "Pete's eight. His dad lives in San Francisco, so he can't always make it for things like Back to School Night and the science fair. I do my best to fill in."

"Your sister's divorced?"

He gave a short nod. Divorces were never a happy situation, Nora reflected. One of her brothers, Kyle, had split up with his wife and it had wiped him out financially and emotionally for a long time.

Sometimes she wondered if marriage merited the risk. At least when you set out to disarm a bomb, you knew it would all be over, one way or the other, within a short time. Marriage meant taking a gamble that could cost you years of heartache.

She hadn't had much interest in the subject since breaking up with Len. And although Nora had reached an age at which some women's biological clocks sounded the alarm, she'd never felt any strong urge to have children. Watching Sam smile at two little girls skipping by tugged at her heart in a funny way, though.

A few steps further, they reached their destination. The woman who met them at the classroom door had dark-blond hair the same color as Sam's, although her eyes were green, rather than gray, and she barely reached her brother's shoulder. Her expression full of curiosity, Mary welcomed them both.

"Sam doesn't usually work on a team," she told Nora. "This is the first I've heard he has a partner."

"We only got the news this morning." Nora followed her into the room, with Sam bringing up the rear.

Two dozen bright faces turned toward them. Little figures wiggled at their desks and a book dropped to the floor with a thump.

Nora made a quick survey of the room. Crayoned pictures festooned the walls, along with a map of the world and posters promoting reading. In one corner, a hamster raced furiously on a wheel.

"This must be Mr. Hamm." Sam crossed the room to examine the rodent. "Did anyone call the paramedics?"

A little girl giggled. A boy said solemnly, "I wanted to call Dr. Ripani. She treats my dog."

"I know Lisa Ripani very well," Sam responded.

"Because of your cats!" cried a pretty Latina girl.

Sam had a reputation in the fire department for rescuing stray cats and finding them homes. Obviously, the children also knew this. Nora gathered that Sam helped out in the classroom more than he'd let on.

She remembered her initial concern about cat hairs in his car. Since there weren't any clinging to her clothing, she as-

sumed he put the animals in a carrier before driving them anywhere. A wise move, since a panicky cat loose in a vehicle
could cause an accident.

"Class, you remember my brother, Investigator Prophet,"
Mary said. "He came here today to explain why Mr. Hamm
got a shock and how you can be careful not to get one yourself. This is his partner…"

"Nora Keyes," she introduced herself. "I'm a bomb squad
specialist."

A murmur of excitement rippled across the room. "Do you
blow things up?" a boy called excitedly.

"Only in practice exercises," she said. "Or if we recover
illegal explosives and have to remote-detonate them so they
can't hurt anyone." She supposed her terminology might be
a bit technical, but she'd found that children preferred being
treated like adults.

"Did you ever get your hand blown off?" asked a little girl
in pigtails. When everyone laughed, she blushed furiously. "I
mean, you could have a bionic hand, couldn't you?"

"Fortunately, I haven't had any significant parts blown off
yet," Nora told her. She decided not to mention one occasion
when she'd assisted her father and brothers in imploding a
building scheduled for demolition and a blasting cap went off
prematurely.

Anytime she started to get overconfident, she had only
to remember the burns she'd suffered and the painful heal-
ing process. So perhaps the accident had been a blessing
in disguise. But she didn't like to parade her mishaps in
public.

"Okay, hold on, guys." Sam opened the suitcase, which he
must carry around for occasions like this.

Out came a stack of fire-safety coloring books and handouts, a tan-and-yellow slicker and a yellow helmet fixed with
a white reflector. When he donned them, Nora could picture

him wearing that gear while dragging a hose up a ladder to rescue someone from a burning building.

She knew how it felt to be thrown over a man's shoulder and carried fireman style; she'd played the role of victim in emergency exercises. Hanging over a guy's shoulder two stories up wasn't her idea of fun, but then, she'd never been carried by a man built quite like Sam.

She could imagine those strong muscles moving beneath her. Exhilaration replaced fear. Sam…smoke…heat…flames…

Obviously, she must be picturing herself in Hell, she reflected wryly.

Nora cleared her mind in time to hear him warning the kids about the dangers of electrical wires and sockets. As he spoke, he took the hamster from its cage and carried it to the front of the room.

"I don't suppose we have to worry about Mr. Hamm playing with lighters or matches," he told the class, "but if he ever ate a cigarette, it could kill him." Heads nodded in understanding.

The little creature poked its way from one large cradling hand to the other, its whiskers twitching. Sam moved his empty hand lower and the hamster stepped onto it as if walking down stairs. One finger stroked the furry head and shoulders gently.

Why had a man who loved animals and clearly enjoyed children backed off when his girlfriend started getting serious? Nora wondered. If she hadn't known better, she'd have pegged Sam as the settling-down type. Which, of course, made him unsuited to her in yet another way.

"Cigarettes are dangerous from a fire standpoint even if you don't smoke or eat them," he went on as the children listened raptly. "A lit cigarette can smolder for hours deep in a chair and burst into flames while everyone's sleeping. Which is why we need—what? Anybody know what we need to wake us up in case a fire starts at night?"

Several children choroused, "Smoke detectors!"

"Very good," Sam said. "And make sure your parents check the batteries twice a year when they change the clocks for Daylight Saving Time." She doubted most of the children would remember, but some might, and she saw that the information was also printed on the handouts he'd given them.

While returning the hamster to its lair, he chatted about emergency exit plans, then took questions until the lunch bell rang. The three adults escorted a line of children to the cafeteria, and found a table apart from the students.

The spaghetti turned out to be overcooked, as advertised, but no worse than Nora herself had done plenty of times. She found the sauce delicious.

"Do they make this from their own recipe?" she asked.

"I think it's the kind you buy in the bottle." Mary named a well-known brand.

"Really? I usually get my sauce from a can. This is much better."

"You're kidding." Sam regarded her in disbelief. "You heat spaghetti sauce out of a can?"

"What are you, a gourmet chef?" she retorted.

"You don't have to be Julia Child to make decent spaghetti sauce."

"You know firefighters," his sister put in. "They have to learn how to cook because they take turns during those twenty-four-hour shifts. Our dad had more skill in the kitchen than our mother."

"My best skill in the kitchen is rapid-dialing the pizza place." Seeing Sam's dubious reaction, Nora added defensively, "I mean, of course I *can* cook."

"Oh, really? What's your best dish?" he demanded.

He *would* have to pose a tough one like that, she thought in annoyance. The term *best dish* implied lots of chopping, baking and sauce-stirring. As if she had time!

"Does making tuna salad count?" she asked.

"Yes," said Mary.

Sam shook his head. "No."

"Wait! I know! My best dish is that freeze-dried Indian food you get at Trader Joe's."

"You don't have to cook that," Sam said. "You just heat it."

Nora refused to accept his objection. "A microwave is an oven. If you put food in the microwave and press the buttons, you're cooking it."

Mary burst out laughing. "You two make quite a pair!"

"We fight all the time," Nora admitted.

"How can you possibly work together?"

"We're still trying to figure that out," Sam said.

In her pocket, Nora's phone rang. After a quick apology, she answered it.

She forgot their silly argument when she heard the police dispatcher's voice. The bomb squad had been summoned to the hospital along with a backup fire truck and paramedics.

An explosion at a medical center presented one of the worst scenarios Nora could imagine. "What's going on? How bad is it?" She tried to keep her voice low, but Mary and Sam both reacted with alarm.

"All I know is we got a call about a possible explosive device," came the response. "I haven't had any reports that it detonated."

"Inside or out?" Carl Garcola lay in the intensive care unit, Nora remembered. They'd posted a guard, but they hadn't considered the possibility that the Trigger might be willing to cause widespread casualties simply to wipe out one target.

"The woman who called said the device was outside," the dispatcher told her.

"Did she give her name?"

"It's Fran Garcola."

The witness had been on her way to the hospital right after

Sam and she had left, Nora recalled. Apparently Fran had run into trouble. "I'm on my way." Nora gave her companions a terse, one-sentence explanation.

Sam jumped to his feet. "Thanks, Mary. We've got to go."

"I understand completely," his sister said. "Thanks for coming."

As the two of them swept out of the cafeteria, Nora saw the children watching with wide, awestruck eyes. She so rarely spent time around kids that she'd forgotten how sweet and funny they could be.

But there were people in this world who didn't hesitate to injure innocent bystanders, children or anyone else, she thought grimly, and broke into a lope.

CHAPTER SIX

As Nora filled Sam in on what she knew, he attached a red light to his car roof and activated the built-in siren. Then he hit the gas.

Her mind zoomed ahead. According to bomb squad procedure, a containment unit should be on its way or already at the scene. If the device hadn't yet exploded, they needed to neutralize it as quickly as possible.

Before her arrival, the city had had the foresight to purchase a Total Containment Vessel capable of providing protection from fragmentation as well as the blast itself. Mounted on a hydraulic transporter and towed on a trailer behind a response vehicle, it could be placed close to the device.

Squad members in protective suits, using a robot if possible, would perform the extremely dangerous job of moving the device into the vessel. Nora needed to be with the team. They would have extra suits on hand, since team members often had to be summoned from other assignments.

The Courage Bay Hospital lay at the north end of the city's central section, just a few blocks from City Hall. The fact that the area was heavily trafficked meant that an outdoor bombing risked widespread injuries.

As Sam steered, Nora activated his fire department radio, which shared a frequency with the police. Although she half expected to hear accounts of major damage, to her relief, the dispatcher indicated emergency teams were now searching for the unexploded device.

Although it hadn't gone off, it might at any second. The searchers were putting their lives on the line.

No one mentioned over the radio exactly what the device looked like, but Nora had a good idea. "Mrs. Garcola phoned in the report. What if the Trigger tampered with her phone, hoping to detonate it while she was with her husband?"

"If he did, he's one step ahead of us," Sam said unhappily. "When could he have gotten to her?"

"I can't imagine she'd have been foolish enough to leave the phone anywhere accessible, not after our discussion." Nora leaned forward as if her body language could speed their way to the hospital.

"Maybe he'd managed to rig it before we interviewed her."

That they might have been blown to pieces in the Garcolas' living room was a chilling thought. But Nora didn't buy it. "This bomber isn't sloppy. If he'd planted the charge too early, someone else might have phoned Mrs. Garcola and set it off accidentally. I'm betting he waited till the last minute."

"How?"

"I don't know," she said. "But obviously, something he did tipped her off. This could be our first real break."

As she'd mentioned to Sam, bombers tended to be smarter than the average criminal, perhaps because their work called for more planning and organization. Despite the possibility that the Trigger had made an error that alerted Fran Garcola to her danger, Nora refused to underestimate him.

So far, he—or possibly she—had moved through the town undetected, coolly choosing his victims and gaining access to targets while blending into the surroundings. He could be monitoring the police radio right now, tracking every move the investigators made. More than ever, Nora felt the urgency of finding and stopping him.

They halted on Poppy Avenue, where a small crowd had gathered behind a line of fire engines and police cruisers. After glancing at their badges, a police officer waved Sam and Nora through. "Stay behind the perimeter unless you plan to suit up." He pointed toward an area of landscaping defined by yellow police tape. "It's somewhere in those bushes."

"Thanks," Nora said.

A bomb tech approached, almost unrecognizable in his full-protection suit. Aside from the clear polycarbonate face shield, the suit swathed his entire body with flexible armor made from aramid fiber, a manmade organic polymer. Although the getup weighed more than sixty pounds, at least it came with a ventilation system. Nora had heard the latest suits were equipped with built-in cooling systems as well. She couldn't wait to try one.

"What have you got so far?" she asked.

"We're looking for a cell phone."

No surprise there. "What happened?"

"We got a call from a woman that someone switched phones on her. I guess you know about her husband—the same thing happened to him. We figured we should take her seriously."

"Good decision," Sam said.

The tech indicated the roped-off area. "She tossed it into the bushes. We're going in as soon as we get the containment unit in position."

"Let's wait," Nora blurted, obeying her instincts, although she hadn't had time to analyze them.

"Why?"

Sam's quirked eyebrow echoed the tech's question.

She searched her mind for the answer, and, mercifully, it came to her. "Because from what I've learned about this bomber, I've got a hunch he's going to activate it any minute."

"But if he waits and detonates it later, we'll miss the chance to capture a fingerprint or DNA evidence," Sam pointed out.

"I don't want to risk somebody getting blown up," she argued. Effective as bomb suits might be, they had limits. At close range, an explosive could still cause severe harm.

"Neither do I." Sam gritted his teeth, obviously frustrated at missing a chance to collect clues.

"Besides, I don't think he'll delay," Nora said. "Either he knows we're here and doesn't want us to get our hands on the evidence, or he's left the scene and is calculating when Mrs. Garcola should reach her husband's room. Which surely she'd have done by now."

"You're right. I'll tell the others." The tech headed toward a couple of heavily suited men waiting for the containment unit to be angled into position.

By luck or instinct, Mrs. Garcola had flung her phone well away from both the building and the sidewalk, Nora noted. "Have you evacuated the building?" she asked a nearby officer.

"All the adjacent areas."

Although usually it was preferable to clear out an entire building, Nora knew it might do more harm than good to relocate so many patients reliant on life-sustaining equipment. Besides, a cell phone didn't hold enough plastic explosive to bring down the structure.

However, glass shards could shoot for long distances, especially outdoors. "We need to move back the perimeter," she told Sam. "I'll go tell the—"

Before she could finish, a boom shook the adjacent fire truck, followed by the shriek of windows shattering and the screams of bystanders. Whatever Nora had meant to say vanished as she stumbled backward and lost her balance.

The shock thrust her into Sam's reassuringly solid form. He enclosed her with one arm as he hung onto a handle projecting from the truck.

Her heart thundered and the breath rasped from her lungs. She could feel Sam's muscles straining as he braced for a secondary blast. You never knew if a bomber had planted an additional charge nearby to increase the damage, distract authorities and spread confusion.

Mercifully, a second blast never came. An eerie silence descended, as if the detonation had frozen everyone in place.

Nora leaned back, unable or unwilling to stir. Although she thrived on excitement, she harbored no illusions as to her own vulnerability. The roar and the sensation of being flung helplessly backward had aroused a primitive fear mechanism—or at least, that's what she blamed for this sudden yearning to take refuge.

Sam's free arm tightened in a protective gesture, holding her close, and his cheek grazed her hair. He seemed in no hurry to release her.

In the silence, she heard the thrum of his blood and the rapidity of his breathing. The relief at finding safe harbor gave way to an unexpected longing to merge into him. For a suspended moment, Nora ached for Sam purely as woman to man.

The wail of an approaching siren broke the spell. Officers sprang into motion, a buzz went up from the bystanders and a woman began loudly demanding how she was supposed to get all this glass out of her hair.

Determined to assess the damage, Nora looked around the edge of the truck. Bushes had been ripped up by their roots and a small crater blasted into the ground. There appeared to be only cosmetic damage to the hospital, and its safety glass had cracked in starburst patterns. The windows of nearby buildings gaped jaggedly.

She let the suited-up squad members approach to check for unexploded ordnance. Some time later, they signaled the all-clear.

While Nora conferred with them, Sam went to talk to firefighters and assess the damage. He returned a short time later. She hated to admit how reassuring she found the sight of his confident figure as he approached.

Her brain told her that this man had no more control over the forces of destruction than she did. Yet right now, with her nerves strained by the blast, she savored the air of strength he projected.

"A few people suffered cuts and some of the vehicles acquired interesting etchings in their paint," he reported. "Other than that, it appears we got lucky. No serious injuries."

"Let's hope not." It would take hours and possibly longer before the total picture emerged. Nora hated to think how much damage the exploding windows must have caused inside adjacent offices, and there remained the possibility of someone experiencing a heart attack from stress. Still, it appeared that well-designed emergency measures and good fortune had blunted the damage.

A short time later, she spied Fran Garcola, blond hair askew and eyes rimmed with red, talking to Chief Max Zirinsky. Catching sight of them, the witness gave a small, self-conscious wave.

Nora and Sam joined her. "Are you all right?"

"I want to thank both of you for saving my life. If you hadn't warned me about the cell phone, I'd be dead by now, and so would Carl." Fran's voice trembled.

Sam caught the woman's arm as she sagged. "You may be suffering from delayed shock."

"You've got to catch this guy. Look what he did!" Fran indicated the scene teeming with emergency personnel, ripped-up vegetation and bits of debris. "All to kill my husband. And if you don't stop him, next time he might succeed."

Max nodded. "We're going to move your husband to a wing that's being remodeled and is closed to the public. All visitors will be searched."

"Thanks. But this guy won't stop, and you can't keep Carl locked up once he recovers," Fran replied.

Sam pulled out his notebook. "I'm sure you've already

told the police what happened, Mrs. Garcola, but we'd like to hear it again. We might pick up details that will tie in with our investigation."

"I'll be glad to tell you anything I can," she said.

With the police chief, the three of them adjourned to an undamaged outdoor picnic area and took seats around a concrete table. Nora was glad to get off her feet. Although she struggled to hide it, her legs had begun to tremble. All her experience notwithstanding, the blast had shocked her.

The others had been similarly affected, she gathered. Both men held themselves more stiffly than usual, as if to keep a tight rein on their emotions, while the color had drained from Fran's face.

Clasping her hands on the table, the witness soldiered on. "I was walking toward the entrance when a man bumped into me. My purse flew into the air and everything spilled on the sidewalk. He stuffed a few things back inside, apologized and hurried away."

"What did he look like?" Sam's eagerness reflected Nora's own excitement at discovering that, at last, someone had seen the Trigger.

"I'm afraid I got distracted picking up my stuff and hardly noticed the guy," she admitted. "He was a big fellow, I remember that."

"By 'big,' do you mean tall or heavyset?" the chief asked.

"Tall and muscular—beefy, I guess you could call him," Fran said. "He wore sunglasses and a dark blue baseball cap. And work gloves."

"What about the rest of his clothing?" Sam put in.

"Jeans and a flannel shirt." Fran blew her nose into a tissue.

Nora knew that most witnesses observed much more than they initially realized. Sometimes bits of information came back to them later. "Any logos on his clothing?"

"I don't think so."

"How about the cap?" Most such headgear bore the name of a sports team.

Fran reflected. "Wait a minute. It did have an emblem. Some kind of black-and-white animal. A skunk—you know, the cartoon type."

Nora made a note. She couldn't immediately associate the symbol with any sports team. "When he spoke, did he have an accent?"

"No."

"Pale skin? Dark? Ruddy?" Sam put in.

"Ruddy, I guess. I'd describe him as some kind of work-man, but it might have been the clothing that made me think that." Fran released an uncertain breath. "He seemed so nor-mal. You could pass him in a crowd and you wouldn't think twice."

Nora had already guessed that. A bizarre-looking man wouldn't have had such an easy time planting his explo-sives. "What made you decide to alert the bomb squad?" she asked.

"You," the witness said.

"Me?"

"Both of you." She included Sam in her wan smile. "See, after I collected the stuff from my purse, I checked around for my cell phone. When I didn't see it, I realized the man had already put it in my pocketbook."

"You remembered our warning," Nora filled in.

"That's right. I took it out and—it wasn't my cell phone." Shudders ran through the woman. "He'd replaced it with an-other one. I was holding it right in my hand. That bomb." Her horrified gaze strayed to the devastation in front of the hospital.

The Trigger must have realized in advance that he wouldn't have time to tinker with Fran's phone, Nora thought, so he'd exchanged it. "He's desperate to make sure your husband doesn't talk."

Fran hugged herself. "I was scared enough already!"

"You used your head," Sam said. "You should be proud. You saved your life and your husband's."

"He won't stop," the witness said. "How long will this go on?"

"The fact that he's stepping up the pace means he's more likely to make a mistake," Max observed. "Today he risked making contact with you. Someone could have recognized him. Next time, maybe they will."

Fran shuddered. "I hope there won't be a next time."

Nora searched for some new angle, some way that today's blast might help lead them to the Trigger. "You don't happen to have a locator in your phone, do you?" Many newer cellular appliances came equipped with Global Positioning Satellite technology. If the killer still had the phone, they might be able to find him.

"I don't think so. It's an older model."

Another slim chance shot down. Nora wasn't ready to give up, though. "Could I get the number anyway? It's worth calling to see if someone answers."

When Sam's jaw worked, she thought for a moment he might argue with her. To her surprise, he merely seconded her suggestion. "If the bomber discarded the phone, perhaps whoever found it could provide some information," he told Fran. "The location could tip us off to his habits. Maybe someone spotted him discarding it."

Fran gave them the number. "I hope it helps."

"I'd like you to come down to headquarters and work with an artist," Max said. "Maybe you'll remember enough for someone to make an ID."

"I'll try." Fran got to her feet. "First I want to see Carl."

"Of course." The chief stood up. "I'll escort you in."

"The paramedics ought to take a look at her first," Nora said. Although the woman appeared in control, Nora had seen people collapse from the effects of delayed shock.

"I'll see that they do," Max assured her. "Then after she visits her husband, I'll drive her to headquarters."

"Thanks, Chief." Nora saw Grant Corbin making his way through the welter of emergency vehicles. She'd almost forgotten about him and the forensics team examining Carl's plane. "Here's someone else we need to talk to."

"I'll leave you to it," Max said, and escorted Mrs. Garcola away.

Grant reached them a moment later. "Are you guys all right? I heard this thing blow halfway across town."

"We're fine." Sam sounded impatient that anyone would question his resilience. To Nora it seemed a typical macho reaction, but perhaps it was a masculine way of rejecting the notion of weakness. "Did you finish searching the plane already?"

"Unless we want to dismantle it, yes," Grant said. "You told me not to do any damage."

"That's right." Nora intended to keep her promise to Fran. "What did you find?"

"Nothing significant," the detective said. "We'll be running tests, but unless we discover a trace of drugs or something unexpected, the thing looks clean."

After a few more questions, she and Sam decided to wait and read Grant's report the following day. If he'd found nothing worth pursuing, they would trust his judgment. She hadn't really believed Carl to be involved in smuggling, anyway.

"Well, I guess it's time we try to have a conversation with a killer, or whoever found his phone," she said.

"We should get it on tape," Sam said.

"Right." She took out her pocket recorder and hooked it up to her cell. "Listen for ringing, in case he's around here."

The Trigger might have decided to blend into the crowd and enjoy the sight of the devastation he'd wreaked. It wouldn't be unusual for a bomber to offer to help bystanders, smugly accepting the thanks of the very people he'd injured.

Grant and Sam separated, stationing themselves some distance off. When both made eye contact with her and nodded, Nora dialed the number Fran had provided.

It buzzed three times. Neither Sam nor Grant signaled that they'd registered a phone ringing in the crowd.

Just when she thought no one was going to answer, the sound stopped abruptly. Nora caught her breath. "Hello?"

The rasp of breathing filled her ear.

She decided to feign ignorance in the hope of hearing a voice. "Fran, is that you?"

In the background, a siren blared. The connection cut off.

Nora could hardly believe it. That might have been the Trigger, right there at the end of the connection. Despite the tantalizing contact, however, she doubted she'd learned anything useful.

"I think I reached him," she said when the men approached. "He or she didn't speak, though."

"Did you hear anything in the background?" Sam asked. Standing close by, his body creating a barrier to passersby, he watched Nora intently.

"A siren. He must still be in the downtown area."

"Not too close," Grant observed.

Sure enough, now that Grant pointed it out, Nora realized that the only sirens were coming from some distance away. So many fire and police workers had already been on site before the detonation that there hadn't been the normal clamor of emergency vehicles afterward.

Frustrated, Nora unloosed a couple of curse words. She'd been so close. She'd actually heard the Trigger breathing, had experienced a link to him, and yet nothing had come of it.

Time to return to good old-fashioned police work. Digging, probing, inspecting and testing. Sam ought to be thrilled.

After Grant left, they spent the rest of the afternoon combing the scene of the bombing and interviewing anyone who might have seen the Trigger before or after he approached Mrs. Garcola. No one recalled a large man with sunglasses and a baseball cap. No one recognized the logo, either.

To eliminate one possible suspect, Sam made a series of calls and tracked the witnesses cited by Bethany's husband. They confirmed that Andrew Peters had been in Houston all day Tuesday.

As she stood there observing Sam's collected manner, Nora wondered how long it would take him to concede that she'd been right about pursuing the Garcola case while it was fresh. Probably as long as it would take her to confess that she appreciated having a partner who knew his job, she thought in silent amusement.

Sam hung up. "He checks out. The guy has my sympathy. Here he is caught up in a murder investigation and all because he has a cheating wife."

"It's sad when people trample on those who care about them." Realizing her comment might apply to Sam's relationship with Elaine, Nora dropped the subject, even though he had no idea she knew his ex-girlfriend.

Nora remembered the comforting sensation of being held against him after the explosion. Sam's naturally protective manner had a certain appeal, she conceded, but only a fool would take it personally.

Around five o'clock, Max stopped by to distribute the artist's sketch based on Fran's recollection. Unlike many chiefs, Max took an active interest in the day-to-day work of his officers, particularly in view of the numerous deaths and near-deaths during the past year.

Nora examined the sketch, fascinated to "meet" her enemy face to face. It showed a middle-aged man with a broad face and weathered skin. Thanks to the sunglasses obscuring his eyes and the cap covering his head, the only other features evident were his mouth and nose, neither especially distinctive.

The artist had produced a couple of other sketches showing how the man might look with longish hair. Nothing rang a bell.

Sam indicated the busy area surrounding them. "He could be half the men here."

"Still, if we assume the Trigger's working alone, we can downplay the likelihood that we're seeking a woman," Nora noted. "The description also eliminates anyone very young or old or short."

"It's a start," Max agreed. "Well, I want to go pass these around. Let me know if you come up with anything new."

"You bet," Nora said.

Sam studied the flyer. "This might fit me," he commented after the chief departed.

"I can vouch for your whereabouts," Nora joked. "Besides, I wouldn't call you beefy."

He spared a wry smile for his flat stomach. "I hope not."

The forensics unit was hauling off bags of evidence. However, unless the Trigger had dropped his wallet or made some other uncharacteristically bonehead mistake, Nora wasn't optimistic about coming up with new clues. Besides, her body ached from hours spent searching the scene.

"We never did get around to reviewing the other unsolved murders," she reminded her partner.

"Why don't we break for dinner to clear our heads and go over everything this evening?" Sam said. "In fact, if you're willing to haul the files over to my house, I volunteer to cook."

A little voice in Nora's head warned that they ought to stick to neutral territory. But they wouldn't be able to spread out their papers in a restaurant, and she didn't fancy spending a long evening in a desk chair plowing through reports.

"Since you made such a point about your culinary skills, I'll let you prove it," she responded.

"No problem."

They drove to the police station. As they exited the car, Sam wrote his address on a pad and handed it to her. "I need to run by my office and stop at the supermarket. Give me an hour."

"Make it an hour and a half." Nora indicated smudges on her clothing and face. Except for removing a few stray bits of glass, she hadn't taken time to clean up. "I need to change."

"Fine." He reached over and plucked a fragment from her hair. As he lifted it away, the pad of his thumb traced a gentle trail along her temple. "You missed something."

Nora relished the warmth of his touch, and scolded herself for her foolishness. "What is it?"

He examined his trophy. "Dead bug."

"Sam!"

"I'm not kidding. It's a ladybug." He extended his finger so she could see. As he did so, the little creature righted itself, wobbled indignantly and popped into the air. "Not so dead, I guess."

"Fly away home," Nora murmured, remembering the children's rhyme.

"Good advice," said Sam. Without so much as a farewell, he turned and strolled across the pavement toward the fire department.

The man had a gift for hip action, Nora mused, watching shamelessly. Not to mention great buns. And he could cook, too.

Now all he had to do was help her catch a murderer.

CHAPTER SEVEN

THREE YEARS AGO, Sam had nearly bought a small, older home in his childhood neighborhood. Then he'd noticed a housing development rising nearby and watched with fascination the daily progress from open field to graded earth. Each time he drove by, something new caught his eye: the curve of a road, the laying of foundations, the completed framework.

It reminded him of a garden growing from seed to mature plants. When the dust settled, he'd stopped by to preview the model homes out of curiosity.

His spirit had expanded at the sight of the high ceilings and arched doorways, the sunny tiled kitchens and expansive master suites. Although the prices might be steep, a little research convinced him that property values were likely to increase in that area, so a three-bedroom home made a good investment.

Since moving into his house, Sam had spent his spare time establishing a garden, furnishing the place and outfitting the garage with a workshop. He'd imagined himself settling down with a wife and raising children to join the kids riding their tricycles and skateboards along the sidewalks.

He didn't know what had gone wrong with Elaine. He'd enjoyed her company and she'd have fitted easily into his life plans, but he'd felt something akin to panic when he realized where they might be heading. Maybe he hadn't loved her enough to get married. Maybe he wasn't capable of loving anyone that much. Or maybe he'd rather not take the risk.

He'd read once that when a man married and had children, he gave hostages to fate. As a firefighter, Sam had seen too often the shattering effects of people suffering unbearable losses. With his father's death, he'd experienced it himself.

Maybe when he met the right woman, he wouldn't worry about such things. In the meantime, he appreciated finding an excuse to cook for someone else tonight. At least with Nora, he didn't have to worry about romance becoming an issue. Attractive as he found her, she had too many sharp edges and *way* too sharp a tongue.

On his swing by the supermarket, he decided to keep things simple. Throw a couple of steaks on the grill along with some fresh corn, add a gourmet salad—fresh out of the bag—on the side, and you had a dinner as good as any restaurant cuisine. He picked up a dozen fresh-baked cookies at the bakery counter for the perfect climax to the meal.

Whoa. Poor word choice, Sam told himself as he carried the sack of groceries in from the garage. Nobody was going to be doing any climaxing here tonight!

If only the scent of Nora's hair, which he'd inhaled while holding her outside the hospital, didn't keep tickling his memory. He'd been seized by an instinctive desire to keep her from harm's way. Later, when she'd called the Trigger, it had disturbed him to think of her having direct contact with a murderer.

Heck, that was her job. And Nora Keyes could take care of herself; nobody knew that better than Sam. Still, he didn't like the idea of her being connected, even by phone, with a killer.

He went outside to fire up the grill. Soon the cooking aromas replaced any lingering romanticism with sheer hunger.

Sam checked his watch, growing impatient when the appointed time came and went. He liked punctuality in a woman. Besides, he wanted to eat.

When the doorbell finally rang, he reined in his impatience. Being tired and hungry didn't excuse a bad temper, he lectured himself, and put on his most sociable manner as he went to the door.

Nora had traded her pantsuit for jeans and a black knit top that contrasted with the rich mahogany of her hair. Even carrying a briefcase stuffed with files, she radiated sensuality.

Trying to concentrate on something other than her shape, Sam blurted the first thing that came to mind. "Is that color natural?"

"You mean my hair?"

"What else would I mean?" Well, that was hardly polite, he reflected with regret.

She marched into the living room and dropped her briefcase on the coffee table. "It's no secret that I dye it. Nature gave me a boring mouse brown."

"I like it," Sam said quickly. "But then, I'm partial to weird colors." Oh, great. That sounded even worse. "I mean, unusual colors, like those." He indicated his mantel, where the selection of pottery shapes ranged from squatty to cylindrical and the glazes included Indian black, Chinese red and celadon green. He'd collected them on vacation trips to New Mexico and Arizona.

"Those are beautiful." Nora didn't spend much time gazing at them, however. Apparently décor wasn't her favorite subject. "Whatever you're cooking, the smell lives up to its billing."

"I decided to barbecue."

After giving the air one more appreciative sniff, she invited herself through the kitchen and onto the back patio. "Typical fireman. You get home and can't wait to light some charcoal."

He followed her out. "What does an explosives expert do when she gets home, make popcorn?"

"You bet." Nora took a moment to study the yard. "You've got quite a spread here."

"Glad you like it." Sam had invested many hours of hard work nurturing the emerald lawn. He'd also designed and installed the meandering flowerbeds, with annual blooms interspersed among ferns and bright-leafed perennials. Geraniums and chrysanthemums in pots that could be moved around as needed provided accents.

A plastic storage shed hid the less aesthetic accessories: feeding dishes and water bowls for the neighborhood stray cats. Fond as he was of the little creatures, Sam didn't want them rubbing his ankles while he entertained. Even now, a curious tabby peered at them from behind the shed.

"You've done a great job with the yard," Nora said.

"Thanks."

If he'd been hoping for further praise, she quickly disabused him of that notion. "But I think it's kind of strange."

"Excuse me?"

"You're nesting. The house, the yard—you've created a cocoon."

"What's wrong with a nice safe place to come home to?" Sam demanded. The few other women he'd brought here had exclaimed in delight.

"Nothing." She chewed thoughtfully on a stray wisp of hair before brushing it away. "Okay, tell me, where does a woman fit in? You've got the house decorated and the yard landscaped down to the Johnny Jump-Ups tucked picturesquely in the corners. There's zero room left for anyone else's taste."

Sam bristled. "I take pride in my home. Some people find that admirable."

"So you don't consider yourself controlling?"

"If you're afraid of strong men, that's your issue, not mine," he said. "Besides, I hardly think my personal life is any of your business."

"You're right. It isn't."

"Good." Sam didn't understand why she'd become so heated about the issue. "How do you like your steak?"

"Not burned." Casting a dubious glance at the barbecue, Nora went inside.

To his dismay, he saw that the steaks verged on being charred. Swearing to himself, he transferred them to plates, along with the corn.

How could she blame him for wanting to control his surroundings when work took him to the brink of disaster? he wondered as he stalked into the house. Perhaps Nora lived comfortably amid chaos. To Sam, the order and harmony of his home offset the unpredictability of his job.

Not that he intended to mention it. He didn't have to justify himself to anyone, especially not his temporary partner.

He found no sign of his guest in the kitchen. A glance into the living room showed her sitting on the floor, Japanese-style, with her files spread across the coffee table.

"Why don't we eat in the kitchen?" Sam called as he stuck pronged holders into the cobs and added salad to the plates.

"Because we can't afford to waste time," her voice drifted back. After a moment, she added, "Man, these are all over the place!"

"What are?" He hoped she hadn't discovered a new invasion of ants. The exterminator had been out only two weeks earlier.

"These other murders. There's a shooting, a strangling, a beating death and a suspicious plane crash. If it's one killer, he's pretty creative." When he entered with the plates, she muttered, without looking up, "Just put those anywhere."

Sam couldn't help it. He started to laugh. "You have the social skills of a bull moose."

"So people tell me."

Amused by her lack of repentance, Sam plopped her dish and tableware in the middle of the coffee table. Taking a seat on the couch, he prepared to dive into murder and mayhem.

NORA KNEW HER MANNERS verged on rudeness. Still, in her present mood, she couldn't bear to sit across a kitchen table from Sam and make polite conversation.

Maybe it was the aftereffects of surviving today's bombing that had made the sight of his tasteful home and charming yard so appealing. To her dismay, she'd experienced a sudden longing to make a nest of her own—to curl up and let a man keep her safe, just for a while.

She didn't want to sit across from him at dinner and risk having her leg brush his beneath the table. What if she did something really stupid like ending up on his lap and stroking that thick blond hair?

Sam would laugh himself sick should he ever suspect that his nemesis-cum-partner had a soft side. Besides, if she searched to the ends of the earth, Nora knew she couldn't find a man less suited to her.

She hadn't been kidding about her reaction to his domestic setting. The whole place shouted "Control freak!"

The aroma from the plate he'd slipped in front of her slowly drove out any negative thoughts. The man had a gift with the senses, she allowed.

She took a bite. Steak a bit overdone but flavorful. Another bite: tasty salad. And out-of-this-world corn.

"Exactly what are we looking at here?" Sam asked from the sofa.

"The cases Max wanted us to consider." Nora dragged her focus away from the food. "The department always has unsolved murders, of course, but I narrowed them down to four that seem to fit together. They all occurred during the past year, and in each case, the victim had previously escaped justice after being accused of a felony."

"You think we've got a vigilante operating here?"

"Possibly. The chief calls these the Avenger cases." After

handing the first folder to Sam, Nora hefted her ear of corn and treated herself to a mouthful.

"I'd use both of those corn holders, if I were you," Sam observed dryly. "Otherwise, if you keep waving that around, it's likely to turn into an unguided missile."

"What? Oh, sorry." She corrected her grip and waited while he read the material.

Sam scanned the preliminary report. "The Trigger's victims aren't suspected of wrongdoing as far as we know, so that's an important distinction."

"But you admit revenge might be his motive?"

"Sure. But revenge and vengeance are a little different. One's specific and the other's more general."

She found herself wanting to argue for the sake of it, but the truth was, she agreed that the Trigger's motivation didn't appear to be the same as the Avenger's. So she kept quiet while he read.

Despite her antipathy to anyone who took the law into his own hands, Nora could understand why the Avenger might have gone after the first victim. A film producer, Dylan Deeb, had been strangled in his home last November. Six months earlier, he'd faced charges of demanding sexual favors from underage actresses in exchange for movie roles. The case had to be dismissed when the young witnesses declined to testify, apparently frightened by Deeb's threats to blackball them in Hollywood.

Sam closed the file thoughtfully. "What an ugly business. This sounds like the work of an angry father or boyfriend."

"If it were an isolated incident, I'd concur." Solving Deeb's murder wasn't their problem, however. "You agree it most likely isn't the work of the Trigger?"

"Absolutely." He polished off more steak before continuing, "Our guy has chosen a method that lets him stay far away from his victims. Strangling someone is about as up close and personal as you can get. And even though he took the chance of making contact with Fran Garcola, he stuck with a cell phone bomb. I don't think this is his work."

"Me either." Honesty prompted Nora, who'd been eating steadily, to add, "This meal is great. I'd forgotten how good barbecue tastes."

"Thanks." Sam favored her with a sideways grin that sent an unwanted thrill through Nora. "I agree. I'm a fabulous cook."

"And modest, too." Knowing he must be fully aware of his effect on women, she moved to the next case. "Tell me what you think of Number Two."

The next victim, Bruce Nepom, had been a dishonest, unlicensed contractor. His defective materials and shoddy work had caused a roof to collapse, killing a retired couple. After the district attorney failed to collect enough evidence to bring criminal charges, Nepom had been found dead in his home in January. At first, a collapsed roof during a storm had taken the blame, until it was discovered at autopsy that he'd died of blunt trauma to the base of his skull.

"That doesn't sound like the Trigger, either," Sam said. "I also don't see any connection between Mr. Nepom and Mr. Deeb, other than the fact that both men appear to have escaped justice."

Nora had heard the homicide detectives voice the same reaction. "Considering how often bad guys go free, someone must have taken these particular cases personally, but I agree, nothing about them points to any one suspect. Well, read on."

"Am I allowed to take a few more mouthfuls first?" Sam teased.

"Sure. Just not too many."

"Thank you, ma'am." He tackled his ear of corn.

Despite Nora's attempt to pretend absorption in the other papers, her peripheral vision tantalized her with glimpses of the way Sam's twill pants hugged his long legs and his gray-green shirt brought out the depths in his eyes. If she'd figured she was safer from temptation in the living room than the kitchen, she'd been fooling herself.

He flipped to the next file, a shooting death. "Lorna Sinke." Sam read the victim's name in a puzzled tone. "That sounds familiar."

"She served as an aide to the city council," Nora prompted.

Recognition dawned. "That hostage situation at city hall a couple of months ago. Now I remember—it made all the papers."

Lorna Sinke, one of the hostages, had been shot and died later in hospital. Surprisingly, ballistics tests had revealed that the lethal bullet hadn't come from the hostage takers' guns.

"She'd been charged with killing her elderly parents for an inheritance." Nora decided to save Sam the trouble of finding the information in the report. "The judge threw out the evidence because of a problem with the search warrant. I have to admit, this case bothers me the most."

"Because the victim was female?"

"No. Because the perpetrator might be someone in law enforcement. I don't like to imagine anyone at the PD resorting to murder, no matter how frustrated we get with the revolving-door system." Nora started to take another forkful of salad and discovered she'd consumed her entire meal. She'd been hungrier than she thought—and it had tasted better than expected.

"I presume someone's checked to see which officers were involved in the original investigations of each of these victims," Sam said. "They'd have reason to get angry about seeing justice denied."

Nora had asked one of the homicide dicks about that. "There's no one who worked all the cases. So maybe I'm wrong about that law-enforcement angle." She hoped so.

"Whoever the Avenger is, he's a crack shot." Sam studied the report for a minute longer before closing it. "He's cool enough to plan and execute his schemes, but inside he's got to be seething. Beating one man to death and strangling another shows tremendous rage. Or we might be dealing with some kind of vigilante group, but in a small city like this, it's hard to imagine they could keep such an organization secret for long."

"The Trigger must be angry, too, but he strikes me as more calculating," Nora observed.

Sam opened another folder. "That brings us to last month." He skimmed the fact sheet. "I remember this one. The plane crashed into the ballroom of the Grand Hotel, killing the pilot."

"Turned out the plane had been tampered with," Nora told him. "Take a look at the man's background."

Carlos Espasito, the pilot of the private plane, had escaped going to trial for smuggling illegal aliens because someone murdered the chief witness.

Sam set the file aside. "You've read these more closely than I have. Do any of the reports mention Wonderworld or its subsidiaries?"

Nora shook her head. "Not one. Even though it's hard to believe we've got two serial killers at one time, that appears to be what's happened. I have to admit, I think we'd be confusing the issue if we spend too much time on this Avenger material."

"Is Max going to accept our decision?" he asked. "You know him better than I do."

Nora had the greatest respect for the chief's common sense. "He trusts us. If he didn't, he'd never have given us such an important case."

"Then, let's get back to the Trigger," Sam said.

Feeling cramped on the floor, Nora moved to a stuffed chair. "At this point I believe we can narrow down the motive. Someone's obviously angry with Wonderworld and certain of its employees."

"How can you be so sure?" Leaning back on the couch, Sam folded his arms.

"You don't agree?"

"It looks that way, but it's too soon to zero in on a motive," he told her. "Jumping to conclusions could make us miss important threads."

Just when she'd started to feel comfortable around him, he'd reverted to type. To Nora, the Trigger's motivation stood out clearly.

"Fine. If you see any other angles, I'm open to hearing them." The long, stressful day had taken its toll on Nora's patience, never her strong point. "Otherwise, I'd say we're wasting time if we *don't* narrow this down."

"I didn't say we should abandon this line of inquiry, only that we need to consider other possibilities," Sam pointed out.

"Have you got a better theory?" she responded grumpily. "It's fine to weigh all the scenarios, but sometimes the most obvious conclusion is the right one."

"And sometimes it isn't." He kept his tone level. His ability to retain his composure in the face of her crabbiness irritated Nora more than if he'd argued with her. "Try this on for size. Suppose someone's laying a trail to mislead us. Maybe the real target is only one of the victims and the rest are a smokescreen."

Wearily, Nora ran a hand through her hair. "It's possible, I suppose. But the fact he's tried to take out Carl twice makes that unlikely."

"What if Bethany's husband is the real culprit?"

"He has an alibi." She refrained, barely, from pointing out that it was Sam who'd tracked the man to his Houston hotel.

"He could have put out a contract hit."

"Contract killers don't spend nearly a year blowing up warehouses, trucks and random people just to cover their trails," Nora fumed. "Look, this guy's not going to stop trying to kill Carl, and if there's anybody else on his list, they're in imminent danger too."

They'd reached an impasse. Sam broke it. "How about this. I'll agree that what you've suggested is the most likely scenario. You agree to keep an open mind in case any evidence contradicts your theory."

"That's reasonable." Of course she would consider any solid leads, wherever they led. What investigator wouldn't?

"Now, why don't we go over what we've learned so far and see if we can dazzle each other with any further insights?" Sam asked.

"You're on." She did like having someone to bounce ideas off, Nora admitted silently. Much as she trusted her own instincts, she wasn't egotistical enough to consider herself infallible.

He cleared away the dishes, Nora tucked the Avenger files into her briefcase, and they sat down to review what they'd learned so far about the Trigger.

A couple of hours later, they hadn't made any breakthroughs. Still, both of them accepted that the thread linking the victims appeared to involve a product under development, probably a computer chip, that had been handled by each of the three local subsidiaries.

"My brain is fogging up." Sagging in her chair, Nora rubbed her eyes and immediately realized she'd smeared her makeup. Well, Sam had seen her with smoke and dirt all over her face, so what difference did it make? "I'm hoping Ramon Nunez can help us tie them together."

"I think we should take a break and then push on." Despite lines of weariness on his face, Sam reached for the preliminary data from the search of Carl Garcola's airplane. "How about some coffee?"

"Not at this hour." When a case required her to stay up all night, Nora drank cup after cup. She'd learned to refrain on other occasions. "Hey, I'm aware of the urgency here, but we've got to pace ourselves."

"We're missing something. I don't intend to go on missing it until it's too late. When's the last time the guard at the hospital checked in?"

"Fifteen minutes ago," Nora reminded him. Carl's condition hadn't changed. "Usually I'm the one who drives everybody crazy by pushing too hard. How come you're so wound up?"

Sam stretched his neck. "I keep thinking I should have considered that the Trigger might take another crack at Carl. Instead, I had to stand there and watch that bomb go off. It's just plain luck that Mrs. Garcola escaped."

"I had the same thoughts but they're not tormenting me. What's this all about?" Dealing with death and destruction put stress on an officer, regardless of how tough-minded he or she was. Nora considered it essential to release tension, and talking was the best way to do that. Well, second best, after making love, but that didn't apply here.

"It's not about anything."

She checked her watch. Nine o'clock. "We've been racing around since early this morning, and we're going to do it again tomorrow. If you're beating yourself up, you need to get it out in the open or it'll eat you alive."

"What're you, my shrink?" Sam snapped.

"I'm your partner." She'd accepted that fact, like it or not. It was time he did, too.

He scrutinized her for a long moment. Deciding whether to trust her? Nora wondered.

"I'll make you a deal," Sam said at last.

"What?"

"You get the kink out of my neck and I'll tell you what's bugging me."

She considered asking whether he would have made a similar suggestion had his partner been a man. On the other hand, she didn't suppose a female partner would have sheltered her during a bomb blast, either. In law enforcement, she'd come to realize that the sexes complemented each other. So why quibble about a little neck rub?

"Okay. But I can't do it while you're sitting on the couch with your back to the wall." She yielded her place in the chair. When he shifted over, she stood behind him and rested her hands lightly on his shoulders.

He hadn't been kidding about the crick, she discovered. A cord of tension ran down his neck, connecting with rock-solid muscles.

Gently, she traced it with her thumb, then pressed harder. Sam closed his eyes and a sigh breezed out of him. Nora worked her way along his back, kneading the tightness until she felt him relax.

He hadn't started talking, though. "Well?" she demanded.

"It's personal," he said.

"You want a massage or not?" She stopped working.

"I just don't see what my personal background has to do with this case," he quibbled.

"Let me be the judge." The soft edges of his hair brushed her hands and, standing so close, Nora tingled with the man's heat.

"Okay."

Taking his assent at face value, she resumed rubbing. Probing the shoulder blades, she waited for him to speak again.

Finally he complied. "You may have heard my father was a firefighter," he began.

"Ben Prophet. His photo's up at the Bar and Grill." She'd heard that he died in a fire.

Sam tilted his head back. The contact felt more intimate than she'd expected, as if his emotions flowed through her.

"To me, he seemed like a force of nature," Sam told her. "Even when I joined the department and understood the risks involved, it never occurred to me he could get killed."

"I know what you mean." She never worried about her father or brothers despite the dangers posed by explosives. It must be a defense mechanism.

"Dad had just gotten off a regular shift." Sam's voice roughened. "On the way home, he spotted a fire in a vacant building and called it in."

Her hands dug into the strained shoulders, then worked upward to the neck. The scent of him enveloped her.

"I arrived with the first unit. Dad called on my cell phone. He said he'd gone inside to look for a homeless woman but she must have escaped." Sam gazed into the distance as if watching a movie roll. "I looked up from the fire truck and there he stood in a third-floor window, waving at me. He went inside to check one more time. A minute later, the roof collapsed."

In Nora's imagination, the scene engulfed her: the harsh smell of smoke, the demonic crackle of fire leaping inside the building, the hustle of firefighters dragging hoses into position. During her police career, she'd assisted with crowd control at several fires and found them both fascinating and repellant.

Flames devoured whatever they encountered, indifferent to pain, driven by an insatiable need for fuel. Once they started, there was no reasoning with them, no possibility of negotiation.

"I replayed the scene in my mind for months," Sam said. "Whenever I'm under stress, it returns. I keep trying to figure out what I could have done differently, how I could have changed the ending, as if somehow I could bring him back."

Nora didn't waste her breath trying to reassure Sam that it hadn't been his fault. Every public safety officer knew that failure came with the territory. That didn't make you impervious to it.

Brushes with death were always traumatic. She remembered the burns she'd suffered that summer during college when she'd helped her father and brothers. "I once had a close encounter with an overeager blasting cap. It made me afraid to take risks for quite a while."

"I'm not afraid to take risks," Sam said. "Is that what you think?"

"I was talking about myself." Gripping his shoulders, she gave him a shake. "You know what? You're stubborn."

"Hey! You're supposed to be getting the kink out, not putting one in!" To her relief, he sounded amused.

"How can I cure you when you're one big pain in the neck?" she joked.

"Oh, yeah?" He whipped out of the chair. She hadn't expected him to move so fast. "Think you can give me a hard time, do you?" He grinned as he advanced on her. "Ever learn how to wrestle?"

"I've got two brothers. You bet I did." She could take down a guy his size, no sweat. "You're not so tough."

One problem: Sam knew the same tricks she did. When Nora tried to knock his leg out from under him, he flipped her around, barely catching her in time to prevent a collision with an end table.

"I guess I should have cleared the floor before we started," he murmured, clasping her in front of him. His breath tickled her cheek and she felt his chest rise and fall. He was breathing a lot harder than she would have expected from such a brief exertion.

But then, so was she.

CHAPTER EIGHT

"BEST TWO OUT OF THREE," Nora said.

His chuckle rumbled through her. "You sure are feisty."

"Spare me!" She hated that word. "Next you'll tell me I'm spunky."

"You're spunky."

"Those are fighting words!"

"It was only one word."

To cut short the argument, she stomped on his foot. Since she'd discarded her shoes, it had little effect except to inspire him to tickle her. Even while trying to wriggle free, Nora found herself appreciating the gentle power in his hands.

"Give up?" Sam asked.

"Not in this lifetime." She paused, weighing whether to throw him flat. Before she reached a decision, Sam grasped her waist and drew her against him.

"Okay, you win," he murmured, and kissed her.

When his lips touched hers, silver sensations coursed through Nora's blood. When his tongue explored the edges of her teeth, she melted into him as she'd wanted to do all evening.

Everything about him tantalized her, from the stubbly skin of his jaw to the hardness brushing her below. With a thrill, she recognized that she had the power to arouse this difficult man, and that she wanted to.

Sam eased her onto the upholstered arm of the chair, his body fitting between her thighs and his arms surrounding her.

Nora traced her mouth across his cheek and neck. Pleasure shimmered through her as Sam groaned.

She kissed his throat and, unworking the buttons on his shirt, moved down to his chest. He slid his hands beneath her top, lifted her bra and cupped her breasts. With a gasp, Nora let him take her nipples between his lips.

His ragged breathing matched her own as he fumbled with the snap on her jeans. She wanted him inside her more than she had ever wanted anything.

Wait a minute. What were they doing?

No matter how powerful the physical chemistry, they didn't belong together. And, perhaps even more importantly, they might not be able to function as a team if they went any further.

"Sam," she whispered.

"Yes?" He spoke distractedly, in the middle of unfastening his belt.

"Sam!" She pushed lightly on his chest. "No."

Dazed, he stopped and stared at her.

What a picture they must make, Nora thought, with her top half off and his shirt wide open, on the verge of doing something irrevocable. "We have to stop."

"Why?" He shifted, bringing his hardened length into contact with her heated core.

She nearly changed her mind right then. Her body pulsed with longing to take him inside her and drive him wild, to twist beneath him and feel him plunge in and out of her as they both lost control. She held herself motionless by an effort of will.

Reluctantly, Sam drew away. "Why do we have to stop?"

He looked great, standing there bare-chested, belt undone, jeans bulging. Why couldn't two people simply take what they wanted without worrying about the consequences? Nora wondered.

She knew the answer. *Because those consequences will make you so miserable, it won't be worth it.*

She didn't hurry to cover herself. What would be the use? "You know why, Sam. It would change everything."

"I told you I'm not afraid of risks. I didn't think you were either." He wasn't issuing a challenge, simply stating a fact.

"Are you telling me you honestly think it's a good idea for us to jump in the sack when we have to show up tomorrow and face each other at work?" Nora demanded.

Sam finger-combed his hair while considering her remark. "Who has time to think that clearly? I'd say we set a new world's record for going from point A to way past point B."

"It was fun while it lasted," Nora admitted.

His mouth worked on a smile and didn't quite make it. "You're a cool customer. It's taking me longer to catch my breath. But then, I should have expected...no, forget I said that."

Beginning to get annoyed, she shifted her clothes into place. "What were you going to say? You should have expected what?"

"Cops and firefighters like to gossip. You've got a reputation as a flirt, you know." He pulled on his shirt.

Anger brought Nora's temperature to a quick simmer. "Wait a minute. Are you claiming I led you on?"

"No," Sam conceded.

"Then are you saying I stopped you because I'm toying with your affections?" she asked sarcastically.

"Certainly not."

"Then what?" Without waiting for an answer, she added, "And for your information, I'm not in the habit of ripping a guy's clothes off and then stopping short."

"I must be pretty special to qualify for that treatment, huh?"

She debated whether to slap him and decided against it. Their first wrestling match had created more than enough trouble already. "Yeah, you inspire me to new heights."

"To return to my original point, if I can remember it..." Sam looked around the floor for his shoes. "I'm not in the habit of assaulting my dinner guests. Obviously, there's something going on between us. I don't understand why you're so quick to deny it."

"Exactly where do you think this would lead?" Nora demanded.

"To bed, obviously."

"And then?"

"Who knows? And you're the one calling me a control freak!"

For an insane instant, she toyed with the idea. A casual affair—well, it wouldn't be all that casual, given their personalities—and then they'd part company. Wasn't that what she wanted from a guy? Come to think of it, commitment-phobic Sam ought to be perfect for a woman who hated to be tied down.

At last Nora identified the problem. An affair with her partner would mean the worst of both worlds. He'd try to control her, because it was in his nature. On the other hand, if they ever worked things out and she actually opened her heart to him, he'd stomp on it.

"You don't really want this any more than I do," she said.

"On what level?" Sam asked, maddeningly.

"On the level of anything more than sheer animal physicality."

"There's a lot to be said for sheer animal physicality." He retrieved a shoe from beneath the couch. It turned out to be hers.

"Is this the real Sam Prophet speaking?"

"Hold on." He went into the bathroom. When he came out, she could see that he'd splashed cold water on his face, dampening the edges of his hair. "What were we talking about?"

"Casual sex," Nora reminded him. "You were in favor of it."

"That must have been my libido talking." He located another shoe beneath the coffee table and tossed it to her.

"This is yours." She pitched it back.

"You see how mixed up I am?"

Nora gave up attempting to argue with him. "We're both too tired to think clearly."

"Roger on that."

This whole situation was preposterous, she reflected as she finished dressing. If anyone had suggested when she woke up this morning that she'd wind up nearly making love with Sam Prophet tonight, she'd have laughed until she fell on the floor. Now she might simply fall on the floor from exhaustion.

"Shall we call it even?" he asked.

"Let's forget it ever happened." Nora picked up her purse and briefcase.

When she turned, she glimpsed something—could that be regret?—on his face. It vanished so quickly, she couldn't be certain.

"Thanks for dinner. I bow to your cooking skills." Without waiting for a response, Nora let herself out. In the cool night air, she hurried to her car.

She didn't know what to make of Sam Prophet. He didn't match her old ideas about him, yet Elaine's tale had made her wary. Also, she could see for herself that while their personalities might make for an exciting combustion, it would be like any blowup: it would generate lots of heat and fire, end quickly and leave widespread devastation.

Exactly what she didn't need. And neither, she had a feeling, did he.

AFTER NORA LEFT, Sam went into the kitchen and made himself a cup of coffee. With the so-called Avenger cases fresh in his mind, he wanted to review his Trigger files to see if any new ideas surfaced.

Instead of concentrating, his tangled brain kept drifting back to Nora. His body burned with a longing to complete what they'd started.

She'd been right, though, much as it had pained him to stop

cold turkey. He'd seen couples work together after a relationship went sour, sinking into pettiness and sniping until one of
them transferred or resigned. It embarrassed him to realize
that, for a change, Nora was the one who'd kept a cool head,
but thank goodness she had.

When the phone rang, Sam almost welcomed the interrup-
tion to his musings, even though evening calls often signaled
an emergency. Hearing his sister Mary's voice happily put that
prospect to rest.

"I'm calling to invite you to a party Friday night," she said.
"Mom and I are throwing a barbecue to celebrate the end of
school." Mary lived with their mother about half a mile from
Sam's place.

"Sounds like fun if I don't have to work. With this case,
you never know." Missing family gatherings formed an un-
avoidable part of being an arson investigator.

"I understand," she responded. "But you've got to take a
break sometime. Bring your new partner if you want to."

Despite the casual phrasing, he knew Mary had made the
suggestion deliberately. "We're not an item, if that's what
you mean." Of course, if Nora hadn't insisted they stop when
they did, that might not be true, Sam reflected.

"Are you sure?"

"What's that supposed to mean? I ought to know whether
I'm dating someone or not!"

"Keep your shirt on." She gave a knowing humph! that
made Sam wish he hadn't flared at her. His sister had a talent
for reading him. "She's cute and it's fun to watch you two joke
around."

"You mean it's amusing to watch us lacerate each other?"
Sam grumped.

"Listen, bro, I've watched you with plenty of women over
the years," Mary said. "Most of them make doe eyes at you,
like you're the big strong male and they can't get enough of

you. Which I don't blame them for, because even if you are my brother, I have to admit you're a hunk."

"Thanks, I think," he said more mildly. He didn't mean to get snarly with his sister, who'd always been one of his favorite people.

"But that kind of woman bores you," she went on. "Half the time, you look like you're ready to fall asleep. If the way you two interacted today is any indication, Nora makes you roar like a grizzly. At least when you're with her, I know you're not hibernating."

"I can't tell you how much I appreciate this in-depth analysis of my love life," Sam muttered.

"So bring her along Friday," Mary said. "As an incentive, I should warn you that Mom's invited several single mothers from the neighborhood."

Angela Prophet, also a teacher at the same elementary school as Mary, hosted a homework club in her garage. Last week when Sam had gone over to fix her garbage disposal, she'd described a couple of the divorced moms with an enthusiasm that could only mean she had matchmaking in mind. If he didn't bring Nora along for self-defense, he'd spend the evening deluged by prospective girlfriends, courtesy of his mother.

"You made your point," he said. "If I can spare the time, I'll come by and give Nora the option of joining me."

"You'll 'give her the option'? With that kind of suave attitude, it's amazing you're not married ten times over," his sister kidded. "Seriously, Sam, don't write her off until you give her a chance. I think there's something there."

"You bet there's something there," he said. "Unfortunately, it's the kind of something that frequently leads to homicide."

"You're really on her case!" Mary hooted.

"Believe me, I know what I'm talking about." So did every frustrated fiber of his manhood.

"Methinks the gentleman doth protest too much." Before he could object, she added, "We're starting at six, but you can come later if necessary. Bring chips and dip or just bring yourself. Bye." The phone clicked in his ear.

Sam wished he hadn't taken Nora to the school with him that morning. It hadn't occurred to him that his sister would read a budding romance into an assigned partnership.

The fact that this evening had proved her right did nothing to soften his mood.

WALKING THROUGH the firehouse on Thursday morning, Nora nodded to some of the men hanging around the TV room. Unlike at a police department, where most officers spent only a short time at the beginning and end of their shifts, firefighters sometimes killed hours waiting for a call.

Of course, they spent a lot of those hours training and cleaning their equipment. The whole place shone.

A fire station became a kind of home as well as a workplace. As Sam had mentioned, the firefighters cooked meals here. They also slept in the bunkrooms and bulked up in the workout room.

As a result, the place sure smelled different from a cop shop. One minute she caught a whiff of cooking scents, the next the sour odor of sweat. Nora tried not to wrinkle her nose, aware that if she did, the firefighters—some of them female—would joke later about her delicate sensibilities.

They wouldn't be laughing the next time she drilled them on how to handle a bomb blast, though, especially when she set off real explosives. Her efforts had been rewarded at the hospital yesterday, not that Nora took more than a small share of credit for the smoothness of the operation. Her reward came from knowing that, aside from minor cuts and bruises, no one had been injured, although this morning's report listed widespread damage to vehicles and one section of the building.

Sam's office, next to the fire chief's, formed a sharp contrast to her cluttered workplace. Neatly labeled in and out baskets and a file holder left a large clear area on the desk. His bookshelves and file cabinets had a similarly tidy appearance.

"Any luck reaching Nunez?" she asked from the doorway. When they'd conferred by phone, Sam had said he planned to contact the Esmee Engines president first thing.

Sam drank her in with slow deliberation. She'd believed herself armored against his appeal, but a tiny skip of her heart gave the lie to that idea. "According to his secretary, he's in conference. I left a message."

"You think he changed his mind about talking to us?" She'd seen it happen many times. People started out wanting to help until they began worrying about bad publicity or a backlash from their employer. As if anything were more important than catching a serial killer!

"Let's hope not," he said.

Although an empty chair beckoned, she remained standing. "We've got two cases that concern Finder Electronics," Nora said. "If Wonderworld has clamped down on information, they might give us the cold shoulder there too, but it's worth a try."

With a nod, Sam got to his feet. "Let's go." Neither of them suggested giving their subjects advance warning.

They also didn't need to confer before taking Sam's sedan. Nora had to admit it was the more practical of their vehicles. They had plenty of room for their files and didn't bump into each other at every curve.

No repeats of last evening, Nora vowed. From now on, they'd keep things strictly business.

She'd awakened during the night in the throes of a passionate dream. Fleeting images had reminded her how delicious it had felt to slip her arms around Sam and explore the hard eagerness of his body. She'd had to switch on the light and read for half an hour before she managed to fall asleep again.

Located about a mile from Esmee Engines, Finder Electronics occupied a tan freestanding building with a blue tile roof. "It used to be a discount furniture outlet," Sam informed her as they parked. "My parents bought a couch here once."

"At least the place has a little personality." She'd been expecting another bland white building like Esmee.

"I kind of liked that couch. Too bad the place went out of business."

As at Esmee, they required clearance from a guard, who made a phone call and instructed them to wait in the foyer. Minutes ticked by, bringing a trickle of employees arriving for work. Since the hour had passed nine, Nora gathered that the company took a casual approach to scheduling.

She had begun to wonder if they were being stonewalled when a short man with thick round glasses hurried in from the parking lot. She immediately noted that, because of his height, he couldn't be the man who'd bumped Fran.

"I'm Rick Tennant, president of Finder." He shook hands with them both. "Sorry for the delay. I was expecting that you might drop by but I didn't know you were coming this morning."

"Sorry for the inconvenience," Sam said. "We don't always know our schedule in advance."

"No problem."

After traversing a series of gray-carpeted hallways, they settled into his ample office. Nora sketched Carl Garcola's situation quickly, aware that Rick probably had already been briefed by Nunez or someone from Wonderworld headquarters.

Sam pointed out that Finder had lost computer chips in a warehouse fire last August, followed by the death of product designer Julius Straus when his cell phone exploded in his car two months later. "We believe these incidents may be connected to the murders and attempted murders of employees at Esmee and Speedman as well. We need your help to find the key."

"I'm not sure what I can add." Tennant folded his hands on the desk. "It's certainly alarming if someone is targeting us."

"Can you think of anyone who might hold a grudge against Finder Electronics or its parent company?" Nora asked.

"People get mad about all sorts of things." Rick blinked owlishly behind his glasses. "For instance, I'm sure you know about the environmental fringe groups that go off the deep end over anything technological, like the Unabomber."

"This doesn't strike us as the work of an environmental extremist," Nora said. "This bomber appears to be picking very specific targets."

"We don't believe he's finished, either," Sam put in.

Rick wiggled in his seat. He didn't offer any more of his bland generalities, Nora noted.

She pressed the point home. "We could see more victims. Judging by his willingness to endanger a large number of lives at the hospital yesterday, an escalation in the scope of the attacks is possible as well. Are you aware that two pounds of a plastic explosive like Semtex can destroy a small building? The attacker could hide that much inside a cassette recorder."

"Or that phone right there." Picking up on her remark, Sam indicated a device on the president's desk.

Rick cleared his throat. "I don't suppose—I mean, he couldn't have rigged *my* phone, could he?"

"He's darn clever," Sam said. "If he really wants to, he can get to almost anyone."

The company president had grown progressively more red-faced as they piled on the warnings. Had the subject not been so serious, Nora would have found it difficult keeping a straight face.

Rick pursed his lips. Finally he said, "We're not supposed to discuss internal company affairs, even with the police."

"Are you willing to die for your company?" Sam's level tone intensified the chilling effect of his words.

The president raised his hands in a gesture of surrender. "I don't know what good it will do, but I'll tell you what I know."

Nora took out her tape recorder. "This is for our records."

Rick stared at the mechanism. "You're sure he hasn't tampered with that?"

"Try not to get paranoid," she advised, although she and Sam had just done their best to make him feel that way.

Slowly, the man began to talk. Julius Straus, he explained, had designed a computer chip, code-named the Chiseler, which improved the fuel efficiency of internal combustion engines by twenty-five percent. He'd received a large bonus.

"That sounds like a valuable discovery," Sam remarked.

"If it had worked properly, it would have been worth hundreds of millions, maybe more." Rick sighed. "Wonderworld kept the whole thing under wraps while it underwent testing. Naturally, we didn't want to be accused of manipulating our stock value until we knew what we had."

"You said *if* it had worked?" Sam queried.

"The thing had some unstable properties. I can't go into detail because it's a trade secret."

"You think Julius Straus became a target because of this?" Nora asked. "Why?"

"Our lawyers will kill me for mentioning this." Rick only hesitated for a moment, however. "A man named Freddie Wayland sued us after word leaked out that we'd begun manufacturing prototypes of the Chiseler."

Wayland, an amateur inventor, claimed to be the real designer of the chip, the president explained. His legal suit, which he'd filed by himself without a lawyer, claimed that he'd discussed his brilliant idea in a chat room on the Internet, where Julius must have learned about it.

"It's nonsense," the president insisted. "The man hadn't patented his device and the one he showed us lacked the sophistication of what Julius came up with. I doubt there's any connection."

"What happened to the lawsuit?" Sam asked.

"The judge dismissed it." Rick shook his head. "The guy didn't have a chance against our lawyers. He got so mad I thought he was going to have a stroke."

"You were there?" Nora hadn't expected this.

"Sure. I'm the company president, after all. Freddie practically pushed Julius into a wall outside the courtroom. He claimed people always steal from geniuses, but nobody could keep him down."

"That sounds like a threat," Sam conceded.

"It didn't concern us at the time. Lots of people get mad, but they calm down as soon as they have a chance to think about it." Rick rubbed his fingers together. "I guess not in this case."

"Do you have a photo of Mr. Wayland?" Nora asked. "An address would help, too."

"I'm not sure I should.... Oh, the heck with it." Rick activated his intercom. After a brief conversation and a pause, his secretary entered with a file. Flipping through it, the president extracted a slightly blurred shot of a chubby, thirtyish man.

Nora guessed it had been taken by a private detective, perhaps trying to dig up dirt on the inventor for the company. That didn't say much for Finder's sense of fair play.

With no one else in the photo, she couldn't judge the man's height. One detail jumped out, however.

Jammed atop Freddie Wayland's head, a dark-blue baseball cap sported the black-and-white emblem of a skunk, exactly as Fran Garcola had described it.

CHAPTER NINE

IT DIDN'T SURPRISE Sam when they learned, later on Thursday, that Freddie Wayland no longer resided at his last known address, an apartment in a large complex. A flaky inventor who discussed his work in chat rooms and filed his own lawsuit probably had to move around a lot to avoid bill collectors.

The manager consulted his records to refresh his memory. "He moved out about a year ago. His neighbors kept complaining about strange noises and smells from his place, so it came as a relief. I don't know where he went."

"Can you describe him?" Sam asked, thinking of Fran's description. "Height, approximate weight, that kind of thing?"

"Tall and heavyset. According to my records, he's in his midthirties." The manager didn't know whether Freddie had any friends or family in the area. He didn't have the man's license plate number, either.

"He's the right size," Nora remarked as she slid into the car. "From the sketch, though, I figured the Trigger to be in his forties."

"Maybe he's got acne scars that make him look older." In Sam's experience, descriptions of a person often varied widely. Studies had repeatedly demonstrated the unreliability of eyewitnesses.

Nora rubbed one eye with a fingertip. She didn't look as if she'd had an easier time sleeping last night than he had.

Weary or not, they both put in a full day. Since talking to

the Finder president that morning, they'd pursued other leads and tried again, in vain, to reach Nunez at Esmee Engines.

They also learned that Carl Garcola appeared to be slipping deeper into a coma. Perhaps the Trigger knew that as well, because he'd refrained from making any further attempts on the victim's life.

A sense of urgency refused to let Sam rest. "While we're chasing shadows, the Trigger could be moving on to his next target. We need to try to figure out what he'll do next."

"If Freddie's the Trigger, a logical target would be Rick Tennant," Nora observed. "I hope he didn't disregard our warning the minute we walked out the door." They'd advised the executive to take precautions after making sure he understood the Trigger's methods.

"Let's hope our guy doesn't decide to change his operating method," Sam said. "He must know we're wise to him." Although killers usually stuck with the same MO, the Avenger hadn't, so why should the Trigger?

When Nora spoke again, Sam could tell she'd been thinking along different lines. "You know, Tennant's so obvious, I keep wondering why Freddie didn't go after him right away," she said. "And why pick people from Esmee and Speedman? They didn't steal his chip."

Although Sam had no answer, another idea came to him. "Since he's an inventor, he must advertise his business somewhere. Where's the best place to find buyers and investors?"

"The Internet," she said.

"Exactly."

When they reached the fire station and accessed the computer, they found that, indeed, Freddie maintained a web site. In gee-whiz prose marked by misspellings and poorly lit photographs, he offered the manufacturing rights to half a dozen devices. At the bottom, the home page provided an e-mail address and a P.O. box.

"Bingo," Nora said. A P.O. box meant his street address would be registered with the post office.

"It's not sexy, but it's a start." Sam noted her startled look at his choice of words. Sexy certainly described Nora right now, with her pupils widened and her lips parted.

They regarded each other for a long moment. "I think we're getting punch-drunk from exhaustion," she said at last.

"I don't feel exhausted. Do you?"

"I feel tired and stimulated at the same time," she admitted. "What do you suggest we do about it?"

"Some people recommend cold showers." Sam refused to bring up the other alternative: consummating their lust. Not only did it not suit either of them, he also had the feeling that once wouldn't be nearly enough.

"I've got a better cure," she said. "Getting Freddie's address."

An alarm shrilled through the fire station. Sam's pulse speeded instinctively. "We'd better find out what it is."

It turned out to be a fire at Finder Electronics.

As they headed for the door, Sam suspected they both entertained the same dismal notion: their warnings to Rick Tennant had been too little, too late.

BLACK SMOKE POURED from the lobby, nearly obscuring the blue roof. The parking lot, which that morning had dozed half-empty in the sunshine, swarmed with fire trucks and police cruisers. Behind a police line, employees waited uncertainly.

To Nora's relief, Rick Tennant stood to one side talking with the fire department's Captain Joe Ripani. Whatever had happened, the company president had escaped without serious harm.

"There they are." The president pointed as Sam and Nora approached. "Those are the people who came to see me this morning."

Joe greeted them. "This must be about the Trigger case. How's it coming?"

"We've got one suspect but he's shaky." Sam's eyes narrowed against the smoke.

"What happened?" Nora asked Rick.

"According to the guard, a man walked into the lobby about half an hour ago wearing something like a space suit and demanded to speak to me." Rick spoke so fast the words tripped over each other. "Since he looked like a nut case and didn't have an appointment, the guard tried to escort him out. He set off some kind of device."

"What did it look like?" Sam asked.

"I don't know. I didn't see it!" He spoke in a high-pitched tone. "The next thing you know, the place filled with smoke. An alarm went off and we evacuated. Is this the bomber? Was he trying to kill me?"

"I doubt it," Nora assured him. "Did you hear an explosion?"

"No, I don't think so. Maybe I missed it."

"I doubt you'd have missed it. Any idea where the intruder is now?" Sam raked the crowd with his gaze. Nora, too, was looking for a man matching the Trigger's description.

"Still inside, I suppose," Rick answered. "I went out the back way. I don't know where he is."

Flint Mauro, the assistant police chief, approached. "We've deployed the SWAT team, and we're trying to make contact with the guy holed up in the lobby, assuming he hasn't managed to sneak out. Are all your employees accounted for?"

"I'm not sure," Rick admitted. "I'll ask around. Maybe one of my managers did a head count." He went off to join a small knot of people in business suits.

The president had been quick to save his own hide without, apparently, a thought for his workers, Nora reflected in disgust. She wondered if the same self-serving philosophy permeated the rest of the company. Ramon Nunez at Esmee hadn't given that impression, but he hadn't yet kept his promise to provide further information, either.

Rick had mentioned that Julius's chip was unstable, Nora recalled, and wondered whether there'd been any safety implications. With a fortune at stake, to what lengths had Wonderworld been willing to go to try to make it work? And had anyone been hurt as a result?

"He's coming out!" an officer shouted.

The onlookers quieted. Rick Tennant ducked behind a fire truck, while the other emergency workers also took cover. Nora and Sam retreated to a spot that still afforded good visibility.

From the entryway waddled one of the strangest sights Nora had ever seen. The man's getup resembled an old-fashioned diving suit altered so it bristled with wires. With one arm, he swung a flexible tube over his head lasso-style, sending a small saucer-shaped object whistling around in a circle.

"What on earth is he doing?" Flint muttered.

"Is that thing going to blow?" Joe asked Nora.

She wished she knew. She'd never seen a bomb like it. "This is a darn weird way to commit suicide, if that's what he's planning," she pointed out. "Frankly, I'm as confused as you are."

The bizarre-looking figure let the saucer clunk to the ground. In a fit of rage, he leaped forward and jumped on it repeatedly until pieces spewed across the parking lot.

"I guess it's not going to blow up," Sam drawled.

Flint stepped cautiously into the man's view. "Courage Bay police! Put your hands up!"

An incomprehensible mumble issued from inside the suit. The man wrestled with his helmet and at last wrenched it off.

The bespectacled face that emerged wore an expression of frustration mixed with alarm. Atop his head, flattened by the helmet, lay a baseball cap with a skunk logo.

If Nora had had any doubts about the man's identity, they vanished. "Freddie Wayland," she said aloud.

"Up close and personal," her partner added for good measure.

Freddie gaped at all the emergency vehicles and the police with their weapons drawn. "Oh, for Pete's sake! It didn't work," he announced. "You might as well all go home."

"Hands in the air!" Flint trained his gun on the man isolated in an expanse of blacktop.

The object of everyone's attention blinked as the officer's meaning sank in. Slowly, as if finally recognizing the gravity of the situation, he raised his hands and let the helmet plunk to the pavement.

The SWAT team raced in and handcuffed the suspect. Behind them, the smoke pouring from the lobby began to dissipate.

"This is ridiculous!" Freddie stared wild-eyed as Sam and Nora approached. "You're making such a fuss."

Rick Tennant held back, probably still afraid for his safety. One of the managers came close enough to listen.

"What's going on?" Nora asked Freddie.

"I'm an inventor." He seemed to think that explained everything. When they continued regarding him dubiously, he said, "I set off a smoke bomb to prove my point. My Smoking-Gone was supposed to clear it up in no time."

"Your smoking gun?" Flint said.

"No!" Freddie cried. "My Smoking-Gone!"

Nora remembered seeing the device on the web site. According to the ad, when activated, it cleared air rapidly of something called large particulates—dust and grime.

"It worked perfectly in my storage unit," the inventor insisted. "You whirl it around and it eats the smoke. I figured Finder Electronics would want to license the rights to it. I mean, they owe me a break."

The onlookers stared as if they'd captured a Martian.

"That's why I released the smoke bomb. So I could prove how it operates." Freddie tried to gesture, but the handcuffs prevented it.

"Tell me about your hat," Nora said.

"What?" He shifted uncomfortably. "Would someone please take these cuffs off me? I explained what I'm doing."

"I'm afraid we're going to have to take you down to the station," Flint said. "Mr. Wayland, there are laws against setting off smoke bombs in occupied buildings."

"You're not going to arrest me, are you?" The words came out in a whine.

Seeing Flint about to advise the man of his rights, Nora held up one hand. She didn't intend to ask an incriminating question, only to find out information that might lead them to someone else. "This is important. Freddie, tell us about the hat. Where did you get it and what's the significance of the logo?"

"I bought it at a gun show," he said.

"What about the logo?" Sam growled. "What does it mean?"

"I don't know," came the perplexed response. "I think some Western-style clothing manufacturer makes them. It's kind of cute, don't you think?"

Nobody answered.

"Are these only sold at gun shows?" Nora asked.

"I've seen them on the Web," Freddie said. "Lots of people sell them."

Great. Another dead end, Nora thought, not exactly surprised. It would be uncharacteristically careless of the Trigger to have worn an identifying insignia when he swapped Fran's cell phone.

Still, although this inept inventor looked less and less likely to be their culprit with every word that issued from his mouth, she and Sam accompanied him to headquarters. At the station, they waited for a court-appointed attorney and participated in the interrogation.

By the time they finished several hours later, they'd crossed Freddie off their list. They'd also missed dinner. "You think there's any point in us reviewing our notes this evening?" Sam asked as the two of them emerged from the interview room.

"I think our most productive move would be to get some sleep," Nora returned.

"Sounds good to me."

A longing tugged at her to go home with this man to his beautifully kept house and let him cook for her. But she could pop a frozen meal in the microwave just fine by herself. Besides, he looked too tired to cook.

"See you tomorrow," Sam said. "We can review in the morning."

"You got it."

He strolled out of the police station, heading across the plaza toward his office. As Nora watched through the window, his rugged, loose-hipped stride put her in mind of a cowboy in the old West. He seemed at home in his own skin, and nice skin it was, too, she remembered wistfully.

"I'm glad to see you two getting along," Max said, stopping beside her.

"Don't count on it lasting, but for now we've established a truce," she told him. "Want an update?"

"I'd appreciate it."

Nora accompanied the chief to his office, where she filled him in on what they'd learned so far. "I wish I could tell you we've got a suspect, but we're still drawing a blank," she concluded.

"At least you're putting the pieces together," Max told her. "I knew you two would make a good team."

"Necessity is the mother of collaboration, I guess," she responded.

On her way out, she also briefed Adam Guthrie, the chief of detectives. Not until she was driving home did Nora recall what she'd been thinking in the parking lot at Finder Electronics. After observing Rick Tennant's callousness toward his employees, she'd wondered how far Wonderworld had been willing to go to try to make the chip work and whether it had harmed an employee further down the line.

Mentally, she made a note to follow up on that point to-morrow.

SAM AWOKE Friday morning convinced that, despite his reluc-tance, he had better take Nora to his sister's party tonight. Not for her company but for protection.

By now, Mary must have filled their mother's ears with the notion that the two of them suited each other. He needed to put the kibosh on that idea right now.

Mary might romanticize his and Nora's bickering, but given direct evidence, Angela would know better. Unlike her daughter, she'd see at once that the two of them were funda-mentally incompatible.

In addition, she'd told Sam once how lucky he was not to be the one waiting at home, worrying while his loved one risked her life at work. Once she recognized how much dan-ger Nora ran as an explosives expert, she'd do everything in her power to discourage Mary's speculation.

"I wouldn't give up my years with your father for anything, but believe me, it's not the kind of marriage I'd choose for my children," she'd once told him. "Your future wife has my sympathy, but at least you'll never have to live with that ter-rible anxiety."

"You mean you wouldn't want Mary to date a firefighter?" he'd asked.

"I'll encourage her to go out with a nice dentist," Angela had responded tartly. "At worst, he might get bite marks on his hand."

So it seemed safe enough—even advisable—to take Nora with him. They could use an evening's relaxation, if events didn't interfere, and he wouldn't mind socializing as long as he had his partner to discourage unwanted female attention.

He dropped by Nora's office and found her talking animat-edly on the phone. Looking around, Sam wondered how she could function amid such disorder, although he suspected she would answer that she knew exactly where to find everything. A lot of investigators worked this way. He didn't happen to be one of them.

No point in moving her stuff aside to clear a place to sit. Judging by her tone of voice, they'd be heading out soon.

When she hung up, she thumped the desk and grinned. Her spontaneous enthusiasm crackled through the air like an electric charge. "That weasel! I knew he was avoiding us!"

One person came immediately to mind. "Ramon Nunez?"

A nod set her dark hair bouncing. "When I called, he picked up the phone because his secretary hadn't come in yet. I demanded an explanation for why he's been refusing our calls, and he admitted Wonderworld didn't want him to talk to us."

"Is he going to?"

"You bet." She grabbed her purse. "I played up that smoke bomb over at Finder yesterday, which shows how easily a loony can gain access to one of their facilities. He sounded like he was having an anxiety attack. Let's hit the road before some honcho slams the lid shut again."

She didn't have to ask twice.

On the drive, they ran through their observations from yesterday. Nora brought up the possibility that the Chiseler might have injured someone during the testing process. Sam had to admit it made sense. If an engine malfunctioned at high speed, it could cause a collision or a fire, or both.

The guard at Esmee Engines admitted them immediately. This time, they didn't need directions to the president's office.

Dark circles shadowed Ramon Nunez's face, Sam noticed when they shook hands. "I'm sorry about stalling you guys yesterday. My bosses in Atlanta figured we should sit tight and this whole thing would blow over."

"Blow over?" Nora barely refrained from commenting on

his unfortunate choice of words. "Let me see. Somebody's made two attempts on Carl Garcola's life and he's lying in a coma. Lance Corker is dead and one of your trucks got blown sky high last December. That's not to mention what's happened to people from Finder and Speedman."

"I'd say the pace is accelerating," Sam added to goose the guy into cooperating. "Exponentially."

The president paled. Sam saw with satisfaction that, coming after the groundwork Nora had laid earlier, his words had achieved the desired impact.

"I found a few things. I hope they help." When Nunez retrieved his notes from a desk drawer, his hand trembled. "They could fire me for telling you this stuff."

"That sounds like Wonderworld, doesn't it?" Nora probed, apparently trying to encourage the president to open up. "They seem to care a lot less about what happens to their employees than what happens to their bottom line, don't they?"

"Businesses have to make a profit," Nunez responded. "But in a case like this...well, a lot of people have made bad decisions. Now they're paying for them. Or someone is."

Sam's instincts went on full alert. At last, they might be close to unraveling the Trigger's true motive. "What do you mean?"

To his dismay, the man backpedaled. "Nothing. I was just speculating."

"We understand that Finder developed a chip code-named the Chiseler that ramps up fuel efficiency," Nora said. "We know that, despite some problems, it won approval for further testing. Did that involve your company and Speedman?"

Nunez nodded. "Esmee Engines did the lab simulations."

"Who handled them?" Sam asked.

"Lance Corker."

Despite his sympathy for the victim, the name gave Sam a jolt of gratification. They were apparently heading in the right direction. "Have you seen the results of his tests?"

Nunez fiddled with his papers. "Yes, I read them yesterday. The Chiseler worked great at the equivalent of normal highway speeds. That means if you were to use it in your personal car commuting to work, you'd save twenty-five percent of your fuel. With gas prices periodically skyrocketing in California, you can imagine how much that would be worth."

"Okay, suppose I didn't put it in my personal car," Nora said. "Suppose I put it in a police cruiser and chased a suspect at a hundred miles per hour."

"There could be a problem." The man seemed to have a hard time getting the words out.

"What kind of problem?" Sam said.

"It might overheat and conk out. The sudden loss of thrust could cause a guidance anomaly." Before anyone requested clarification, Nunez volunteered, "At high speeds, if you lose power, you lose control."

"You'd crash," Sam summarized.

"Possibly."

"So it would work great in golf carts," Nora put in, "but that's not exactly a huge share of the automotive market."

"We're not irresponsible," Ramon said. "We didn't just throw the thing into production. Lance proposed that we develop a system to cool the chip when the engine heats up. We figured it merited further investigation."

"In the lab?" Nora asked.

"Well, sure, but we got inconclusive results," he admitted. "We couldn't be sure the cooling system would function under real-world conditions. Lance's supervisor recommended that we build a prototype, install it in one of our race cars and test it on a track."

Carl Garcola had been Lance's supervisor, Sam recalled with a chill. He could almost hear the pieces falling into place.

"What happened when they tested the chip on the track?" Nora demanded.

"I don't know," Nunez said. "Honest. All this went down a couple of years ago, before I arrived, so I don't personally recall it, and the records are either over at Speedman or at headquarters. One thing I can tell you is that we aren't manufacturing the Chiseler, so I assume it failed."

"And Wonderworld refuses to release any further information, I gather." Nora frowned. "We might be able to get a search warrant, but we'd have to know exactly what we were looking for and where it is."

"We need to talk to someone at the top." For all Sam knew, some midlevel executive might be responsible for trying to hush things up.

"Before you tangle with the hierarchy in Atlanta, I'd suggest you talk to Rose Chang, the president of Speedman," Ramon said. "Since she could be on this maniac's firing line just like me, she might want to cooperate."

"Do you mind if we mention that we talked to you?" Sam asked.

"I'd rather you didn't."

"We'll work around it," Nora promised.

Ramon wrote down Ms. Chang's name and phone number for them. "Good luck. I hope you catch this guy soon."

"One more thing," Nora said. "If you had to guess who the Trigger planned to go after next, who would it be?"

He didn't hesitate. "The president of Speedman."

"Then we'd better get hold of her fast." Sam stood up. This time when they shook hands, Nunez looked marginally less frightened, as if talking to them had removed a burden from his shoulders.

Outside, Sam dialed Ms. Chang's number. Her assistant, a woman with a voice strident enough to pound nails, informed them that her boss had left for the weekend and didn't wish to be disturbed. Trying to convey the urgency of the situation got him nowhere.

"We'll have to track her down some other way," Nora said. "I'm not comfortable waiting until Monday."

"Me either."

An afternoon spent tracing Ms. Chang revealed that she owned a cabin in the mountains, but none of her Courage Bay neighbors knew the address or her cell phone number. On the chance that she might check her home answering machine for messages, Nora left a detailed one explaining that her life could be in danger.

Six o'clock had slipped past, Sam noted when he checked his watch. He got up to stretch his legs. As long as he was getting the blood flowing, he collected the coffee cups and candy wrappers that had accumulated around Nora's office. "Listen, I have a favor to ask," he said.

"Oh?" She quirked one eyebrow. Maybe she lifted the other one, too, but a sweep of hair hid it from view.

He explained about his sister's party. "I'm sure they'll have plenty to eat, so it's a free meal. Plus you can help me kill these persistent rumors about you and me being an item." He couldn't bring himself to admit he wanted protection from overeager females. A guy didn't like to show weakness in front of his colleagues.

"Persistent as in, your sister likes me?" she teased.

"In spite of being divorced, she's a romantic at heart." It was kinder than saying that Mary must be suffering from delusions.

"Misguided, in this case."

"Precisely."

When Nora scrunched her nose, he thought she meant to refuse. Disappointment arrowed through Sam. Although they'd spent the entire day in each other's company, there'd been little time for joking. He would enjoy seeing Nora in a playful mood. In fact, if she didn't go, he wasn't sure he should bother.

Not that he wanted a date. Rather, he preferred a companion who wouldn't ask stupid questions about whether he handled safety inspections at the supermarket, which was the fire marshal's job. Or whether an arson investigator carried a gun, and then request to see it when he admitted he did.

"So you want me to come to a party with you in order to convince everyone we can't stand each other," Nora summed up.

"Basically."

"I don't see how any woman could resist an invitation like that," she said. "You're on."

She grinned. And just like that, Sam found himself looking forward to the party.

CHAPTER TEN

NORA HAD SPENT more than enough time poking along in Sam's sedan that week. She insisted on picking him up in her sports car, a condition he accepted with outward calm. At least he didn't mind letting her take the wheel, she thought appreciatively. Her ex-fiancé would never have agreed to ride in the passenger seat.

When she made the demand, however, she'd forgotten how Sam's hip and leg kept pressing against hers after he folded himself into the tight interior. The short spin to his mother's house proved a challenge to her self-control.

She wanted to run her hand up his thigh and hear his breath quicken. The more she reflected on what had happened between them Wednesday night, the more tempting it became to pull over in a secluded glen for a make-out session. Of course, just their luck, some cop would come along and embarrass the heck out of them, not to mention spreading the news all over the department.

Besides, she'd promised herself not to get that close to Sam again. So what if his heat enveloped her like liquid silk? Chalk it up to the enforced intimacy of working all day and half the night together, plus the minuscule size of her car.

Trying to put temptation behind her, Nora hit the gas, and in the process nearly shot by the turnoff to his mother's home. Sam, who'd been watching her with a trace of amusement, said, "Eucalyptus Lane, remember?"

Hoping the diminishing light didn't betray her flaming cheeks, Nora slammed her foot against the brake pedal and cornered onto the residential street. Only the seat belt kept Sam from landing in her lap, and even so, he made solid contact that fell just short of bruising.

"Sorry." Remembering that she had once endorsed the motto *Never apologize, never surrender,* Nora added, "The car needs to get the kinks out. It's been sitting around too much this week."

"It's not the only thing that has kinks." He flexed his leg muscles, a movement that pressed his knee against her stocking-clad thigh. "This seems to be a contact sports car."

"Do that again and I might wreak havoc on a few mailboxes," Nora warned.

"I hope you're paid up on your insurance." He didn't retreat. "Besides, I think you already took out a couple back at the corner."

"Not even close!" Nevertheless, she slowed down, because they'd run out of road.

The ranch-style house lay at the end of a cul-de-sac. Since cars already filled the curbside, he directed her to park in the curved driveway.

As Nora killed the engine, she caught a tantalizing aroma drifting from a breezeway set at a right angle to the house, connecting it to a freestanding garage. A trim middle-aged woman in a red apron looked up from flipping burgers on a grill and waved. Sam returned the gesture.

To Nora's surprise, a wave of homesickness filled her. She'd accepted Sam's invitation on a lark and because she had no other plans for tonight. Now she realized how much she missed family get-togethers.

When she'd moved to Courage Bay, she'd told herself she would make the drive down to see her family in L.A. at least once a month. In truth, she only made it down for major holidays and special events, and not always then if work intervened. Each time she saw her brother's kids, it amazed her how much they'd grown.

When they reached the breezeway, Sam gave his mother a big hug, dwarfing her, then turned to make introductions. "I guess you've heard about my new partner. Mom, this is Nora Keyes."

"Pleased to meet you, Mrs. Prophet." Nora extended her hand.

"Call me Angela." The warmth in the words and firm handshake made her guest feel at home.

"I really appreciate your including me," Nora responded. "I miss my own family."

"Oh? Don't they live around here?"

She explained about her background. As they chatted, Sam beamed at them both until he obviously realized what he was doing and rearranged his features into a more reserved expression.

Voices drifted through the breezeway from the rear yard, which lay out of sight around a corner. Suddenly a young boy about eight years old pelted into view. "Hey! Uncle Sam!" He flung himself forward and laughed in delight when Sam hoisted him into the air.

"How's my favorite nephew?" Sam demanded.

"I'm your only nephew!"

"Well, you're still my favorite." He lowered the boy to the ground. "Pete, come meet a lady who blows things up."

The boy regarded Nora dubiously. "He's kidding, right?"

"No. I'm a bomb squad specialist." She couldn't help noting how much the boy resembled Sam, especially the straight shoulders and thoughtful air, although Pete's hair was a lighter shade of blond and his green eyes resembled his mother's. "My family owns a company that blows up buildings. Legally, of course."

"Why do they do that?"

"Sometimes the owner wants to tear it down and build something else," she answered. "Or maybe the place has been damaged and they're afraid it might fall and hurt someone. We plant the explosives in just the right places and set them off in a special sequence so the walls fall inward. Boom! It's exciting."

"Can I watch sometime?" Pete asked.

"If you're ever in Los Angeles, I'll take you," she said. "But right now I only set off little practice bombs to help train firefighters and police officers. And I hunt down people who blow things up illegally."

"Like terrorists?" He sounded thrilled. "Are you on the trail of some right now?"

Nora caught Sam's eye. "We sure are."

"Pete, would you carry this plate of hamburgers to the back yard?" his grandmother asked.

"You bet. I'm starved!" Balancing the plate carefully, the boy retreated through the breezeway.

"I'm glad to see you like kids," Angela commented as she laid more patties on the grill.

Sam caught Nora's arm before she could respond. "If you don't mind, Mom, we're going to join the crowd, unless you'd like us to stay and help you?"

"No, I'm fine by myself." She began humming a melody that Nora recognized as an old show tune—"People Will Say We're in Love."

She hoped that wasn't meant as an observation about her and Sam. The fact that they no longer drew blood every time they interacted shouldn't give people the wrong idea.

"Pete's cute," Nora commented as they walked. Not having much experience around kids, she couldn't think of anything else to say except, "He kind of looks like you."

Sam didn't miss the implied compliment. "You think I'm cute?"

She didn't intend to admit anything of the kind. "Not when you're grumpy."

"Me?" he protested. "When am I ever grumpy?"

"Only in the mornings." She paused as if weighing the matter seriously. "And—let me see—the afternoons and evenings."

"I have an earnest manner, that's all." If he'd meant to say more, he held back as they rounded a corner into the rear yard.

On a deck rimmed with potted flowers, guests lined up to fill plates from a buffet table. Nearby, a group of children played ball in the grass and a couple of toddlers scrambled over a large shaggy dog. It lay placidly surveying the scene as if unaware of the munchkins assaulting its flanks.

"That's Carmichael," Sam said.

"I've never heard of a dog named Carmichael." Nora had grown up with two pooches named Tawny and Spot.

"My mother named him after a retired principal from the elementary school," he explained. "Apparently there's a resemblance."

She chuckled. "Is the real Mr. Carmichael aware of his namesake?"

"I doubt the subject ever came up."

Mary strolled over. "Hi! I'm glad you could make it." Sam gently removed his hand from Nora's arm as if he'd finally remembered that the point of coming tonight had been to convince his family they were nothing more than partners.

"I'm delighted to be here." Nora glanced at the guests helping themselves to food. "Are all these people teachers?"

"Quite a few. Plus some neighbors and other friends. Let me introduce you." She escorted Nora around, with Sam strolling beside them.

Nora caught curious glances from several young women and wondered if they'd attended in hopes of catching Sam's attention. Well, he was free to flirt if he wanted to.

But she hoped he'd enjoyed their playful conversation enough to want more of it. Letting off steam was easiest with other peace officers or with old friends who didn't require explanations about what she did or why she did it.

To her satisfaction, Sam stuck with her, although he and a couple of other men at their table spent most of the meal debating the merits of the Dodgers versus the Giants. Thanks to having grown up in a mostly male household, Nora had no trouble following the conversation. In fact, she frequently won the police department's informal betting pool.

Sam cleared her plate and brought dessert without being asked. He had staked a claim to her without acting possessive, Nora noticed, and wondered if he even realized what he was doing. She would have warned him off except that, after a hard week, she relished being waited on.

Nora didn't get a chance to speak to Mary again until later, when she went in the kitchen to help clean up. "This is a great party." She stored some condiments in the refrigerator door. "I'm having a wonderful time."

"So is my brother," Mary said with a knowing smile.

"I hope so. He's worked hard all week." Nora intended to do her best to keep the conversation impersonal.

"That's not what I meant." Beating around the bush obviously didn't suit Sam's sister.

Since they were alone, Nora answered frankly. "If you assume there's anything going on between us, there isn't."

"So you think." Her hostess fixed plastic wrap over a casserole dish.

Nora knew she ought to drop the subject, but she couldn't. "What does that mean?"

"I've watched Sam around a fair number of women over the years," his sister said. "He's affable and good-natured with them, but…"

"Sam? Affable and good-natured?"

"You don't see him that way?" Mary asked, distracted from her point.

"We fight all the time." Come to think of it, that was no longer entirely true, Nora had to admit. "At least, we did at first."

"Is that a bad thing? I mean, it shows he has strong feelings, doesn't it?" Mary filled the sink with sudsy hot water.

"Strong *negative* feelings," Nora said.

"Do you really think so?" Mary scrubbed potato salad remnants from a bowl. "I think my brother needs a strong woman."

"But she has to be the *right* strong woman. Someone compatible." Taking a dish towel, Nora dried the bowl as Mary immersed a glass baking dish into the soapy water. "More domestic than I am, for one thing."

"I'm not sure men put such a high priority on a woman's cooking and cleaning skills," her hostess said. "You know...well, maybe I shouldn't mention this—"

"What is it?"

"His gaze follows you. He always knows exactly where you are." She handed Nora the now clean baking dish for drying.

Nora didn't know whether to be flattered or perturbed that Mary had noticed so much. "I'm sure it doesn't mean anything."

"Maybe not. It's just that I'm close to my brother, and the two times I've seen you together, he seems different. I thought maybe you could shed some light on it."

"I'm afraid I know less than nothing about how Sam interacts with women." Impulsively, Nora seized on the chance to satisfy her curiosity. "Do you have any idea why he broke up with Elaine Warner? She happens to be a friend of mine."

"Mine, too." Mary considered before replying. "I'm sure he enjoyed her company, but I don't think he had any idea how serious she was getting. When it dawned on him, well, my brother doesn't have the world's smoothest social skills. I guess he figured he needed to make a break before things went any further."

The explanation made sense but didn't entirely explain what had gone wrong. "I'm different from Elaine," Nora said. "I back off from guys who try to move in on me because I don't want anyone running my life."

"Does that mean you prefer to stay single?" Mary worked her way through a set of glasses, handing each carefully to Nora.

"Not exactly." She'd always assumed that eventually she'd get married. "But I'm a risk-taker. I don't like being tied down or taking the safe way out."

"In what way?" came the response.

"I don't want some guy telling me I can't go scuba diving or rock climbing," Nora said. "I tried bungee jumping once, too. It was great, although my muscles hurt for a week afterward."

"That could be a problem for my brother, I mean, if you two were to get more involved," Mary said. "He's very protective of people he cares about. If he learns I'm dating someone, he manages to show up and look the guy over."

"Doesn't that make you feel smothered?"

"No, because I understand. He took it hard when Dad died. We all did, but it was worse for Sam because he kept thinking he should have saved Dad." Mary let the water out of the sink and dried her hands on a dish towel.

"I know. He told me."

"He talked about Dad? That's unusual." One task completed, she poured water into the coffeemaker. "Anyway, the department insisted on counseling, which helped, but he's always checking the house for safety problems. He paid for us to install an alarm system, too."

Would she feel cared for or stifled if Sam started coming around her apartment making repairs? Nora wondered. It might be fun for a while, but then she'd probably resent it.

"There's nothing wrong with taking care of your family," she said. "But I don't need anyone watching over me."

"Well, good luck. Unless I miss my guess, Sam may start playing knight in shining armor any day now." After measuring coffee grounds into the basket, Mary flipped the Brew switch.

"Relationships can develop fast when people work together practically day and night, but I know better than to read too much into it." Nora had seen it happen between other officers. "Even if he starts liking me, I wouldn't expect it to last beyond the end of this investigation."

"I suppose it's good that you have such a healthy perspective." Mary set out a stack of disposable cups. "You understand his work. Most women don't have a clue."

"Most men can't figure me out, either," Nora conceded.

"Do you think it puts them off? Your being a bomb specialist, I mean." Mary leaned against the counter. "It's not exactly what guys expect from a woman."

"Some of them start edging away as soon as I mention it," Nora said. "Others see it as a turn-on. But they always assume it's a passing phase, that I'd take a safer job if I were married and had kids."

"Wouldn't you?" Mary asked.

Nora shrugged. "Any guy who's interested in me has to take the whole package. If he can't handle what I do for a living, he's Mr. Wrong."

Her hostess didn't answer. As they walked outside, Nora wondered if Mary had decided she was the wrong woman for Sam, and was annoyed to discover it bothered her.

SAM FIGURED HE OUGHT to be disappointed. This evening had been a failure, at least in terms of his original goal: to convince his mother and sister that he and Nora had nothing in common.

He hadn't missed his mother's comment about Nora liking children. And for heaven's sake, did his sister have to corner her in the kitchen and give her the third degree? At least, that's what it had looked like to him through the window.

He'd expected everyone to understand that, as partners, they fell naturally into a kind of comradeship. Sure, there might be a few male-female sparks, but that didn't mean anything.

"What did you and Mary talk about for so long?" he asked afterward in the car.

She didn't beat around the bush. "You."

"Any aspect of my charming self in particular or just me in general?" He hoped his light tone hid the depth of his curiosity.

Nora took a corner so fast he had to hang onto the armrest. "She described you as very protective."

"That's true." What guy worth his salt didn't take care of the people who mattered to him? "What else?"

Nora kept her eyes trained on the road. A good thing, especially at these speeds. "She takes the fact that we argue as a good sign."

"A good sign for what?" Sam asked, although he already had a suspicion.

His partner sighed. "Your sister thinks you like me."

He decided to ignore the romantic implications, since that was what he'd expected his sister to look for. "I do like you. Most of the time we work well together, when you aren't jumping to conclusions or trying to rush things."

"I never rush things!" Reaching a stop sign, she tapped the brake just long enough to survey approaching traffic, and then shot forward.

"Or when you aren't running stop signs," he put in.

"I did not!" She gave her hair a shake for emphasis.

"Rolling stops don't count."

"I came to a complete stop for at least one nanosecond." In the convertible, she had to raise her voice to be heard over the road noise. "I'm careful about these things. As a matter of fact, I've never received a ticket."

"Ever get stopped?"

"Once or twice, but that doesn't count."

He decided not to pursue the matter. Maybe the car really had suspended its forward momentum for a fraction of a second. And maybe Nora got away with flouting rules because cops were suckers for good-looking women in convertibles.

Too quickly for his taste, they reached Sam's house. He didn't like the idea of Nora driving the rest of the way home alone in the dark, but he had to admit that an armed policewoman wasn't exactly helpless.

At the curb, she put the car into park. Sam felt in no hurry to get out. Even though they'd be working together on Saturday, he wanted to linger for reasons he didn't care to examine.

For lack of anything better to say, he ventured, "You never answered my question about why Mary thinks it's a good sign that we argue. If she's trying to play matchmaker, you'd think she'd get the point that she's wasting her time."

"She said it shows I arouse your passions." Nora slanted him a mischievous look. "I claimed to doubt you had any passions."

He reached out to finger a wind-tangled strand of her hair, relishing the soft texture against his work-roughened skin. "You're right. I don't."

"You could have fooled me the other night." She tilted her head as if enjoying the contact.

Sam leaned across the gearshift. "I didn't need to fool you. As I recall, you met me halfway."

"I've been known to act without thinking. Surely by now you know I'm impulsive." Her eyes widened, daring him to answer.

Her suggestive tone and relaxed body language issued an invitation that Sam couldn't resist. And didn't want to.

He slid his mouth onto hers in a gentle kiss that left the door open. If he'd misread the signals, she could pull away or pass it off with a joke.

Instead, Nora angled toward him and touched the hollow of his shoulder. The kiss intensified, exhilarating Sam. His hand traced the curve of her throat above her blouse and moved down to cup her breast.

The intimacy of the contact jolted through him. It took strength of will not to hurry as his desire flamed.

Sam lifted his head. "Shall we continue this inside?" The words barely made it through his suddenly dry throat.

Nora caught her breath. "We'd be tempting fate."

"That's not all we're tempting."

In the moonlight, her eyes glittered. "It would be...un-professional."

"Who cares?" He couldn't think about that right now. Sam ached to trace the sheen of her naked body with his tongue, to lift himself over her and unite them with long, slow thrusts. He wouldn't have been surprised if the intensity of his longing made him glow molten red in the darkness.

"I can't," she whispered.

"Why not?" His voice came out raspy with frustration.

"Because if it doesn't work, we'll make each other very, very miserable," she said regretfully. "It happened to me before. It's the reason I left the LAPD and moved to Courage Bay."

"Ex-boyfriend?"

"Ex-fiancé," she confirmed. "When things didn't work out, he blamed me for the breakup and let everybody know."

"That's not my style. In fact, I'm known for my good nature." Remembering their earlier discussion, Sam added, "Except for mornings, afternoons and evenings."

"I just can't."

He drew back. "Okay. Some things I'll argue over, but either this happens spontaneously or it doesn't."

"Thank you." Nora sounded shaky but relieved.

In a way, he was, too. An unplanned sexual liaison might thrill them both for a while, but now that rational thought intruded, Sam had to admit it could create painful problems in the long run.

He'd never felt such a tangle of opposing emotions with a woman before. When Dan ordered him to team up with Nora, he'd known she was going to drive him crazy. He just hadn't figured it would happen quite like this.

Disentangling himself from the gearshift, he uncoiled from his seat. He did so not without reluctance, even though he knew she was right. But he recognized the time for a rapid exit, so he made one.

IF ONLY SHE COULD HAVE said yes, Nora thought.

She'd have raced Sam into the house and left a trail of clothes through the living room. They'd have steamed up the bedroom windows in record time. How delicious to feel that powerful man throbbing inside her.

And then, sooner or later, ugly reality would rear its head. Demands. Arguments. Recriminations. She'd been there once, and she remembered all too vividly how it felt. When she found the right man, surely she wouldn't have these reservations.

Nevertheless, that night Nora had a hard time falling asleep. She kept thinking about Sam, missing his scent and the rumble of his voice. Liquid heat stirred inside when she remembered his palm closing over her breast in the car.

Better not to think about that. Better to distract herself by counting sheep or police cruisers.

Finally she went to sleep. The next thing she knew, the cell phone shrilled on the nightstand.

Nora groped for it, registering at the same time that somehow the night had passed and now morning light filled her bedroom. Saturday. No wonder her alarm hadn't gone off.

"Keyes here," she answered.

"Sergeant Keyes?" a frightened female voice said into her ear. "Please help me. I don't want to die."

CHAPTER ELEVEN

ON SATURDAY MORNING, the sharp jab of his doorbell brought Sam out of a sound sleep. This had better be good, he thought irritably. Although he'd planned to work today, he didn't appreciate being rousted at—he checked the clock—7:46 a.m.

Clad only in striped pajama bottoms, he stumbled into the front room as his uninvited visitor began pounding on the door. What the heck?

Sam opened up blearily. "Yes?"

A much-too-perky Nora, clad in businesslike slacks and a jacket, studied him with interest. "Nice sleeping duds, Prophet."

He scratched his bare chest. Let her ogle to her heart's content; he refused to retreat. "What gives?"

"Ever heard of answering your cell phone?" she demanded.

"I always answer my…" He stopped, remembering that he'd left it on vibrate and tossed it on the couch. "Sorry. You could have called my other line."

"It's unlisted." Nora didn't bother to tear her gaze away from his naked torso. "Never mind. Rose Chang's meeting us at the station in half an hour. My message scared the dickens out of her."

So the president of Speedman had decided to help save her own life. With luck, she could save some other people's lives as well.

"Good," he said. "Come on in while I clean up."

As Nora edged past him, Sam registered her light herbal fragrance and his own state of undress. He remembered holding her last night, feeling her body throb against his. Heat washed over him.

Rose Chang. The station. Right.

Within fifteen minutes, Sam and Nora were on their way, caravanning in their cars. He noticed how peacefully the city of Courage Bay dozed in the June sunshine, giving no hint of the disasters that too often struck this idyllic setting.

The ten-mile half-moon strip of beach and coastal plain, which gave way inland to forested mountains, had earned its name back in 1848. After a warship called the *Ranger* caught on fire and sank in the bay, Native Americans had defied a storm in their small boats to rescue the sailors.

Local legend held that every one of the braves who'd set sail that day had returned safely to shore. He wished the same were true for all the men and women who'd followed in their symbolic footsteps, especially his father. At the same time, he was proud to be part of such a noble tradition and knew his dad had been, too.

When they reached the police station, they found a woman in jeans and a sweatshirt sitting stiffly on one of the lobby benches. She got to her feet when she spotted them.

The president of Speedman Company, fortyish, with chin-length black hair, gripped her purse so tightly her fingertips turned white. Nora made introductions and they adjourned to her office.

"I didn't dare go home to put on business clothes," Ms. Chang told them.

Sam remained standing, since there was only one guest chair. "The main danger isn't a direct assault." He explained about the bombs being placed inside cell phones.

Ms. Chang quickly handed hers to Nora, who checked

the battery compartment and found it clean. Their visitor relaxed slightly. "What does this mean?" she asked. "What can I do?"

"We'd like you to help us narrow down a motive," he said. "We need to identify this guy."

"How much do you know about the killings?" Nora provided cups of coffee for her two visitors.

"I must seem ignorant, but I don't pay much attention to crime news," Rose said after thanking her. "The first time I realized there was a problem was this week when Atlanta sent out an e-mail. They told us not to provide local authorities with any of the company's inside information unless we cleared it with headquarters."

"They didn't give details of the attacks?" Sam asked.

"I had no idea my life might be in danger until I heard your message." She shuddered.

"I'm glad you're willing to cooperate." Nora picked up a file from her desk. "We'd like to run over some information with you that might help us figure out who's doing this and why."

"Sure thing."

"What can you tell us about Patty Reese?" she asked. "We understand she used to work for you."

"Patty was murdered?" Rose regarded them in alarm. "I heard she died in a fire."

"She did." Sam could still see and smell the smoky, bomb-scarred basement littered with glass from the artificial lights installed to nurture orchids. "A plastic explosive hidden in her phone ignited a fire. We didn't discover the cause of the blaze until later."

"We believe her death had something to do with a computer chip Speedman was testing," Nora said. "It was called the Chiseler."

"Oh, yes." Now that she no longer felt immediately threatened, Rose spoke with more ease. "It was developed and tested shortly before I moved here from a Wonderworld subsidiary in New York."

"What was Patty's involvement with the chip?" Sam asked.

Ms. Chang placed her empty coffee cup on the desk. "I wish I could give you more detail from memory, but as I said, it occurred before I arrived. If you like, we can swing by my office to access the records."

No need to confer. Both Sam and Nora knew it had to be done. "What are we waiting for?" Nora said.

TOO BAD SAM COULDN'T spend all day driving around in his pajamas, she reflected mischievously as they followed Rose's SUV to the Speedman facility. He'd looked so touchable this morning in his pajama bottoms and bare chest that she'd nearly pushed him straight into the bedroom.

Nora kept her eyes trained ahead, although Sam was the one at the wheel. She didn't want to risk having her gaze stray to any of the more intriguing parts of his anatomy. It had been embarrassing enough the way she'd eyed him earlier.

Not that she intended to follow up on last night's reckless embrace. But couldn't a woman appreciate a man from a purely aesthetic perspective?

At the Speedman gate, a guard spoke to Rose and then waved them through. As they drove across the empty lot and around the side, Nora saw that the grounds included a racing track and what appeared to be airplane hangars.

Rose parked in a space marked Reserved and indicated the one beside it, which bore an identical sign. Sam pulled in.

"We can enter this way." The president pointed to a small door nearby. "It's more convenient than the front."

"What's in the hangars?" Sam asked.

"Cars." She strode briskly along the walkway. "We used to develop civilian airplane engines, but the market's been weak. The big buzz is in automobile hybrids, alternative fuels, that sort of thing."

Producing a key, she ushered them inside, down a hallway and into her office. It had a lived-in feel, with engine diagrams tacked to the walls between framed posters of racing cars.

"Let me fire up my computer and I'll answer your questions." Rose seemed to have recovered from her earlier attack of nerves.

"If you need anyone to test your racers, I'd be happy to volunteer." Nora studied the posters admiringly. "I've always wanted to do something like that." She and her brothers used to go hot-rodding in the desert during vacations, to the dismay of their mother.

"I'm afraid our insurance wouldn't allow it." After a few more keyboard clicks, Rose said, "Okay, here's Patty Reese's file. Now, what were you looking for?"

"The chip," Sam said. "Was she directly involved with it?"

As it turned out, she had been. According to the file, Patty Reese had concurred with Esmee Engines' recommendation that the company install the Chiseler and the questionable cooling system in a car despite the risk of a failure at high speeds. To her, the potential profits had made it worth a try.

"In light of what happened, I consider the experiment ill-advised," Rose admitted. "Had I been in charge at the time, I'd have recommended trials in a remote-operated vehicle first. However, we were under a time constraint."

Nora hadn't heard about this before. "Why?"

"Rumor had it that one of our competitors was testing a similar chip." Rose made a wry face. "Apparently theirs didn't work out, either, because it's never come on the market."

"You said, 'In light of what happened,'" Sam said. "What do you mean?"

Nora pushed Play on her tape recorder. She didn't want to risk missing any details.

"During the first trial on our test track, the chip shut down," Rose explained. "The car was going maybe ninety miles per hour, faster than most motorists would drive, but of course a failure is still unacceptable."

Nora cared more about casualties than about the car's speed. "You said it shut down. Was anyone injured?"

"I'm afraid so." Rose paused as she read the file. "The racer spun out of control, ran off the course and hit someone in a group of employees who'd gathered to watch. They were in a restricted area, but security must have been lax," she added.

"Who got hurt and how badly?" Sam asked.

"One woman suffered permanent disabilities." Rose frowned at the screen. "I believe she's a paraplegic, although this information isn't current."

At last they had a victim whose suffering might have stirred someone to seek revenge. "What's her name?" Sam queried.

"I'll have that for you in a minute. There's a hold on the information, but I think I can obtain it a different way." Rose zipped through computer files so fast that Nora, watching over her shoulder, could barely track them. "Here we go. Ginny Stone."

According to a legal department file, Mrs. Stone had been run over and knocked unconscious. Hospitalized for months, the thirty-eight-year-old woman remained partially paralyzed despite extensive physical therapy.

She and her husband, Arthur, had sued. Because she'd ignored warning signs and broken company rules to watch the trial, the company's lawyers had forced a lowball settlement.

"Is there a physical description of her husband?" Sam asked. "I'd like to compare it to what we know about the Trigger."

"Sorry, nothing like that." Rose read for a moment longer before looking up. "It says here he's a plumber."

"Good with his hands," Nora noted. That much at least was consistent with a bomber.

"He'd be able to move around town without raising questions, as well," Sam added. "No one lifts an eyebrow about seeing a plumber on the premises."

Rose printed out some data. "Here's their address and phone number, along with the name of the company Arthur Stone works for. At least, where he worked as of about a year ago." Task accomplished, she released a long breath. "Now what should I do? I don't want to spend the rest of my life waiting for this fellow to come after me."

"You said you moved to Courage Bay after this happened, right?" Nora asked.

The president nodded.

"It's worth taking precautions, but my guess is the Trigger's after the people directly involved," she said. "Who *was* president of Speedman at the time?"

"Barbara Noot," Rose said. "She got promoted and moved to Atlanta. If anything's happened to her, I haven't heard about it."

Nora got a prickly sensation, as if the hairs on her neck were standing on end. If the Trigger hadn't already found Barbara Noot, she was willing to bet he wouldn't rest until he did. "Is there anyone else Arthur Stone might blame, that he might go after? What about the driver?"

"The lawsuit doesn't name the driver," the president answered after checking the computer. "If I recall correctly, he suffered minor injuries."

"We'd like to talk to him," Sam said.

Rose studied him uneasily. "You know, I could get in big trouble for giving out this much. Unless the driver's a suspect, I can't release that."

"Everyone's a suspect," Nora put in.

"That isn't good enough." The woman reacted with narrowed eyes and an outthrust jaw. She'd just switched into get-a-subpoena-or-leave-me-alone mode. She'd seen witnesses clam up that way plenty of times before.

"Ms. Chang…"

The president didn't give her a chance to finish. "Not only is headquarters likely to reprimand me for defying their orders, but these people could sue me for releasing confidential information. You've got what you came for. That's enough."

"What about Barbara Noot?" Nora said. "How do we reach her?"

"I'll send her an e-mail and let her know what's going on. I'd appreciate it if you didn't tell her how much I've disclosed." Rose tapped her way to an e-mail program. "I think you'll agree I've been cooperative."

"Yes, you have." Not as much as Nora had wished, but they'd made significant progress. Now they had a suspect with motive and, possibly, opportunity.

Despite Rose's offer, Nora intended to try to reach Barbara directly. She hoped the Trigger didn't already have her in his sights.

"We can arrange for a patrolman to escort you home," Sam told the president. "This guy's into blowing people up at a distance, so I'd advise you to keep a tight grip on your cell phone and your purse. Keep your car and house locked and report suspicious contact with anyone immediately."

"I'll do that," Rose said. "And I'd appreciate that patrolman."

While they waited for the officer to arrive, Nora notified Max about the latest developments. "Good work," the chief said. "Let's find this guy fast."

She also checked on Carl Garcola's condition. There was good news—his coma hadn't deepened as feared—and bad: he showed no sign of waking up.

For the rest of the day, they tried to trace Arthur and Ginny Stone. Their phone number had been disconnected and, according to his boss, Arthur had quit his job four days earlier, saying he and his wife planned to move to the desert. Nora and Sam found one telling connection to the Trigger cases:

according to the plumbing contractor, Arthur had done some repair work for Patty Reese shortly before her death.

After obtaining a license number from the Stones' landlord, Nora issued an All Points Bulletin for Arthur Stone's van. Four days! If she and Sam had reached Rose Chang at Speedman earlier, they might have caught the man by now, Nora reflected in frustration.

Barbara Noot didn't call. Worried that Arthur's destination might be Atlanta, Nora checked with information and learned there was no phone number for Barbara in that area, listed or unlisted.

Perhaps she relied exclusively on a cell phone or lived with someone who had a different last name. After consulting with Sam, Nora put in a call to advise the Atlanta PD of the situation and asked them to try to locate Ms. Noot for her own safety.

By seven o'clock, Nora was ready to call it a day, or rather, a night. Sandwich wrappers and soft-drink cans lay strewn around her office, and Sam had stretched out on the utility carpet to review his notes. She doubted either of them could concentrate well enough at this point to come up with any bright ideas.

When her cell phone rang, they both gave a start. "Boom." Sam accompanied his graveyard humor with a crooked grin.

Nora grabbed the instrument. "Keyes."

"Hey, little sis!" her brother Kyle saluted her. "Randy and I are going to vaporize the old Sunset Shores Hotel tomorrow morning. Wanna watch?"

"What time?" It would take most of Sunday morning to drive the round trip to the aging resort north of Malibu. Her mind clicked, trying to decide if she dared take off a few hours.

"Eight o'clock. We're going to wake up the neighborhood so everybody can get to church on time." In reality, the day and hour had most likely been chosen to minimize the risk to passersby.

Nora couldn't resist. "Unless there's a major development in the case I'm working on, I wouldn't miss it."

"Great!" After giving her directions, Kyle signed off.

"What was that about?" Sam gathered his papers together.

"My brothers are imploding an old hotel down the coast tomorrow morning," she said. "Want to go with me?"

"Why not?" he said.

"Be at my place by six-thirty."

"A.m.?" he asked in disbelief.

"We have to get an early start," Nora warned.

"Okay, I'll be there." After a moment, he added, "And we're taking my car."

Nora didn't argue. She had no wish to rub against the man during the drive. "Ever seen a demolition before?"

"Once for training purposes, but it was on the small side."

"It's fun!" She gave a little bounce, feeling revitalized by the prospect.

"I can hardly wait." Sam finished assembling the files. "Need any help cleaning up?"

"Who's cleaning?" Nora brushed some crumbs off her blouse. "The janitor knows me. He'll muck out the worst of it." She knew for a fact that her office was neat compared with some of the others in the PD.

"What if you'd written down a vital clue on a take-out bag?" Sam asked as he shrugged into his jacket.

"That would be my tough luck." She waited for him to precede her out the door before switching off the light.

As he went by, she repressed the urge to touch him. Just a little caress. He'd turn toward her questioningly, perhaps brush a quick kiss across her mouth. And then...

And then they might not be able to stop. Better to leave well enough alone.

If they'd gone to bed last night, it would have changed all the dynamics. Okay, so she wouldn't feel this restless need every time she looked at him, or if she did, she'd know it was going to be deliciously fulfilled.

But she'd done the right thing. And any minute now, Nora mused as she reluctantly parted from Sam, she was going to remember exactly why.

ON SUNDAY MORNING, Nora radiated enthusiasm from the moment she slid into Sam's car. She'd poured her taut figure into jeans and a denim jacket and twisted her hair into a loose chignon. Did the woman simply get better-looking every day or was that Sam's imagination?

They didn't talk much on the drive, yet the silence felt comfortable. He'd never before considered watching a building get blown up as R&R, but he was looking forward to it.

The Sunset Shores Hotel, located on a bluff above the beach, had been a glamorous vacation spot during the 1930s before it began a slide into obscurity. In the 1950s, a new owner had spiffed it up for the tourist crowd, but since the 1970s it had descended into a haven for transients. Time to clear it away and erect something new, Sam supposed. It probably didn't meet the latest earthquake standards, and the cost of retrofitting something of this size would be prohibitive.

The Keyes brothers had obviously been at work for several days, surrounding the isolated hotel with advance notices and taping up the windows of nearby buildings. As he and Nora walked toward their destination, Sam noted that all the glass had been removed from the hotel itself.

"You bet," Nora said when he mentioned it. "In a typical blast, eighty percent of injuries are caused by glass shards. You probably noticed that the other day."

"I didn't go around counting the injuries, but it sounds right."

Local police maintaining a perimeter checked Nora's name against a list before letting them through. A few dozen people had gathered to watch, many carrying cameras. Most of the small beach-related stores and restaurants were closed and shuttered, although a vendor did a brisk business selling coffee and doughnuts.

The command post had been established some distance from the castlelike structure, which stood silhouetted against the ocean below. Kyle Keyes, two years older than Nora, proved to be a tall, outgoing fellow who welcomed his sister with a hug.

He gave Sam a more than cursory glance when they shook hands, but accepted without comment Nora's introduction of him as her partner. "Randy's doing a last-minute check." Kyle indicated a figure across the parking lot that appeared to be inspecting the wires leading from the hotel.

"Does he need any help?" Nora asked.

She wasn't seriously thinking of going into the blast zone, was she? Sam knew Nora had assisted at this kind of thing in the past, but their investigation needed her. If she insisted on going in there, he supposed he'd have to go along himself. Not that he felt obliged to protect her, but partners backed each other up.

"I'm sure he's fine." Kyle went on to explain for Sam's benefit that they'd already removed salvageable or dangerous materials, drilled holes in the building's supports and filled them with tubes of magnesium. These would be ignited by electrical sparks from the wires that connected to a small electrical box at the command post.

"The idea is to blow the building off its base, like jerking out the legs of a table, so it falls straight down," he said.

Surveying the surroundings, Sam noticed a couple of video cameras facing the site. Behind them and across the street, a third peered from a different angle high in a building. "What are the cameras for?"

"We always tape our blasts," Nora said. "We review the

video to see what worked and what didn't. If there's ever a problem, they may be the only way to figure out exactly what went wrong."

"Besides, I like to show them to dates," her brother added. "You wouldn't believe what a turn-on it is." Despite his light manner, Sam suspected he was only half kidding.

"Sometimes TV stations borrow the footage for their newscasts." Nora waved to Randy, who'd just noticed them and signaled his greetings in return. "It's great publicity for the firm."

"And useful in case of lawsuits," Kyle put in. "Once we had a guy threaten to sue, claiming he'd been hit with debris in a blast zone. The videos showed he wasn't even there. He probably inflicted the wounds on himself."

Sam didn't want to get started on the galling subject of lawsuits. Although some legal actions were justified, the frivolous variety threatened every public safety officer's peace of mind. Instead, he switched to a neutral topic. "It must be hard getting the charges positioned right."

"You bet! The explosion follows the path of least resistance unless it's directed. If we don't get it spot-on, the whole structure might tumble over the cliff. That would be a real mess." Kyle handed them each a set of earplugs. "Make sure you wear these."

Nora regarded the plugs dubiously, as if reluctant to miss any of the excitement. "Every building is designed differently and you have to take into account the type of materials as well," she added. "But when we get it right, it's incredibly efficient."

Sam didn't need her to explain that trying to bring down a large structure with a crane was even more dangerous and messy than using explosives. And the noise lasted a lot longer.

At last, satisfied with the electrical connections, Randy joined them. He hugged Nora and, in response to her questions, assured her that his little boys were fine. "They wanted to come but my wife objected." To Sam, he noted, "She's not keen on them joining the family business, but my ten-year-old's a real buff."

"I know how he feels." Nora performed a couple of jumping jacks in place. "This is great!"

"Okay, everybody take your places," Randy announced.

Sam checked his watch. Five minutes to go. He put in his earplugs and watched Nora reluctantly insert hers.

Her brothers were talking on their phones, making sure the area had been cleared. Then the countdown began. Fuzzily, through the plugs, he heard the elder brother chant, "Ten! Nine! Eight! Seven! Six!" Randy skipped a beat instead of saying five because, Sam knew, it might be confused with an order to fire. "Four! Three! Two! One!"

Eagerly, Kyle pushed the plunger.

CHAPTER TWELVE

THE FLASHES STARTED on the left side of the hotel, sending black smoke billowing into the clear morning sky. Despite his earplugs, Sam heard a series of booms and felt the jolt of a shock wave.

In front of him, the castle's towers and high walls seemed to fragment in slow motion. They hung suspended for the space of a breath and then, like a house of cards, collapsed inward. Dark dust spewed from the base as a mountain of shabby grandeur shrank into a pile of rubble.

Sam coughed as he removed his plugs. Only then did he notice Nora leaping into the air and high-fiving her brothers.

"Perfect!" she exulted. After impatiently suffering through a bout of coughing when another wave of dust hit, she gave Sam a flying hug that nearly knocked him off his feet. "Did you see that? Wasn't it great?"

"Fantastic." His blood still raced, he had to admit.

"I wish we could do it again!" Nora exclaimed. "Kyle, send me a copy of the video, will you?"

"You bet!" Her brother grinned, his teeth white against a smudged face. Nora too had acquired a layer of grime, which she obviously didn't mind. Sam supposed he must look the same way.

Every inch of her frame radiated exhilaration. At this moment, Nora appeared more alive than he'd ever seen her. More alive than most people he knew, too.

How could a man ever hope to protect a woman like that? Risk-taking formed an essential part of her character, Sam thought. Nora thrilled him more than any other woman he'd ever met, and scared the heck out of him at the same time. Thank goodness he only had to watch her back as her work partner.

"Do you realize people can feel that blast for half a mile?" she asked him. "And here we are at ground zero. I love this!"

"I'm glad you've decided to get your kicks on the right side of the law," he teased. As they both knew, arsonists and bombers often became addicted to creating devastating spectacles.

"Nobody with a heart would unleash this kind of destruction against the innocent," Nora said. "Although I suppose the Trigger tells himself that his victims are guilty."

"The Trigger?" Randy asked.

They explained about the serial bomber apparently seeking some kind of twisted revenge. Her brothers seemed intrigued, and Nora clearly had a hard time tearing herself away.

At last, after cleaning up in the bathroom of the Keyes' on-site trailer, Nora and Sam headed back to Courage Bay. "I'm surprised you didn't go into the family business," Sam said.

"When I was growing up, I thought it involved too much paperwork." Nora laughed. "Can you believe that? I had no idea police spend half their time writing reports."

"You got that right."

They had reached the outskirts of town when Sam's radio crackled. After a few brief, coded exchanges between the dispatcher and officers about a pursuit, he caught the license number. "That's the Stones's plate!"

He activated his siren and swung a U-turn. Sometimes it paid to be out and about early on a Sunday. They might even arrive in time to help take down the suspect.

THE STONES'S VAN HAD pulled into the blind end of a canyon road and halted beneath a rock face. A couple of police cruisers and a motorcycle blocked the escape, Nora saw as Sam parked and the two of them got out. Overhead, a helicopter buzzed.

With Sam at her side, Nora hurried to join Officer Tank Gordon, who crouched behind a car. She saw the driver sitting inside his vehicle, although she couldn't make him out clearly. "What happened?"

"I spotted the license plate on Pacific Coast Highway." The three of them kept their heads and voices low. "When I tried to pull him over, he hit the gas."

"Any shots fired?" Sam asked.

Tank shook his head. "No. He took off at about eighty miles per hour. I guess he hoped to lose us in these canyons, but he didn't know them as well as he thought."

"Anyone with him?" Nora thought of Ginny Stone, crippled and possibly strapped helplessly inside. "The man we're seeking has a handicapped wife."

"We haven't seen any sign of her." The officer picked up an electronic megaphone and called, "Come out with your hands in the air! If you have a weapon, set it on the pavement!"

No response.

"If he's the guy we're looking for, his name is Arthur Stone," Sam said.

"Ask him if Ginny's in the van," Nora suggested. "That's his wife."

"Mr. Stone, is your wife in the van?" the officer called over the amplifier. "We don't want her to be harmed." Receiving no response, Tank took a tougher approach. "Don't make us go in after you, Mr. Stone. Come out with your hands up and let's talk about this."

After a moment, the driver's door opened. Behind the

cruisers, the peace officers tensed, aiming their weapons in case the suspect opened fire.

A dark-skinned man appeared, hands in the air. No sign of a gun.

"Don't shoot," he called. "I'm not armed."

"Mr. Stone?" Tank demanded.

"That's me."

"Lie down spread-eagled on the pavement."

He obeyed. Officers moved in swiftly.

Nora exchanged a puzzled glance with Sam. No one had mentioned that Arthur Stone was African-American. He certainly didn't fit the description of the fellow who'd planted a bomb on Fran Garcola outside the hospital.

They waited until officers finished patting down the suspect and checking for accomplices in the van. Once they received the all-clear, they went to talk to their captive.

Handcuffed and seated in the back of a cruiser, the disgruntled suspect eyed them through the open door. "I can't believe I did something so stupid. All I've got is an expired license and an outstanding speeding ticket. I just didn't want to get hauled in on a warrant."

"I'm afraid you're going to face more serious charges now," Nora said. "But there's something else we want to talk to you about."

"What do you mean, 'something else'?" Arthur asked warily.

"I think we'd better continue this discussion at the station." She nodded at Tank. "Go ahead and book him. We'll meet you there."

An hour later, they faced Mr. Stone in Interrogation Room C. He waived having an attorney present. "I don't want to wait until you can dig somebody up on a Sunday morning. I'm hoping I can get out of here. I had to leave Ginny by herself."

"Is she all right?" Nora asked. "We can send a patrol-man over."

"She can manage alone for a few hours." Her husband stared gloomily into space. "I don't know what she'll do if I go to prison."

"We understand you two are moving to the desert," Sam said.

"Yeah, but we decided to take a break at a motel by the beach first," their subject explained. "I was running into town to pick up a few things."

Carefully, they guided him through a series of questions. When they mentioned Patty Reese, he seemed sympathetic rather than angry.

"My wife used to work with her," he said. "Man, that was awful, her dying down there in that fire. We got really upset when we read about it."

"You did some plumbing work for her?" Sam prompted.

"She had a leak in the basement pipes, where she raised all those flowers," Stone explained. "She had plenty of water down there. I can't understand how a fire got so out of hand."

"You weren't angry with her about what happened to your wife?" Nora asked.

"Angry with Ms Reese?" Arthur said. "Why would I blame her?"

"She was one of the people who approved testing the chip in that race car," Sam said.

"So what? They were always testing things." Arthur seemed genuinely puzzled. If he was faking his response, Nora thought, he was as talented as an Academy-Award-winning actor.

"But you're angry with Wonderworld," she suggested.

"Sure, because they don't take care of their employees. At least, I *was* mad at them, but I've come to accept that some-times things happen for reasons we don't understand. Because my wife's in a wheelchair, she's found a whole new career as an artist. We're making a lot of changes for the better in our lives." The plumber shifted uncomfortably, his wrists still cuffed. "Any chance of you taking these things off?"

"Just a few more questions." Sam leaned forward. "How much do you know about plastic explosives?"

"What?" The man stared at him in disbelief. "I'm a plumber. I don't blow things up, at least not on purpose."

From further probing, they learned that he intended to establish his own plumbing business in a desert town where an informal artists' colony had sprung up. Nora was becoming more and more dubious about him as a suspect, and she could see that Sam had the same reaction.

By late afternoon, searches of the van and the Stones's motel room, along with an interview with his wife, failed to connect Arthur to the Trigger. In fact, they learned that far from holding a grudge, Ginny had painted a series of still-lifes inspired by Patty's orchids.

"Does he have to go to prison?" his wife asked anxiously after the police brought her to the station at her request. "I need my husband."

"He'll face charges related to the pursuit, but no one got hurt, and aside from the speeding ticket, he doesn't have a record," Nora assured her. "I'm guessing that under the circumstances, he'll get a suspended sentence and a fine."

After arranging for Ginny to stay with a friend, Nora and Sam dragged themselves out for dinner at the Bar and Grill. She couldn't face eating one more sandwich at her desk, and neither could he.

The shrimp and scallops Alfredo gave Nora a boost after a rough day. Sam treated himself to a filet mignon coated with peppercorns and laced with brandy.

The meal finished, he leaned back and regarded his partner. "Looks like we're back to square one."

Nora had to agree. The long, wearying day had resulted in one suspect cleared and no new evidence.

At least she and Sam had made progress in meshing as a team. During the interrogation, she'd noticed how readily they reinforced each other's questions, their attitudes dovetailing rather than clashing.

Spending time together at his mother's house and at the detonation had helped, she supposed. In a way, so did the frisson of excitement she felt every time she looked at him. She liked having him as her partner as long as neither of them took the personal side of it too seriously.

She hoped this mellowing on Sam's part turned out to be permanent. If he ever started trying to boss her around again, she'd straighten him out in a hurry.

"Nora?" he prompted.

"Hmm?"

"A whole parade of emotions just marched across your face," Sam said. "What's going on?"

Instead of responding with the awkward truth, Nora seized on an idea that came to her. "There's something puzzling me."

"What's that?" In the soft light of the restaurant dining room, Sam's expression appeared almost tender.

"Everyone at Wonderworld's local subsidiaries has to be scared out of their wits about the Trigger," she said. "Surely they'd come forward if they had any clear idea who was doing this. How can someone hold such a big grudge against the company without anyone knowing about it?"

"Maybe there isn't an obvious connection," he said. "Maybe it's a disgruntled former worker who coincidentally happened to hit these particular targets."

"If that's so, we've got a lot more legwork to do." Nora didn't relish the prospect of broadening their investigation, but it went with the territory.

Sam stretched his shoulders. "If Barbara Noot can't or won't help us, I propose we subpoena the personnel files from Finder, Esmee and Speedman."

Nora permitted herself a groan. The fact that he was right didn't ease the prospect of wading through vast amounts of data, searching for a needle in a haystack. "I guess we'll have to. But what if we're missing some vital clue that's right in front of us?"

"Part of the problem seems to be that Speedman promoted one president and replaced her with a new one shortly after the accident," Sam pointed out. "Whatever happened may have fallen between the cracks."

Nora tried to flog her weary brain into action. "Whoever the Trigger is, he must have something specific against Carl Garcola or else believe he knows enough to identify his attacker. Otherwise, why risk planting that second bomb in Mrs. Garcola's purse?"

Sam rested his elbows on the table. "I think we should go back to Esmee Engines tomorrow and reinterview Ramon Nunez and Bethany Peters. Let's take a second look at her husband, too."

The possibility that over the past year a jealous spouse had blown up a warehouse and truck and murdered employees of other subsidiaries to cover his trail before attacking his rival gave new dimensions to the term far-fetched. They'd reached the point of grasping at straws, Nora reflected wearily.

"I think we need to sleep on it," she said.

"Alone?" Sam teased.

"That was *not* an invitation!"

"You can't blame a fella for asking." A half smile played around his mouth. She didn't know whether she wanted to slap away the smugness or lean across the table and kiss him.

Nora caught sight of Fire Chief Dan Egan and his wife, Natalie, a burn specialist at the hospital, gazing lovingly at each other a few tables away. The pair appeared absorbed in each other, and Nora realized that any public displays of affection between her and Sam would attract notice.

"Dream on," she said.

"I intend to."

Nora chose not to respond. Sometimes it was best to let Sam have the last word.

Since she hadn't had a chance all day to retrieve her car, he drove her home after dinner. Outside her apartment, she considered inviting him in for a cup of coffee. If he kept a pair of trunks in his car, they might even enjoy relaxing in the spa.

After that smart-aleck remark about sleeping together? Not a bright idea.

"Parting is such sweet sorrow," Sam joked.

"I beg your pardon?"

"You've been sitting there staring through the windshield. I would take this as a tribute to my charming company, except that I haven't said a word."

"I'm too tired to move." Not far from the truth.

"Think of all the fun we're going to have on Monday, filling out the paperwork for those subpoenas." Sam let out a weary breath. "I'm almost sorry I came up with the idea."

"Maybe we should get Bud Patchett to break into Wonderworld's computers and steal the employee files," Nora joked.

The firehouse mechanic, who had a knack for computers, often helped fix software glitches for both the fire and police stations. Although the city's technical department was responsible for servicing the computers, the techs tended to be overworked and not always immediately available.

The humor vanished from her partner's face. "Why'd you happen to mention Bud?"

"Is there a problem?" Nora asked in surprise.

"He thinks you're sexy."

"Bud?" Although she'd always found the fortysomething mechanic pleasant and helpful, Nora didn't see him in a romantic light. "Sam, are you jealous?"

"Definitely not. Besides, he's too old for you. And too bald. Are you saying you had no idea?"

"He did volunteer to tune up my car once." Nora had almost forgotten about that. "I declined. But what's wrong with bald men? Some women think they're cute."

Sam bristled. "If you need help, I'm not a bad mechanic myself."

She didn't know whether to be flattered or annoyed by this masculine display of possessiveness. Best not to dwell on it. "Thanks, I'll take it under consideration. See you tomorrow." She slid out of the car.

"I wasn't kidding about the tune-up," his deep voice rumbled after her.

"I can change my own spark plugs. But anytime you want to cook dinner, you're on. Thanks for the ride." Nora hurried away without looking back.

Because if she did, she suspected she'd see him watching her all the way into the building.

SAM ARRIVED HOME to see his sister walking toward her car at the curb. When she spotted him, she waved.

"What's going on?" he asked as he got out.

"I was trying to return these." Mary handed him two DVDs she'd borrowed a week ago. "I forgot to give them to you Friday night."

"No hurry." He had a weakness for old movies and liked sharing them with his mother and sister.

"How was your weekend?" Hands on hips, she regarded him expectantly.

"Busy." Sam saw no reason to go into detail.

He should have known Mary wouldn't be put off that easily. "See any more of Nora?"

"You mean other than working together all day yesterday and today? Not much." He pretended an interest in the DVDs, although he could barely read the cases in the dim light.

"Mom likes her."

"Everybody likes her." Again, Sam kept his response terse and read his sister's frustration in the way her jogging shoe tapped the sidewalk.

"She asked me about Elaine Warner."

That got his attention. As he stared at Mary, he noticed her starting to squirm and guessed that she hadn't meant to betray a confidence. Her intense need to spark a reaction must have tempted her too far. "How does she know Elaine?"

"Apparently they're friends."

Sam had almost forgotten that Elaine lived in the same apartment building as Nora. It hadn't occurred to him that the two women might know each other.

If Nora had brought up his name with Elaine, that might indicate she took more interest in him than she let on—a tantalizing thought. On the other hand, since he doubted she had any more long-term intentions toward him than he did toward her, it might have been Elaine who'd yakked.

At the memory of the way he'd broken up with his former girlfriend, guilt nipped at him. Sam knew he'd handled it badly.

At the time, he'd believed honesty was the best policy, but afterward, the hurt in Elaine's eyes had disturbed him so much, he'd made a quick getaway. Later, he'd chided himself for his cowardice, but hadn't gone back to try to soften the blow, because he doubted it would help.

"Nora knows I'd never treat her that way, on the unlikely chance we ever got involved," he said. "She'd clobber me."

"Yes, I gather she's more likely to do the dumping than to get dumped." Mary's comment bordered on a taunt.

"Nobody's dumping anybody," Sam told her. "We're partners. We work together."

She didn't respond. For a moment, he dared to hope that his sister might simply wish him well and make her departure. Instead…

"I tried to drop off the DVDs at eight o'clock this morning on the way to church. You weren't home."

Aha. Now he understood her intense curiosity. She suspected him of having spent the night elsewhere. "I got an early start. Nora and I drove down to Malibu to watch her brothers blow up the Sunset Shores Hotel."

"They blew up a hotel?"

"They're in the demolition business."

"She rousted you, the soundest sleeper in the West, out of bed early on a Sunday to...never mind." Mary shook her head. "This woman is way ahead of you. Sam, I think you've met your match."

"She can hold her own." He refused to concede any more.

"Don't let her get away," his sister said. "You'll never find anyone like her again. Well, thanks for the DVDs."

At last, an exit line. "Thanks for bringing them back."

"Sure thing."

As she started away, warmth rushed through him. Irksome as he might find being given the third degree, Sam would hate it even more if nobody cared. "Mary?"

"Yes?"

"I love you."

Turning back, his sister wound her arms around his neck and hugged tight. He could have sworn he felt a trace of moisture from her eyelashes. "Love you too."

They held each other for a moment before separating. As she drove off, Sam reflected how vital family was. He certainly wouldn't want to live without one.

NORA DIDN'T DREAD Monday mornings. She loved her work.

Plus, today, arriving at the department meant seeing Sam again. Being around him energized her. Maybe she'd been wrong all these years to prefer working alone.

As if they'd prearranged taking turns, she carted her stuff

to his office without bothering to call first. At least he had plenty of empty space on his desk to spread out their files.

A night's rest had removed the trace of darkness from beneath his gray eyes, and he grinned when he saw her armful of files. "Going to mess up my place for me, are you?"

"Too much neatness is the sign of a diseased mind." She plopped her papers on the near side of the desk.

"You call this order?" He indicated two tidy piles of notes and documents occupying a formerly empty corner. "Stuff's really starting to pile up around here."

"You know, they can treat obsessive-compulsive disorder with medication these days," Nora cracked.

"Unfortunately, as far as I know, there's no cure for sloppiness," he retorted.

"Sloppiness?" She frowned at a loose sheet of paper floating to the floor. Which file had that fallen from?

While she was figuring it out, Dan Egan dropped by. "I saw you guys working over dinner last night. How's it going?"

"We're going to try to subpoena the employment records from the three companies involved." Sam offered the fire chief a cup of coffee, which he politely declined. "We're hoping to find something we've overlooked."

"If you need any help, let me know," Dan said. "I can't help taking this case personally." He'd suffered burns in the warehouse explosion that had also injured Sam, Nora recalled. Dan's injuries had produced one positive result: his marriage to the burn specialist who'd treated him.

"Thanks," she said. "We'll do that."

After he left, they divided up the morning's chores. For the sake of efficiency, Sam agreed to fill out forms while Nora made a round of calls. First she checked to make sure no one had disturbed Rose Chang or Carl Garcola. After that, she called the Atlanta police. So far, they hadn't had any luck locating Barbara Noot.

Her next project: following tips phoned in by the public. After Carl's case got front-page treatment in the *Sentinel*, residents had flooded the desk with suggestions. Nora set about prioritizing them.

Top rank went to those that provided the most details, such as the names and addresses of possible suspects. Unfortunately, most of the tips were vague suspicions. One concerned a neighbor who'd blasted some gophers out of his yard. Another cited a coworker who railed against drivers using cell phones. Everything had to be evaluated.

About 10:00 a.m., the jail notified her that Arthur Stone was being released on bail. Although Nora no longer considered him a suspect, she appreciated the information.

The next time she glanced at her watch, noon had arrived. Another morning shot, a lot of work done, and yet they were no closer to catching the Trigger. What was he doing right now? Was he planning another attack?

From across the desk, Sam watched her levelly. Nora's expression must have given away her frustration, because he said, "Don't worry. We'll get him."

"I hate sitting around," she admitted. "I prefer action."

He glanced at the candy wrappers and coffee cups that seemed to have materialized out of nowhere. "At least the place looks lived-in now. Care to take back that remark about my being obsessive-compulsive?"

Before she could muster a reply, Nora's cell phone rang. She flipped it open. "Keyes."

"This is Barbara Noot at Wonderworld in Atlanta." The voice had a hoarse edge. "My superiors don't want me getting involved, but I just found out I have to fly to Courage Bay for a family emergency, and frankly, I'm terrified."

Thank goodness she'd contacted them. Nora had been half-afraid that when the police did locate her, they'd find the woman already dead.

"When are you arriving?" To Sam, she mouthed the woman's name.

"Tomorrow afternoon. My mother's critically ill. I can't take the chance of her dying without seeing her."

"I'm so sorry." What a terrible situation for Barbara, to have to weigh risking her life against saying goodbye to her mother. "We'll move her to a secure area at the hospital. What's her name?" Nora jotted down the information, along with Barbara's phone number.

"You don't think the bomber would go after her, do you?" the woman asked worriedly.

"Unlikely, but let's not take any chances." Now that she had Barbara on the line, she needed to learn as much as possible. "We're trying to pin down who might have a grudge against the victims. We think the situation is related to the Chiseler chip." She mentioned the two people they'd already cleared.

"They're the only ones I can think of with a motive," Barbara said.

"What about the driver of the race car?" Nora asked. "Rose Chang believed he suffered minor injuries but she didn't give us his name."

"Oh, for heaven's sakes, I don't remember," Barbara said. "But I was there and he walked away from the crash. He looked fine to me."

"Do you have any other suggestions?"

"I still can't think about the crash without getting upset, especially about that poor woman who was crippled," the executive said. "Then Wonderworld announced my promotion and I got caught up in moving."

"The accident didn't affect your promotion?" she asked.

"They didn't see it as my fault," Barbara said sharply. "I don't either. I'm just sorry about the consequences."

Nora switched to the most pressing issue: Barbara's upcoming trip to Courage Bay. "Let's discuss your visit. We'll be happy to provide protection while you're here."

"How can you be sure the guy won't get to me anyway?" the woman demanded. "If he's determined enough, all he has to do is slip a cell phone into my purse or my luggage, which wouldn't be that hard now that we're not allowed to lock our suitcases. How can you possibly protect me against everything?"

They couldn't.

Then Nora got a brainstorm. Adrenaline started pumping. Not only could she protect Barbara, she might be able to draw the Trigger into a trap.

"I have an idea," she said. "But first, describe what you look like."

CHAPTER THIRTEEN

WHY WAS NORA ASKING Ms. Noot for her description? Sam wondered uneasily. He didn't like the idea that came to him, because it was far too dangerous.

"That's great," she said into the phone. "You're just an inch shorter than me. How long's your hair? What color?"

Sam opened his mouth to object. His partner's eyes flashed in response. They could hardly get into an argument while she had Barbara on the phone. "Call her back," he said.

"Barbara? Listen, I need to brief my partner. I'll call you back this afternoon." Nora quivered with what Sam could swear must be excitement. Whatever she had in mind, it clearly involved risk, and probably lots of it. "Don't tell anyone you've spoken to me, okay?"

A moment later, she rang off. From the way she folded her arms, Sam could see he was in for a fight. He didn't care, because he'd already figured out what she was planning.

"You are *not* going to act as a decoy," he said. "If we can't devise any other way to handle this than to have someone pose as Barbara, Max can assign one of the patrol officers."

"We don't have another policewoman close to my size. Besides, we need someone who knows this case and understands the Trigger the way I do. Sam, it's perfect."

He snatched at the next argument that came to him. "Don't forget that the Trigger probably knows what Barbara Noot looks like."

"She's been living in Atlanta for a couple of years, so he's likely to be fuzzy on the details," she returned with spirit. "And he probably didn't know her personally in the first place, unless by some chance he worked at the company."

"Which he might have done!"

Nora pulled a small mirror from her purse and regarded her hair critically. "She's a blonde. I wish there were some way to bleach my hair fast."

"Are you listening to me?" Sam demanded.

"On the other hand, if the Trigger's watching us and saw me with blonde hair, he'd know what we're up to," Nora said. "Besides, there's no practical way to strip the color out myself, and I don't have time to go to a salon. I'll need to rustle up a wig."

Sam suppressed an urge to grip her by the shoulders and force her to meet his gaze. "You're forgetting that the Trigger probably knows what you look like. He might recognize you."

"That's a chance we have to take."

No, they didn't. "You can do a better job of protecting Barbara by watching her, not trying to be her."

"Sam! We have to chance it!" Nora insisted. At least she wasn't babbling about hair color anymore, he thought irrelevantly. "This guy is running rings around us. Here's our chance to set a trap. And you know we can't put a civilian's life in jeopardy by using Barbara as bait."

"He'll be watching from the moment she gets off that plane."

"She won't get off the plane—I will," Nora said. "I'll slip in among the passengers as they exit. We'll have plainclothes cops all over the place. And if anyone can spot this guy trying to plant a phone, it's me."

If she was wrong, she might pay with her life. A wave of something near despair swept over Sam, but was quickly replaced by sheer outrage.

"You're jumping into this without considering alternatives," he told her. "You're being impulsive and foolhardy."

"We've tried every way we can to nail the Trigger." Nora regarded him with a stubbornness that further irritated him. "Now that Barbara's flying out, we don't have time to subpoena records and sort through paperwork. It's time to let go of the safety net, Sam. If this case is moving too fast for you, hop off the train!"

He refused to get sidetracked. "Ms. Noot needs a guard, not a double!"

"Do you honestly think I'd be any safer guarding her than pretending to be her?" his partner shot back. "Sam, I can't watch her every single minute, but I can certainly watch myself! She's more likely to end up with a tampered phone than I am, and anyone close to her would get blown to kingdom come."

"What's the Trigger going to do, slip a phone in her purse in a ladies' rest room stall?" he demanded.

"Suppose our perp has a woman accomplice? She might manage it." Nora's chin came up and her mouth tightened.

He wanted to keep arguing but he couldn't. And he knew why...because Nora was right.

It absolutely killed Sam to admit that. No way would he say it aloud.

"I'll tell you what," he said. "Before you make the final arrangements, let me make one more attempt to track the Trigger. Something we haven't tried yet."

"Such as?" Her eyebrows lifted in an almost comical gesture of skepticism that made him want to tell her how precious she was and how dark and grim the world would be without her. As his partner, of course.

Sam didn't trust his feelings at this moment, so he said nothing. Anyway, he needed to come up with an idea, something they hadn't considered before that might actually work.

Miraculously, one occurred to him. "The Trigger is keeping tabs on his victims, right? Maybe he's doing it through computers."

"A hacker?"

"Exactly." Sam wished he had more skills in that area. He knew how to use the department's databases, but he couldn't hack his way out of a paper bag. "Let me see if Bud Patchett's got any ideas. You were joking about having him break into Wonderworld's computers and steal their personnel files. Maybe we can use him for real."

"I thought you didn't like Bud." The corners of Nora's mouth twitched with amusement.

"I don't like him around you," Sam answered honestly. "That's why I should be the one to talk to him."

She nodded wryly. "Okay. You go pick Bud's brain and I'll call around to see who sells wigs. But remember, I promised to get back to Barbara this afternoon, and it's three hours later in Atlanta."

Sam glanced at his watch. Half past noon. "I'll hurry."

The maintenance department occupied half of Bay 4 at the fire station. Despite rigorous cleanliness standards, the place smelled of oil and brake fluid. A radio tuned to a country station echoed off the array of welding and automotive repair equipment and the racks of spare parts.

One of the mechanics directed Sam outside to the plaza, where firefighters and officers often ate on pleasant days. He found his brawny target with a group of fellow workers at a picnic table, consuming a sack lunch.

When Sam asked to speak to him alone, Bud complied amiably. "What can I help you with?" he asked when they were out of earshot of the others.

"It's these cases Nora and I are working on." Sam paused, unsure how much he needed to explain.

"The Trigger," Bud supplied.

"You keep up with the department's cases."

The mechanic shrugged. "I may not be a firefighter myself, but I care about what's going on."

"We figure this guy might be tracing his victims by hacking into the companies' computers," Sam said.

Bud frowned. "It's possible, but more likely he used to work there and has the passwords. You'd think people would change them, but you'd be amazed how rarely they do."

"I can believe it." Having once forgotten his own password, Sam understood how embarrassing it was to have to call on tech support. He hadn't changed his password since then. "Is there a way to backtrack and find out if somebody's reading other people's e-mail?"

"You'd have to access their computer system to do it," Bud said.

"We might be able to get permission."

"Given enough time, sure, it's possible." The mechanic considered a moment "It's not really my job, but I'd enjoy the challenge."

"Will you do it if Chief Egan agrees? And if we get the company's okay?"

"I'd be glad to," Bud said.

"Thanks." Sam clapped him on the shoulder. "I'll see what I can set up."

"Anything else I can do, just let me know."

When Sam dropped by the chief's office, Egan said it was fine with him if Bud wanted to try it. After returning to his desk, Sam placed a call to Rose Chang at Speedman.

"I'm sorry, but we've got confidential information in our system," she said. "You'll need a court order."

"You realize that Barbara Noot is arriving tomorrow. We're trying to catch this guy before he has a chance to hurt anyone else." Sam could see Nora watching him guardedly.

"It isn't up to me, it's up to my superiors at Wonderworld, and they've clamped down," Rose said. "It's the usual corporate knee-jerk reaction. In this case, however, there are also legal restrictions on who can access personnel files."

Although a court order could be obtained quickly in an emergency, Sam doubted a judge would move that fast in this case, if he agreed at all. Without Wonderworld's cooperation, Sam knew he didn't have a chance of accomplishing his goal before tomorrow.

"It's not going to fly," he told Nora after hanging up, and put in a call to let Bud know the bad news.

"You did your best," the mechanic said. "I was kind of looking forward to the challenge."

"We have more than enough challenges facing us." Sam didn't go into detail. "I'll catch you later." They both rang off.

"Thanks. It was a good idea about the computers. I'm sorry it didn't work out." Nora tried to look solemn, but her eyes began sparkling. "Won't it be exciting? I haven't done anything this adventuresome in ages!"

"Almost as good as blowing up a hotel." Sam's effort to make a joke fell flat, mostly because he didn't feel particularly humorous.

"Let's get started." Nora cited the need for a backup team and a couple of officers to act as bodyguards. There were logistics to work out with Barbara, the airlines and the airport authorities. "And, of course, I'll have to get Max to spring for a wig," she finished with a grin. "I'll send him an e-mail right now."

Since the scheme appeared inevitable, Sam determined to do everything possible to make sure it went off smoothly. "Count on me to be right beside you."

"I will, believe me." Despite her obvious eagerness to spring into action, Nora paused. "Sam, I'm not taking your concerns lightly. I know this is dangerous. But it's who I am. I've never hesitated to put myself on the front lines if that's what the situation calls for, and this time it does."

"Then let's make sure we've covered all the bases. It's not

enough just to keep you and Barbara safe. We've also got to catch this guy," Sam said.

"Agreed."

Time to bring in Max, Dan and Adam Guthrie, the chief of detectives. From now on, there'd be no turning back.

AT LEAST WONDERWORLD COOPERATED in one respect: Barbara's bosses agreed to fly her secretly from L.A. on a corporate jet, landing at the Courage Bay Airport away from the main terminal. In addition, she booked a seat on a commercial flight scheduled to arrive several hours later, and e-mailed Rose Chang with the fake plans as if they were real. With luck, if the Trigger had access to Speedman's in-house computer, he would read it and take the bait.

That gave Nora time to meet Barbara and make sure her disguise looked good enough to fool a casual observer. After a quick lunch, they would join Barbara's bodyguards, who could transfer her to the hospital through a side entrance. Meanwhile, Nora, watched by an undercover backup team, would make a show of arriving with the commercial passengers and proceed to the hospital in a taxi secretly driven by another officer.

With so much to arrange, they didn't knock off work until after nine o'clock. However, lights still blazed at the firehouse, where the rec room echoed with the hollow thunk-thunk of a table tennis ball. In addition, a couple of firefighters were playing video games in one corner.

Energy zapped through Nora. She didn't want to go home and try to sleep. She needed to work off her excess energy.

"Let's go dancing," she said to Sam.

He nearly ran into a door frame.

"Are you okay?"

"I'm fine." He sidestepped smoothly. "Did you say dancing?"

"I'll never get to sleep if I don't exercise," Nora said. "I feel like I'm about to explode."

"Your terminology leaves something to be desired," Sam muttered.

"Sorry." It occurred to Nora that the rooftop patio at the Courage Bay Bar and Grill was probably the only place in town that offered dancing on a Monday night. If they showed up there together again, tongues would wag. "I guess I'll go for a swim at my complex."

"Alone?" Sam asked as they exited the building. "That's not safe."

On the point of arguing, Nora conceded that she knew as well as he did that people should never swim alone. "You're right."

"Besides, I'm not convinced exercise is the best way to release your tension," he said. "I seem to recall owing you a massage."

She remembered the neck rub she'd given him at his apartment—and the wrestling match that had followed. "That might get me more worked up than relaxed," she pointed out.

They both halted. Above the plaza, the starry June night vibrated with unspoken questions.

"Would that be a problem?" Sam asked quietly.

Drawing closer to him against the cool of evening, Nora tried to remember all the reasons why she'd put him off earlier. The concern that once he engaged her emotions, he might dump her the way he'd dumped Elaine. The fierce resistance to opening herself to a man who might try to control her. The looming catastrophe whenever two co-workers got involved.

They all made sense. But her back felt stiff as a board.

"Let's see how it goes." Immediately, she recognized that she'd given out a mixed signal. "I mean..."

"You mean, let's see how it goes," Sam said, cutting off her attempt at clarification. "I'll pick up some food on the way. From what you've told me about your approach to cooking, we'll need it." They'd bought snacks out of the vending machine earlier as a substitute for dinner.

"So we're going to my place this time?" A small inner voice warned that this might be a really bad idea. Nora ignored it.

"We take turns with our offices. Why not our houses?"

She chuckled. "Makes sense."

"See you." Sam strolled away toward his car. He wasn't acting overprotective now, Nora thought appreciatively.

Reaching her sports car, she left the top down and zoomed home with the wind streaming through her hair. All her senses on full alert, she noted the sweet scent of a flowering bush and caught an arc of melody soaring through the open window of a passing pickup.

Tomorrow, she planned to risk her life. Tomorrow night, she might not be here. That made every prick of sensation sharper.

What would it be like to make love to Sam? Nora wondered.

She remembered the teasing pressure of his lips against hers. His muscular buttocks beneath her grip. The deep voice that murmured straight into her soul when he spoke close to her ear.

She yearned to explore him without reserve. And yet, she knew she'd better not. Because after making love to Sam, she might *not* die tomorrow, Nora reflected, and then she'd have to live with the consequences.

AS HE PICKED OUT a roasted chicken, fruit salad and fresh-baked French bread at the supermarket deli, Sam acknowledged that his offer of a massage hadn't been intended as a come-on. Although the idea of engaging in window-steaming sex with Nora appealed to him at many levels, he didn't want to make assumptions.

At the checkout, he took his place in line. Ahead, a rack of magazines celebrated the start of summer with a throng—or was the appropriate word a thong?—of bikini-clad cover models. Nipped-in waists. Swelling bosoms. Long bare legs.

Not one of them stirred him like a single smile from Nora. Tonight, the only waist he wanted to circle with his hands belonged to her. The only curving female body he yearned to feel yielding beneath him was Nora's.

An ache in his groin warned that he was letting his fantasies run away with him. Grimly, Sam tried to distract himself by reading the labels on the packets of chewing gum and candy displayed above the magazines. Juicy. Chewy. Sweet. Tart.

Well, that certainly didn't help.

By the time he reached Nora's apartment, the scent of broiled chicken had stirred a different appetite. Sam congratulated himself on overcoming his supermarket lust. Also, he understood now why prudes over the ages had pasted fig leaves onto nude statues. Sometimes a guy had a hard time resisting visual stimuli.

Nora had changed into jeans, a knit top and moccasins. Her new blond wig sat atop a mannequin head in the middle of the coffee table. She nodded toward it as she whisked away the tub of ice cream he'd added to his purchases at the last minute.

"I think I'll call her Babs, in Barbara's honor," she said.

"How come you brought that wig in here?" Carrying the rest of the food, he followed her across the living room.

"It didn't seem right to leave her in the trunk of my car. Besides, she has a faint chemical smell. I want to air it out."

Sam thought the thing looked ridiculously artificial. Obviously, Max hadn't sprung for an expensive model made of real hair. "Are you sure it's the right style?"

"It matches the description Barbara gave me. In any case, she'll have a chance to help me fix it tomorrow." Nora led the way into the kitchen, where she tucked the ice cream into a half-empty freezer compartment. "I'm glad there's time for me to have lunch with her. I want to observe the way she moves and holds herself. I'm no actress but I'm not a bad mimic."

"Where'd you learn how to do that?" he asked. "I don't think I could walk like some other guy."

"I took some acting classes in college. It seemed like fun." From a drawer, she removed two place settings of flatware. "I'm looking forward to dressing up as someone else."

"I might suggest that's due to your feminine instincts, but you've got a knife in your hand," he teased as he removed the food from the sack.

"A dull knife."

"They hurt the most."

She plopped the flatware onto the table. "You're scared of me. Good. I like that in a man."

"Not that scared," Sam said amiably. "Just sensible."

While the food vanished, both of them pretended not to notice how often their calves and ankles brushed in the tight space. The conversation skated across a variety of topics, occasionally veering into the personal, but Sam quickly returned to the other thing on his mind: the investigation.

"I wonder whether the Trigger's read the e-mails we sent announcing Barbara's arrival," he said.

"It's strange to be hoping he really is clever enough to track her—or rather, me." Nora dug into a second helping of fruit salad.

"But not so clever he recognizes the substitution," Sam noted. "Or figures out she's coming earlier."

Because they couldn't discount the possibility of an inside job, they purposely hadn't advised anyone at the local Wonderworld subsidiaries, even by phone, of Barbara's true arrival time. She'd assured them headquarters had agreed to keep the secret as well.

Wonderworld executives still showed no signs of cooperating with the police department. However, they'd apparently decided they had an obligation to Barbara to help protect her during this visit.

"Time for ice cream." Nora tossed the carry-out containers in the trash and Sam added the paper plates. "Let's see what toppings I've got." She prowled over to the pantry.

"Hot fudge sauce?" Sam asked hopefully. "Cherries and whipped cream?"

"I used to have some, but I ate them the last time I got the late-night munchies." Nora tucked her hair behind one ear as she peered inside. "How about this?" She whisked out a bottle of cream sherry.

"Perfect." Sam would have preferred the hot fudge sauce, but this was almost as good.

The sherry went down smoothly on top of the ice cream. Nevertheless, he declined a second helping. He didn't want to overeat and feel sluggish tomorrow.

"It won't go to waste," Nora assured him. "I'll enjoy the leftovers for breakfast."

"You drink sherry in the morning?"

"I meant the ice cream." Settling back in her chair, she flexed her shoulders, a motion that threw her figure into jaw-dropping relief. To Sam's dismay, the desire he'd worked so hard to suppress rebounded enthusiastically. To his frustration, she added, "Maybe we should skip the massage."

"I hate to be accused of not paying a debt." His hands itched to touch those slim, straight shoulders.

She debated with herself briefly before breaking into a smile. "Well, if you insist."

They cleared away what remained of the dishes. All the while, Sam tried to tell himself that he would give her a quick back rub and then head home. But he kept wanting to bury his face in the pulse of her throat and trace his tongue across the velvety skin of her jaw.

It seemed to him that Nora moved more sensuously than

usual tonight. She kept sneaking sideways glances at him, and when he allowed himself to glance downward, he saw erect nipples poking beneath her knit top.

"Well, that's done." Sam wrung out the sponge. The counter and sink gleamed.

"Good job," Nora said. "Where do you want to do this?"

His breath caught. "Do what?" When she chuckled, he remembered the subject at hand. "Oh, the back rub. On the couch, I guess."

"Sounds good to me."

They made it halfway across the living room. He was about to ask whether Nora preferred to lie down or have him stand behind her, when she said, "The heck with that. Why not go for it?"

Before Sam could figure out what she meant, she grabbed him by the belt and tugged him toward the bedroom.

CHAPTER FOURTEEN

"GO FOR IT?" Sam repeated as they crossed the living room.

Not until she heard his words did Nora realize he'd misinterpreted her intentions. "That couch is uncomfortable and I want a proper massage," she explained. "That means skin lotion and lying down."

"So that's what you meant," he choked out. "You, uh, want your massage in bed."

"Sure. What did you think I wanted?" As if she didn't know!

"The fact that you're pulling off my belt gave me a different impression."

Glancing down, Nora saw that she'd partly undone his buckle. "That's because you aren't wearing a tie."

"Excuse me?"

"I wanted to pull you in by the tie but you're not wearing one," she explained. "Sam, I'm sorry if it comes as a disappointment, but I'm not planning to undress you."

Crinkles of amusement formed around his eyes. "I hope you left your gun in your purse."

She paused in the entrance to the bedroom. "Why?"

"Because I presume you're not planning to shoot me, either. On the other hand, if you don't shoot me like you're not undressing me, I could be in trouble."

He gave her a wry smile that wrapped itself around her heart. It made her want to hold him and laugh with him, and maybe fight with him a little, and then drive him completely, thrillingly, soaringly out of his mind.

Starting now.

Why be shy about this? Nora thought. Tomorrow they would both be flirting with death. If anything went wrong, they might never get this chance again.

"Okay, I'm officially undressing you," she said, and yanked open the buckle.

"Ow." Sam's eyebrows shot straight up.

"Did that hurt?"

"Are we going into the bedroom? Because I need to decide which way to collapse." He staggered a little for emphasis.

"You know," Nora said as she steered him inside, "nobody told me you had a sense of humor."

"Nobody told me either," he admitted.

She found his shirt buttons and released them as she leaned against him, inhaling a sensory brew of pure Sam. He nuzzled her neck and, at the same time, unfastened her bra.

Nora kissed the corner of his mouth, he kissed the pulse of her throat, and then their lips and tongues met and they melted into each other. Clothes showered around them like a fall of golden leaves. Nothing had ever felt so right as the silken whisper of his skin against hers.

Sam drew her onto the bed, pushing aside the quilt and stretching beside her on the sheets. Nora couldn't get enough of touching him, of their bodies exploring each other.

There was no need for a slow seduction. They'd been seducing each other the entire past week, she acknowledged silently. Every word, every gesture had promised lovemaking.

Sam propped himself on one elbow. "I hate to mention it, but what about protection?"

"Don't worry. I'm prepared." She reached for the drawer of the bedside table.

He regarded her with a hint of amusement as she handed him a small packet. "Care to help me lock and load?"

"You bet!"

Nora slid the protection into place, enjoying his firmness in her hands. Sam leaned back against the pillows, eyes half-shut, breath coming fast. When she stroked him, a moan wrenched from his depths.

She loved drawing him out this way, giving him pleasure and watching him yield. Gently, Nora pressed with her thumbs.

"Whoa." He caught her wrists. "Slow down. I'm only human. Besides, I'd like to do this the old-fashioned way."

"How about both ways?" Much as she ached to take him into herself, Nora also wanted to bring him to climax with her hands and mouth. She wanted to give him joy and watch him fly with it.

"Maybe later." Catching her unexpectedly, Sam flipped her onto her back. "I'm calling the shots now, my little vixen."

"That's what you think."

"That's what I know." Pinning her lightly, he trailed his tongue along the valley between her breasts and then lower until heat enveloped her. A moment later, he stopped.

"I want us to do this together," he said.

"We are doing it together."

He ignored her words and lifted himself over her. "Tell me how you like it."

"I like it this way." Grasping his hips, Nora pulled him into her.

Sensations rocketed through her as she fused with Sam all the way to the cellular level. She found herself transported to a vaster, freer world, like an eagle spreading its wings on the edge of the Grand Canyon.

Stroking firmly in and out, Sam arced down for another kiss. As they completed the circuit, electricity sparked through Nora.

They teased and enjoyed each other, but soon their longing proved too strong for delay. When she shifted her hips sensuously, Sam gasped, tried to restrain himself, and lost.

He pressed himself into her with long fluid motions. The delicious pressure transformed Nora's body into pure energy.

Fireworks burst against a dark sky, soaring, exploding, and filling the world with light. There was only Sam, only their glittering response to each other.

When she came down to earth, Nora was almost surprised to discover they still lay on her bed in the familiar room. It had felt like they'd landed on a cloud.

After moving away to remove the protection, Sam returned. And cradled her in his arms. Close to her hair, he murmured, "That was spectacular."

"Fireworks," Nora said dreamily. "The Fourth of July."

"And it's only June. Just imagine what lies ahead." He traced the shape of her breast with his finger.

"I can't wait to find out." Nora rested her cheek against his shoulder.

"Let's not wait too long," he said.

She felt his hardness stirring against her hip. "I guess we won't have to."

Sure enough, they didn't.

SAM HADN'T HAD the dream for a long time. Even in his sleep, he recognized the details: smoke rising in the distance, the wail of a siren throbbing through his head, the sway of the fire truck as it raced along the streets.

Ahead, he saw a black cloud pouring from an abandoned three-story building. At the curb sat a familiar car—his father's.

It didn't look right. In his sleep, Sam peered harder through the haze. Not his father's sedan, after all, but a red sports car.

No, no, no.

He took out his phone and dialed Nora's number. When he heard her voice, he shouted at her to get out now.

Through the billowing smoke, he saw a slender figure silhouetted in a third-story window. Phone pressed to her ear, Nora waved gaily.

He shouted into the phone, *Get out!* She went on waving, oblivious.

As the fire truck halted at the curb, Sam heard a terrible cracking sound. In the window, the figure disappeared.

Someone shouted that the roof was down. The front of the building still stood, but through the gaping windows, he saw only empty space. It was like film footage of ancient ruins.

Everything inside had vanished. Crumbled, fallen, turned to ash and rubble.

Nora, where are you?

Sam hit the sidewalk with a jolt and lit out running. He had to go into the flames and save her. But other firefighters grabbed at him and pulled him back. He couldn't break free.

Sam woke with a sickening tightness in his stomach. Morning light seeped through the blinds of Nora's bedroom.

Beside him, she slept with her back to him, hair curving across the pillow. Nora, safe and sound.

Today, she was going to risk her life. Today, Sam had to make sure she survived.

NORA AWOKE full of excitement and a little jumpy. More than ever, she appreciated Sam's presence. He understood what lay ahead in ways that no outsider could.

What had happened last night when they made love? she mused dreamily. She'd never experienced that kind of merging before.

When she leaned down to kiss his cheek, he stretched. After blinking for a moment in the sunlight, Sam sat up and studied her, frowning. "I had a dream about my father. Only it was really about you."

Nora didn't like the sound of that. "You mean about dying in a fire?"

"The roof falling in. The whole mess." His chest rose and fell heavily. "Nora, I hope this isn't a bad omen."

"When did you get superstitious?" She swung her legs out of bed, eager to get moving before this conversation became any more burdensome.

He placed a restraining hand on her arm. "I know it would be hard to change our plans with so many people involved. But let's find another way to handle this."

She couldn't believe it. He was trying to control her, just like Len. Okay, that might not be fair, but what gave him the right to smother her just because he'd had a bad dream?

"Stop right there." Nora pulled away. "Whatever you think happened between us last night, here are the facts: we went to bed. Now we're back to being partners. Separate people who do our jobs." She gestured toward the window. "See that? It's the light of day. Reality. Take a good look."

Irked, she grabbed a robe off a chair and stalked into the bathroom.

When she came out, he was dressing. Sam's face had a shadowed, reserved look. "Nora, I'm not trying to push you around."

"No, you're trying to protect me. But I can't be who I am with some guy treating me like a china doll."

His eyes narrowed. "Maybe I can't stop you," he said. "But I'm going to watch over you whether you like it or not."

"Just keep out of my way," she answered.

"See you at the office, then. I'll shower at home."

"Okay."

He hesitated as if he wanted to kiss her. In a way, Nora wanted him to, but she couldn't stop bristling. Finally Sam gave a nod and left.

She didn't have time to sort through what had just passed

between them or why it left her with a hollow sensation. Her mind was too busy racing ahead, sorting out plans for the day ahead.

After scarfing up the leftover ice cream for breakfast, she put on a suit appropriate for a business executive, although she decided not to don the wig until after she picked up Barbara. Then Nora headed for the station.

Once she arrived, she finalized details with Max. The corporate plane was due at about 11:30 and Barbara's official flight arrived at 2:47. The backup officers were to meet her and Barbara at one o'clock at the Sunscape Coffee Shop. The cheerful glass-fronted restaurant lay along the route from the airport into town, and Nora had reserved its private room.

From there, some officers in uniform would take Ms. Noot to the hospital. The rest of the team, in plain clothes, would trail Nora. Although Sam tried to insist on riding with the police, Max nixed the idea.

"We're already risking the possibility that the Trigger might recognize Nora, but at least she'll be in disguise," the chief said. "If he spots you, we'll have zero chance of catching him."

"But I know his methods," Sam argued. "And this is my case."

"That's why we want you here at the station, monitoring all information as it comes in," said Adam Guthrie, who was supervising the team. "We'll need your objective input."

Sam's mouth closed in a hard, stubborn line. Although he didn't argue further, Nora hoped he wasn't going to make himself a pain in the neck.

She should have anticipated this. She should have maintained a distance between them. Maybe, after today, there'd be nothing left *but* distance between them. Although the prospect dismayed her, it couldn't be helped.

Afterward, Sam stayed behind for a word with Adam. Nora went upstairs with Max.

"Danger must agree with you," the chief said as he stepped into his office. "You don't seem nervous."

"This kind of work excites me," Nora admitted. "I know it's risky. There's a part of my brain that tells me I must be crazy to do this. But it gives me an adrenaline rush."

At that moment, Sam ambled out of the stairwell into the second-floor hallway. Whatever might be running through his mind, he'd resumed his usual easygoing demeanor. "Hey, Nora, I must have left my belt at your place. You didn't happen to bring it, did you?"

Heat rushed to her face. "It's in my purse."

"Thanks." Coming abreast, he spotted the chief's open door and Max's interested expression. "Oh."

No need to say anything more, she reflected, and hurried away with Sam on her heels. In a low voice, she scolded, "Did you really say that by accident? Or are you trying to stake out your territory?"

"Don't read too much into it," he returned coolly. "I goofed, that's all."

Rounding a corner, she nearly collided with Bud Patchett. "Sorry." Silently, Nora chided herself for getting distracted.

"No harm done. Actually, I was looking for Sam." The mechanic switched his attention to the man behind her. "Oh, there you are. You know that suggestion you made earlier about finding out who's been tapping into those computers? I came up with an idea."

"That's great." While the two of them conferred, Nora went into the office, retrieved the belt and set it on a chair.

A short time later, Sam entered. "He could catch the hacker, I'm almost sure of it. Unfortunately, I had to explain that Wonderworld still won't give permission."

"Let's hope we don't need it." Nora didn't say the obvious:

if things went seriously wrong today, searching Wonder-world's computer records might be like closing the barn door after the horse escaped.

He slid the belt through his pant loops. What would he have done if she hadn't brought it? Nora wondered, and decided not to ask.

"Listen, I'm sorry I shot my mouth off in front of your boss," Sam said.

She saw no point in worrying over what couldn't be changed. "He'll get over it. We're both consenting adults."

They stood facing each other for a long moment, and then Sam touched her hand lightly. "I still wish I could talk you out of this."

"Don't even try," Nora said.

"I know."

Keeping their focus on work, they reviewed the final details. Just when Nora believed they'd settled everything, Sam added, "I'm going to follow the backup team in my car. I'll be monitoring the information, as we discussed, but I can also provide an extra set of eyes and ears."

"The chief wants you at the station."

"The Trigger's smart, which means he might pull something we don't expect. There's also a possibility he has an accomplice and, if so, the others might not spot him or her." He spoke with such quiet reason she couldn't help seeing his point.

Besides, she didn't want another fight. "You'd better clear it with Max, or at least with Adam."

"I'll make sure to apprise them of the situation."

He intended to wait until he'd set his plan in motion, Nora guessed. Well, she'd always believed in trusting one's instincts, so how could she ask Sam to ignore his?

Besides, she felt safer with him nearby. While emotions could cloud a person's judgment, they could also, as he'd pointed out, make him extra sensitive to details the others might miss.

"Okay," she said. "But no crowding me, no moving in because you're afraid I'll get hurt. It's my job to be out there."

A muscle jumped in his jaw. "Nora, I won't kid you. Letting you go is the hardest thing I've ever done. Part of me wants to haul you off and keep you under guard, but I'll do my best to respect who you are."

She hoped he meant it. "I'll be fine."

"Just in case you're not, I've got your back."

She checked her watch. Close to eleven. "I'd better get going. We wouldn't want to keep Barbara waiting."

The office phone rang. Nora lifted the receiver. "Keyes."

"This is Officer Cruz at the hospital," the man said. "You asked me to notify you when Carl Garcola woke up. Well, he opened his eyes a few minutes ago."

That could be a major break. "Has he said anything about who attacked him?"

"The nurse sent for a doctor. She won't let me disturb him."

"Someone will be right over." They couldn't afford to delay, Nora reflected as she rang off. To Sam, she said, "Garcola's awake. He needs to be debriefed. The sooner the better."

Conflict warred in his face. It didn't take more than a moment for him to see the priority, however. "I'll get right on it."

Nora discounted a twist of apprehension at the knowledge that he wouldn't be following her. "Call me when you know anything." She picked up her purse, making sure to zip it shut. She didn't intend to give the Trigger a chance to drop anything inside.

Sam gave her a tight nod. "See you."

"See you." It hardly seemed an adequate response, but right now, it was the best she could do.

THE AIR IN HIS CAR hinted of Nora's light fragrance, Sam noticed as he drove the short distance to the hospital. He also

could have sworn the front passenger seat retained a slight in-
dentation from her tantalizing rump.

Without intending to, she'd moved into every corner of his
life. Unfortunately, that didn't appear to be what she wanted.
After today, Sam wasn't sure the two of them had a future together, but he did know one thing.

He couldn't change his fundamental nature any more than
she could. That meant looking out for people he cared about,
and whether she liked it or not, right now that included Nora.

But first, he had to question Carl Garcola. If he could identify the culprit who'd planted the bomb in his cell phone,
Sam might be able to short-circuit the afternoon's charade and
pull Nora out of harm's way.

Mentally, he reviewed what he knew about the subject. Carl
was in his late forties, he cheated on his wife and he worked
as a supervisor at Esmee Engines. That wasn't a lot to go on,
but Sam didn't need to establish a personality profile, just to
ask the right questions in the right way.

Assuming the Trigger had been angered by the Chiseler
chip, Carl's connection was clear. Garcola had reviewed
Lance Corker's simulation tests and, although they'd shown
the chip could fail at high speeds, had recommended testing
it in a race car.

The problem was, the only person seriously injured had
been Ginny Stone, and her husband gave no sign of being the
Trigger. Yet *someone* had been vengeful enough to kill Lance
and Julius Straus and Patty Reese, and to attempt twice to kill
Carl. Who and why? What had he and Nora missed?

As he parked in the hospital lot, Sam couldn't shake the
feeling that the truth had been right under their noses all
along. He wished they'd been able to learn the identity of the
race-car driver. Maybe he knew something that no one else
had mentioned.

Another possibility suggested itself. Wonderworld headquarters had blocked the investigation several times. That appeared to be due to a natural corporate instinct toward secrecy, but was it actually the work of an executive with a hidden agenda? If so, he or she might know about Barbara's alternate plan.

One way or another, Sam reflected as he strode into the hospital, he desperately needed to learn the truth.

AT THE COURAGE BAY AIRPORT, Nora drove through a rear entrance and whipped along a road to a small, unmarked terminal. Out of sight of the general public, it served private jets carrying corporate passengers and the occasional VIP.

A guard checked her ID before admitting her. Inside, she spotted a man in a chauffeur's uniform who presumably went with the limousine parked outside. Only a handful of other people, including a janitor and a woman staffing the counter, occupied the lobby. No one looked familiar, and no one paid her any particular attention.

A few minutes remained before Barbara's scheduled arrival, although with a private jet, the timetable might not be exact. Through a rear window, she saw a jet bearing a computer company's logo taxi toward the terminal. After it stopped, a worker drove a motorized staircase into place, the plane's door unlatched, and a couple in business suits descended.

The limo driver stood up. The newcomers came into the terminal, shook hands with some of the waiting people and departed through the front door, accompanied by the driver. That left only Nora, the janitor and the woman at the counter.

Finding it impossible to keep still, Nora paced in a long, looping path. So many things could go wrong. Suppose the Trigger had tracked Barbara from Atlanta to Los Angeles and managed to tamper with her cell phone? After the attempt to plant a bomb in Fran Garcola's purse at the hospital, Nora didn't doubt the killer's willingness to blow a jet out of the sky.

Thinking about Fran reminded her that Carl had awakened. Glad to refocus her thoughts, Nora pictured Sam striding through the hospital to the restricted area. She smiled at
the image of his tight muscular build and the memory of how
that body felt in her arms. If only he weren't so obstinate.
She'd sworn never to let a man control her again, and that
hadn't changed.

Outside, a small jet droned into view above the airport. As
she watched, it banked for a final approach.

If the Trigger had planted a bomb, he might set it off now,
when he could see for himself that the job was done. Nora
braced herself.

Maybe their ruse was about to end before it even began.

CHAPTER FIFTEEN

CARL GARCOLA LAY attached to tubes and wires, including an IV and a heart monitor. After a week in bed, his skin looked pallid, and although he was clearly awake, his expression had a vague, confused quality.

"Don't overtire him," the nurse warned. "His wife should be here any minute. The physician on duty says he may not stay awake long, and I'm sure he'll want to save his energy for her. Also, the neurologist needs to examine him."

Normally, Sam would have backed off. Today, he didn't have that option. "Lives may depend on what he knows. Possibly including his own."

The nurse bit her lip and refrained from instructing him further. After she left, Sam pulled a chair to the bedside.

"Mr. Garcola?" He noted with relief that the man's eyes fixed on him. "My name is Sam Prophet. I'm an arson investigator here in Courage Bay."

The patient managed a nod.

"Someone planted a bomb in your cell phone." Sam went on to sketch the connection to the death of Lance Corker and other Wonderworld employees. "We believe whoever did this held a grudge because of a chip you tested, code-named the Chiseler. Do you remember it?"

Again, he received a nod.

"Do you know who might have tampered with your cell

phone?" The importance of the question made Sam want to hurry the witness, but he forced himself to wait patiently.

A furrow formed between Carl's brows. After a cough, he rasped out, "Not sure."

"You didn't see anything suspicious before it happened? You didn't lend your phone to anyone?"

A weak head shake.

"We've talked to a man who claims to have invented the chip and the husband of the woman injured by the race car, but we don't believe either of them was involved," Sam said. "We wondered if anyone else might have reason to…"

He stopped, hearing the guard in the hallway demanding someone's identification. It was only a formality, since whoever approached should have already cleared an earlier checkpoint, but Sam took nothing for granted. If the Trigger had learned that Carl was awake, the chance to get revenge on Barbara Noot might not be enough to keep him away.

Rising quietly, he drew his gun and took a position behind the door.

THE SMALL JET VANISHED from sight. Nora moved to the other side of the window, craning her neck until it reappeared on a runway.

If the Trigger intended to detonate a bomb on board, he'd probably have done so in the air. Nevertheless, she didn't breathe easily until it halted, the door opened and a woman of medium height descended the movable staircase, her blond hair bouncing and a pair of sunglasses shielding her from the California sunlight.

Nora made a quick assessment. Medium height, a slightly chunky figure, tailored suit. A friend would have no difficulty telling the difference between the two women, but they had a good chance of fooling anyone else.

As soon as Barbara entered, Nora introduced herself and

shook hands. When the executive removed her sunglasses, a tracing of laugh lines showed her age to be late forties. That could present a problem up close, but it wouldn't be evident from a distance.

"I'm glad you're here," Barbara said. "I'm terribly nervous."

"How's your mother?" Nora asked.

"Holding up, but very frail, according to my sister. I wish my daughter could have come—she's twenty-two—but I refuse to expose her to danger." She exhaled deeply. "Where do we go from here?"

"I've reserved a private room at a restaurant," Nora told her as they walked through the small lobby. "That way you can help me adjust my disguise and we can catch a bite to eat, too."

"Your disguise?"

"I've got a wig in the car." After checking through the glass and seeing no one in the area, she held the door.

As they exited the terminal, Barbara looked distinctly unimpressed. "I'm afraid you don't resemble me much."

"You should see how I look without this wild red mane." In the store mirror yesterday, the change had been startling. "Do you have luggage?"

The executive indicated the slim suitcase in her hand. "Just this."

"Good. My car's trunk isn't exactly huge." Nora clicked her key holder. With a cheerful beep, the red sports car flashed its lights and unlocked the doors.

Barbara halted in dismay. "Surely you don't expect me to ride in that!"

"I'll put the top up, of course." She moved around to the driver's side.

"I hate being cramped." The older woman brushed at her skirt. "This rayon creases horribly. Besides, that car's so distinctive, people will stare at us. I thought the point was to avoid attracting attention."

For once in her life, Nora wished she drove a stodgy department-issue sedan. "If it bothers you, I'll rent a car."

Barbara's frown deepened. "I want to get away from the airport. Waiting around makes me feel so helpless. I'm going to call a cab and you can follow me over."

"I'll ride with you." As soon as she said it, Nora realized that wouldn't work. Without a car on the premises, she'd have no way of whisking Barbara to safety in an emergency. "No, I guess not. Look, it's only a few miles. Why don't you hop in and we'll be there in no time?"

The executive wavered. Just when Nora thought she might agree, a taxi pulled to the curb, discharging a couple of Asian businessmen.

Barbara made a beeline for the cab.

"Wait!" Nora cried. "You can't do that!"

"Give the driver the name of the place, would you, please?" Her charge slid inside, cutting off the argument.

Short of physically wrestling the woman from the taxi, Nora didn't see what choice she had. "Sunscape Coffee Shop," she said.

"Yes, ma'am." The cabbie, a young man with blond highlights in his brown hair, wrenched the wheel and pulled away.

"Wait!" Nora wanted to make sure he had the right address. Apparently, he failed to hear her.

She trotted to her car, jumped in and shot away from the curb, barely taking the time to fasten her seat belt. Ahead, the taxi made a swift right and merged into traffic.

Heavy cross traffic held Nora back. By the time she made it onto the main road, the other car had vanished.

Zipping in and out at top speed, Nora squeaked through a light as it turned red and snapped around the next corner. The cab should be straight ahead of her.

There was no sign of it.

Although the cabby's posted license had appeared to be in

order, Nora hadn't had time to give him or the photograph more than a quick glance. If she had planned to disguise herself, maybe the Trigger had done the same thing.

She hit the gas and started to pray.

IN THE HALL, Sam heard the guard say, "Thank you, Mrs. Garcola, you can go in."

He holstered his gun but kept his hand ready and stayed out of sight. He and Nora hadn't ruled out the possibility that the Trigger might be female.

A middle-aged woman with short blond hair entered hesitantly, her back to him as she concentrated on the figure in the bed. "Carl?" Recognizing Fran Garcola's voice, Sam relaxed.

The patient stared at his wife. "Fran. Oh, lord. I was at the motel…I was…I'm so sorry."

"We'll deal with that when you're better." She stood awkwardly behind the chair. "I'm glad you're awake. I've been terribly worried."

"Mrs. Garcola?" Sam saw her start as he moved into view. "I hate to intrude, but I have some vital questions to ask your husband. Time is of the essence."

Her strained face showed relief. It must be difficult to face a man who'd been injured while betraying her, he reflected. "Of course. I just wanted to see for myself that he's okay. I'll wait outside."

"Thank you." After she left, Sam sat down again. "I'm sorry to interrupt."

"Don't be." Carl's words came out in a croak. "I'm a real louse, aren't I?"

"I'm sure you two will work it out." When it came to people's morals, Sam kept his opinions to himself. If an investigator started judging his witnesses, he'd never get anywhere. "We were talking about the chip."

"Chiseler." The word was slightly slurred.

"That's right. Did the accident harm anyone other than Mrs. Stone?" he asked.

"Bethany?"

Confused, Sam tried to make sense of the response. "Was she present during the testing?"

"No." The patient struggled to explain. "Is she hurt?"

Realizing Carl was concerned about the blast at the motel, Sam reassured him. "She escaped without harm. You helped her out the window."

"Don't remember."

That wasn't encouraging. However, people who suffered head trauma often lost their short-term memories of the moments before the injury. That didn't mean Carl couldn't help with information on the chip.

"The bomber may not be finished attacking people." Sam needed to emphasize the urgency before this man got too tired. "We have to catch him before he strikes again. You may be the only one who can help us."

It took Carl a moment to clear his throat. "Sure. How?"

"Did the race car hit anyone other than Ginny Stone?"

"Hit? No."

The way he responded alerted Sam that he might have phrased his question too narrowly. "Was anyone else involved in the accident?"

"Yes." Before Carl could continue, he burst into a fit of coughing. When it abated, he leaned back against the pillow and closed his eyes.

"Mr. Garcola?" Sam demanded.

He received no answer.

NORA ZOOMED PAST a self-storage yard, made a right next to a concrete-block wall and circled the restaurant parking lot. She was about to call the dispatcher on her hand-held radio when, on the far side of the cafe, she spotted the cab beneath a clump of trees.

She shot toward it, arriving in time to see Barbara pay the driver and collect her suitcase. Thankful to see her safe, Nora whipped into a parking space.

"You're right—this wasn't far," the executive said when they met up. "But I hope I'm not expected to ride around on those little bucket seats for the rest of the day."

"No, you'll be in a police cruiser," she assured the woman.

They entered through a side door, Barbara toting her suitcase and Nora with a large bag slung over one shoulder. Inside, diners crowded the tables. She noted a small family with children, some people in business suits and a group of older ladies in red hats and purple dresses.

One man sitting alone appeared to be studying them. "Please take a look around without being too obvious and see if you recognize anyone."

Barbara swept the crowd with an imperious gaze. "No."

"What about that fellow over there?"

The man had returned his attention to his menu. "Him? No."

"Good." Still, Nora made a note of where he sat and what he wore in case she needed to describe him later.

She led the way into the private room, where a small table had been set up for them. It wasn't exactly an elegant setting, but quiet. "Would you rather eat first or help me with my disguise? We've got almost an hour till the backup team arrives."

Barbara scrutinized Nora skeptically. "I think we'd better start with the hair and makeup," she said. "This could take a while."

"MR. GARCOLA," Sam repeated. "Right at this minute, Barbara Noot's life is in danger. You remember her?"

Slowly the man's eyes blinked open. For a moment, he didn't appear to understand. Then, to Sam's relief, he said, "Yes."

"Who else was involved in the accident?" he pressed.

"Driver."

Sam already knew that, but now at last he might be able to learn more. "I understand he walked away from the crash."

"Yes."

Again, Sam had to rein in his impatience. Harassing Carl wouldn't help either of them. If they were going to get anywhere within a reasonable time frame, he surmised, he'd better start filling in the blanks himself instead of relying on open-ended questions. "So the driver got hurt?"

A nod.

"His wounds turned out to be more serious than expected?"

"No treatment," the patient rasped. "Said he was okay."

"Is he still alive?"

"No."

Since Sam couldn't read minds, he had to keep drawing out the facts one at a time. "He died later? Was it that same day?"

"Uh-huh…went surfing," came the labored response.

"After work?" Seeing a nod, Sam added, "Did he drown?"

"Yes."

The picture began to come clear. "So the company claimed it was a surfing accident unrelated to the car crash?"

The troubling memories apparently spurred Carl to make an extra effort. "Left a pregnant wife. Not much insurance."

"She sued and lost?" Wonderworld's lawyers had won again. "I'm guessing the autopsy showed a head injury that might have come either from the crash or from hitting his head on a surfboard?"

"Right."

Maybe the driver really had died from a surfing mishap, but Sam suspected there was more to it. Enough to convince someone that the driver and his family had been terribly wronged. But who?

Although a woman could have planted the cell phone devices, Sam didn't see the widowed mother of a baby risking her life that way. He also imagined she would have been more consumed by grief than by a thirst for vengeance.

"Was there someone else involved with the case who might seek revenge?" he asked.

The one word that broke through Carl's dry lips chilled Sam to the core. "Brother."

"YOU KNOW WHAT?" Nora told Barbara. "If you don't mind, I'd like to check the contents of your purse and suitcase before we go any further."

"I didn't bring my cell phone." The blond woman handed over her sleek designer purse. "I hate not having it, but I figured it posed too much of a risk. People will just have to leave messages with my sister."

"Nevertheless, the Trigger might have slipped a phone inside. You probably wouldn't notice the extra weight." Nora removed the contents of the purse one item at a time. "You don't have a tape recorder or anything else containing a battery? Plastic explosives require an ignition source."

"No, I don't think so." Barbara frowned as she watched.

"Any pockets in your suit?"

The executive patted her lightweight jacket. "Yes, but they're empty."

After removing everything from the pocketbook, Nora checked its compartments. Nothing.

"I'll put the stuff back," Barbara said. "You go ahead and look in the suitcase."

Nora went through it carefully. No sign of danger. "You're clean."

"He hasn't found us yet." The woman allowed herself a weak smile. "That's good. You know what? I'm actually hungry. Let's order, and then we can fix you up while we wait."

"Fine with me." Nora was about to go in search of a waitress when one came in.

"Sorry. I didn't see you arrive." Briskly, the young woman handed them menus. "Would you like to hear our specials?"

The two of them nodded.

From memory, the waitress recited, "Today we've got fried clams, shrimp and scallops—that's the Chef's Seafood Blowout. Our other special is a steak sandwich, fries and a shake. We call that our Blast From the Past."

Nora met Barbara's startled gaze. To the waitress's confusion, they both started to laugh.

It wasn't really funny. But the break in tension made Nora feel better, all the same.

"DO YOU REMEMBER the brother's name?" Sam asked.

A shake of the head. Carl's pallor didn't bode well, although according to the monitors, his vital signs appeared stable.

"Do you know what he looks like or where he works?" Sam went on.

"Can't recall."

The door opened and a doctor entered, clipboard in hand. The neurologist, apparently. "I'm sorry, but I need to examine the patient."

"I'm almost finished." They'd come too close to the truth for Sam to give up now. "At least you must remember the driver's name, don't you?"   He hoped the test driver hadn't been hired from an outside company. If that was the case, it could take hours to track him down.

"Tim," Carl said.

"Tim what?"

The doctor opened his mouth to speak again. Sam glared so hard the man closed it silently.

Carl's jaw worked. At first nothing came out, and then Sam heard a name so familiar that it almost didn't register. The name was Patchett.

CHAPTER SIXTEEN

As HE RACED THROUGH the hospital, Sam dialed Nora's number. It rang three times, and then a recording told him the phone was out of service.

Nora never turned off her phone while working.

The battery might have died. She might have left it at home by mistake. But Sam knew neither of those things was true.

Vividly, he saw Bud Patchett in the corridor outside Nora's office this morning. He'd distracted Sam with his suggestion of how to hack into computer systems.

The trick had worked. Sam hadn't registered the fact that this man had had the opportunity to duck inside Nora's office and switch the cell phone in her purse.

Since he worked on the police and fire computer systems, Bud must have been following their investigation every step of the way. Sam had even sought his help. The memory of Bud's feigned solicitude repelled him.

A couple of years ago, he'd heard that Patchett had lost his brother, although until now, Sam hadn't had any reason to connect that fact with the Trigger case. Many of his colleagues had even attended the funeral, although Sam had had to go out on a case that day. Understandably moody for weeks afterward, Bud had appeared to recover over time.

No matter how upset the mechanic must have been, there was no excuse for the violence, lies and hypocrisy that had followed. The Trigger had played his co-workers for fools, using their trust against them as he racked up victims. So great had his obsession grown that he'd become willing to sacrifice anyone who could further his purpose.

Sam couldn't bear the thought of losing Nora, with her stubbornness and blazing courage. Her quick mind and ready smile lit up his life.

He'd yearned to protect her, and now, it seemed, he couldn't. What a monstrous ego Bud must possess, to believe his own sorrow justified devastating other people's lives.

Sam forced himself to concentrate. Surely the Trigger meant to activate the bomb as soon as he saw the two women drive off together. In the confined space of an automobile, they'd both be torn apart. If it hadn't already happened, there wasn't a moment to waste.

He called the dispatcher, tensely relating what he knew. She immediately ordered patrol officers and the backup team into action and put out an All Points Bulletin for Bud.

There'd been no report of an explosion so far. Sam wondered if Barbara's plane had been late. The Trigger might still be waiting for the pair to get into the little red sports car.

In that open vehicle, he'd be able to see them clearly when they left the airport. Then he could place his cowardly, murderous call.

Sam told the dispatcher to call the supervisor at the VIP terminal and ask him or her to relay a warning to Nora. Next, he asked her to notify the restaurant manager, just in case somehow they'd made it there alive. Someone had to be able to reach the women.

Sam loped out of the building past the roped-off area where a bomb had detonated less than a week ago. The devastation only underscored today's deadly peril.

At his car, a painful reality hit him. Without knowing the women's exact location, he had no idea how to save them.

A dozen years ago, he'd been helpless to rescue his father.

Last night in the dream, he'd had the same horrifying experience with Nora. Now it was happening in real life.

Yet Sam had to take action, any action. The restaurant lay half a mile away, en route to the airport. He decided to go there first.

Keeping his attention on the traffic, Sam activated his light and siren, hit the gas and drove like a maniac.

IN THE BATHROOM MIRROR, Barbara watched Nora tuck her hair beneath the wig. "You still don't look like me."

"I'm not trying to trick your friends, just create a general impression," Nora reminded her. "We don't believe the Trigger necessarily knew his targets personally. Some of them, he may never have seen in person before he...contacted them."

The executive shuddered. "It's so cold-blooded, killing total strangers because they once made the wrong decision."

"We don't even know for sure that that's his motivation," Nora added. "He could be a disgruntled former employee."

"No matter who he is, I'm glad you're the one going out there today and not me." Barbara produced a brush. "Let me fix that. It may sound vain, but I wouldn't be caught dead with my hair in that outdated flip."

"Thanks." Nora submitted to a faint tugging at her scalp as the wig shifted. "Are your sunglasses prescription? It might help if I wear them."

"Be my guest." Barbara handed them over, and Nora put them away for later. "Do you have a different lipstick? This shade works better for a brunette than a blonde. I don't want people to think I'm losing my touch."

Just her luck, Nora reflected, to pose as a woman who seemed almost as worried about her image as her safety. "Sorry. I didn't bring any other color."

"Take this one." Barbara fished out a tube and gave it to her.

"Okay if I save it till after we have lunch?"

"I suppose so." The executive returned the brush to her bag. "I'm getting nervous again. When do those other officers arrive?"

Nora checked her watch. "Half an hour. Let's go eat." To her, the exciting prospect ahead inspired an appetite. Besides, she'd ordered the Blowout, and she loved seafood.

As they exited the ladies' room, Nora heard a siren in the distance. Heart attack victim? Car chase? Right now, she had her own work to do.

It occurred to her that Sam must have arrived at the hospital nearly an hour ago. Had he learned anything from Carl Garcola? Surely he'd have called if the man had revealed the Trigger's identity.

Maybe she ought to check in with Sam anyway, to be on the safe side. Distressed at nearly losing Barbara in traffic and preoccupied with keeping her safe, Nora hadn't reported in, since the undercover operation wasn't yet officially under-way. She resolved to make the call as soon as they resumed their seats.

First, however, they had to pass through the open part of the restaurant. Again, Nora surveyed the occupants. Although she saw no one suspicious, a worry nagged at her.

The Trigger did his dirty work from a distance. If he'd learned of their arrangements and planted a bomb in the pri-vate room, he wouldn't be sitting here in plain view, risking injury. He'd be outside with binoculars, watching through the window until they went back in.

Subliminally, she noted the siren's wail growing louder as it approached. The sound increased her uneasiness.

Nora believed in intuition.

"You know what?" she told Barbara. "I want to make a tour of the parking lot."

"I thought we were safe here," the executive said disap-provingly.

"I believe we are, but…well, it's just a hunch." And probably a fruitless one, Nora conceded. Besides, she could hardly leave Barbara unescorted while she circled the lot. "I suppose it doesn't matter."

Far from acting reassured, the woman beside her stiffened. "What's that man doing in our room?"

A thirtyish fellow in a blazer emerged from the reserved area, his expression puzzled. He didn't match the description of the man outside the hospital, but perhaps the Trigger had persuaded him to leave a cell phone on the table on a pretext. It would certainly seem like an innocent request.

"Let's play it safe. We'll go to my car. Keep it natural but move fast." As she caught Barbara's arm and turned, they nearly collided with the waitress carrying their plates.

"Is something wrong?" the woman asked.

"Do you know that man?" Nora pointed.

"Sure, that's Brad. Our manager."

The young man caught their gaze. As he started toward them, the siren blared directly outside the restaurant. Once it fell silent, Nora heard other sirens further off.

"What's going on?" Barbara gazed wildly from the approaching manager to the flashing red light visible through the front window. "That isn't a police car."

With a sense of relief, Nora recognized the sedan. "It's my partner."

"Is either of you Sergeant Keyes?" the manager said.

"That's me."

"The police dispatcher just called." He glanced around uneasily. "Maybe we should discuss this somewhere private."

As he hesitated, Nora caught a glimpse of Sam, his face hard with resolve. Shoving the glass front door so hard it snapped open, he barreled toward them.

Her pleasure at seeing him changed to apprehension tinged with annoyance. If something was wrong, why hadn't he called? Did he have to barge in here and take over?

Before she could speak, he ripped her purse off her shoulder. "The Trigger is Bud Patchett!" To Barbara, Sam said, "Just a precaution." Snatching the pocketbook from her hand, he fled.

Other diners stared after him. A couple buzzed angrily, apparently under the impression that they'd witnessed a purse snatching.

Bud Patchett. Nora stood rooted to the spot, stunned.

She visualized the tall, muscular figure outside her office this morning. Bud, who'd always seemed friendly and outgoing, must have sneaked into her office and set up her murder.

It gave her the chills. But not for her own sake.

Her purse might blow at any moment. Sam had put himself in harm's way to save her.

Nora's heart squeezed. She'd never felt more than mild fear for herself, no matter the danger. A new kind of terror gripped her at the possibility of losing this man.

She wanted Sam to live long enough for her to tell him that even though he sometimes infuriated her, she loved being his partner. Long enough to hold him again. Long enough to at least say goodbye.

Abruptly, her mind jerked out of its daze. If the bomb went off, it could smash the front window. "Everybody down!" she roared, so loud that Barbara and the manager both flinched. "Courage Bay Police Department! There's a bomb on the premises. Get under the tables!"

Some people obeyed. Others simply stared at her.

"Down!" Nora shouted. "Under your tables! Right now!"

Mercifully, the remaining diners complied, but Barbara stood motionless. Pulling her to the floor, Nora threw herself over the woman.

SAM ZIGZAGGED between parked cars, gripping both purses by their straps. He didn't dare pitch them where the explosion could ignite gas tanks and magnify the damage.

He registered more vulnerabilities at every turn. Across the lot, a young couple were lifting a baby from a car seat. To his right, a fuel tanker pulled into the corner gas station.

Was Bud watching? Sam had to assume that even if the killer realized his plot had failed, he'd behave as he had at the hospital. That meant detonating the bomb to destroy evidence no matter who got hurt.

The only hope lay to his left, where a cinder-block wall separated the Sunscape Coffee Shop from a self-storage facility. Praying that no unlucky soul was walking or driving out of sight behind the barrier, Sam swung the pocketbooks around his head and lobbed them full-force over the wall.

They didn't quite make it.

They were still in midair when the blast went off with a force that smashed him backward into a parked van. The last thing he felt was a painful throbbing in his head and the sting of glass against his cheeks.

THE BOOM ROCKED the restaurant, shattering windows and sending dishes, glasses and food flying. Something thudded painfully into Nora's hip and she felt the wig fly from her head. The harsh scent of smoke mingled with the odors of spilled coffee and splattered food. Keeping down, she couldn't tell how strong or how close the explosion had been.

As the shock faded, a baby began to cry. Nora finally dared to look up. Although the damage appeared extensive, the walls and ceiling remained intact. Around her, people stirred.

"Please stay down!" She had to consider the possibility of a second explosion, either from a bomb or from one of the cars. "Is anyone seriously hurt?"

No one answered, and, mercifully, she didn't see any inert figures or major bleeding. If only she knew what had happened to Sam! Had he had time to toss the purses before the detonation?

Nora couldn't allow herself to yield to emotions. A woman under her protection and a restaurant full of people needed directions.

Shaking off some stray utensils that had landed on her, she pulled herself from atop Barbara. "Are you all right?"

"A little shaken," her charge said hoarsely. "How about you?"

"I'm fine." Ignoring the pain in her hip, Nora stood up. Through the gaping front window, she saw red lights flash into the parking lot.

If only Sam would come striding in here and give her his lopsided grin. But she couldn't wait for that. Despite the apparent sturdiness of the building, the danger of structural collapse remained.

"We need to evacuate," she announced in an authoritative voice. "Proceed in an orderly manner through the door to my left." She indicated the undamaged side of the building. "Remain on the premises until an officer gives you the all clear. Does anyone require medical treatment?"

Heads shook in the negative as the diners followed her directions. A few had suffered cuts from flying glass, but everyone seemed able to move without assistance. They left behind a restaurant in shambles: overturned tables, broken dishes, and scattered food.

Battling her impulse to run in search of Sam, Nora shepherded everyone outside. She made a visual sweep of the restaurant to confirm that no one lay unnoticed and unconscious.

A squad car rolled alongside. "Please don't leave," Nora requested as she joined the diners on the walkway. "We need you all as witnesses. Also, it may not be safe to start your cars yet. Please wait until the officers clear you."

Paramedics, a fire truck and other cruisers had arrived in front of the building. "I need to coordinate with the bomb squad," she told Barbara. "Can you wait here for me?"

The executive nodded, apparently reassured by the presence of uniformed officers. "No problem."

Nora pointed her out to an officer she knew. He promised to keep an eye on her.

Her heart in her throat, she sprinted toward the front of the restaurant. The fact that Sam hadn't come to assess the situation scared the wits out of her.

As she rounded the corner, Nora slowed to navigate the debris. A paramedic van blocked the center of the lot, where a couple of techs knelt beside a motionless form on the pavement.

Nora's throat clamped shut.

She came closer. Blood covered the man's face but she knew those broad shoulders and that rumpled dark-blond hair. Sam.

Nora willed him to sit up. He had to be all right.

He didn't move.

She wanted to grab the nearest medic and force him to say that Sam was going to be fine. She understood now why families rushed up to doctors demanding information when it was clearly too soon.

"Nora?" One of the bomb squad members approached. "Have you done a Render Safe?"

"No," she said. "But we evacuated." For good measure, she added, "Bud Patchett put a cell phone in my purse and Sam carried it outside."

"I'll handle the Render Safe." The man indicated a point on her neck. "You should have the paramedics take a look at your cut."

Until that moment, Nora hadn't noticed the smarting. "It's nothing. Thanks." She preferred to let the paramedics work on Sam and help a young couple who'd suffered gashes. The baby in the woman's arms appeared unharmed.

Nora could see from the blast pattern that the bomb had gone off near the block wall. A few seconds later and the impact might have been absorbed by the concrete, but they hadn't been that lucky.

Sam still didn't stir.

This isn't over.

Nora heard the thought as clearly as if someone had spoken in her ear. Because of her focus on the bomb and on Sam, she'd allowed herself to become distracted from her primary purpose.

To protect Barbara. And to catch the Trigger.

This semi-chaotic scene was exactly what he needed to provide cover. And she'd left Barbara with officers who had crowd control, not bodyguard duty, uppermost in their minds.

Furious with herself, she hurried back the way she'd come. She found a patrolman writing down the names of the witnesses while the other photographed them. In case someone gave a false name or left unnoticed, the shots could verify who'd been there.

She didn't see Barbara.

Nora hurried toward the group, silently cursing herself for a fool. "Bill!" she called to the officer she'd spoken with earlier. "Where's Barbara Noot? The blond woman in the business suit."

He surveyed the area. "She was standing by your car a minute ago."

Not anymore.

Nora didn't waste time scolding him. Barbara had been her responsibility. "We've got to find her, right now. Bud Patchett planted this bomb to kill her and he's not giving up."

"I'll call for backup."

"You do that."

Leaving Bill to radio the dispatcher, Nora tried to recreate what might have happened. Assuming that Bud had lured Barbara away on a pretext, they wouldn't have gone inside the building or to the front. The gas station next door offered no cover. That left the rear, largely empty section of pavement behind the café.

A landscaped row of trees screened the farthest area. Peering through them, she saw two figures. With a shout to Bill, Nora took off running.

Although she sometimes carried her gun in a shoulder holster, she'd put it in her purse today because of the disguise, which meant it had been blown to smithereens. She had to hope Bud wasn't armed, either.

By the time she arrived at Barbara's side, the large man in slacks and a blue work shirt had taken off running. Recognizing Bud's powerful shape from behind, Nora realized that until this moment, she had hoped against hope it wasn't him.

"Stop! You're under arrest!" she shouted.

Bud turned but kept moving backward. Madness glittered in his black eyes. "So shoot me," he taunted. "They already killed my brother and got away with it."

"How could you do this?" The words burst out of her. "How could you set up your friends?"

"You're all part of the system—you've been protecting the murderers," he snarled, and pointed to Barbara. "She's going to die. Count on it."

Then he broke into a run toward a black pickup truck.

"He said he was a detective." Barbara shivered. "Thank goodness you showed up."

"It isn't over yet." Cursing herself for the delay, Nora patted down the woman's jacket. When she felt a lump in one pocket, she yanked out a cell phone. Barbara stared at it in dismay.

As soon as Bud reached a safe distance, he'd detonate. And he'd just started his motor.

"Run!" Nora ordered Barbara, and headed the other way. Acting on instinct, she pitched the cell phone as hard as she could toward a clear area far from the restaurant.

At the last minute, the truck swerved in the same direction. Maybe Bud had misjudged Nora's reaction, or perhaps he briefly lost control while placing the fatal call. Whatever his reason, the movement put him right in the path of the cell phone.

It bounced into the truck bed. Nora turned and shouted to Barbara, who took shelter behind the trees. Before Nora could retreat more than a dozen feet, the shock wave hit.

As she smashed forward onto the pavement, she found herself thinking, *Two bombs in one day is really too much.*

Then, behind her, she heard Bud's gas tank explode.

CHAPTER SEVENTEEN

"I'M GLAD TO SEE neither of us is dead," Sam joked from where he reclined on the hospital examining table.

He'd suffered a spectacular array of cuts and contusions, some of which were already turning purple. Even wearing a hospital gown and covered with bandages, he still managed to look gorgeous, in Nora's opinion.

"You scared the heck out of me." She wanted to hug him, except she knew how painful that would be—for both of them.

She'd never been so happy in her life as when she'd seen him limping toward her to investigate the results of the blast. What a pair they must have made, her bleeding from her scraped hands and covered with grime, him stiff as a board in the paramedics' neck brace as he helped her to her feet.

There'd been no chance for private conversation. Fire trucks had rushed over to extinguish the remains of what had been Bud's truck, while other emergency personnel crowded around. And of course Nora's first responsibility had been to make sure Barbara was delivered safely into the hands of her escort team.

"Thank you for saving my life," Barbara had said before she left. "I wish I could do more to show my gratitude, but I'm too worried about my mom."

"Please don't let me stop you." Nora had dusted herself off as best she could before allowing a paramedic to clean the scrapes on her palms. "My prayers go with you."

Despite the Trigger's demise, the case hadn't yet been closed, so Barbara's team had carried out the assigned guard duty. As for Nora, after she received a clean bill of health and gave a statement to the officer in charge, she'd driven to the hospital. Thank goodness she kept her keys, driver's license and badge tucked into a pocket.

She'd found Sam in a curtained-off cubicle awaiting the doctor's verdict. It seemed to her that they should both be brimming with meaningful things to say, yet aside from a superficial greeting, she hardly knew where to start.

The emotions that had rushed in on her were still too raw to sort out. The sight of him lying motionless on the pavement had taught Nora at the gut level what fear meant.

While her thoughts raced, Sam stared at the ceiling. When he spoke, all he said was, "I keep reviewing the clues, trying to figure out how we could have found the Trigger's identity sooner."

"I'm not worried about what could have been," Nora said. "I'm just glad you found out when you did. He nearly got us."

"I had no idea it was Bud." He grimaced. "That jerk had us all fooled."

A part of Nora grieved for the robust, seemingly good-natured man who'd been so helpful to others and who, but for his brother's death, might have led a long and productive life. But Bud had chosen his own path. "I'll leave it to the psychologists to explain how someone can become so corrupted by vengeance that he'd murder his own friends."

"It's up to us to finish determining how he did it." Sam levered himself to a sitting position. "I'm going back to work."

"You can't!"

He grimaced. "What I can't do is sit around. We've got important ends to tie up."

"I'll take care of it," she promised.

"You're flying a desk until further notice and you know it."

Officers involved in fatalities had to be cleared before returning to active duty.

"Regardless, you're in no condition to work," she told him. "Not with a concussion."

"I'm fine."

"You're as muleheaded as ever," she conceded. "That hasn't changed, anyway."

The curtain parted and Max Zirinsky poked his head inside. "Is this a private argument or can anyone join?"

"He's being stubborn," she said. "He thinks he's Superman."

The police chief studied Sam, who tugged irritably at the inadequate hospital garment. "I have Dan's okay to give you the day off. More if you need it."

"I don't," he said. "Thanks anyway."

"Forensics is searching Bud's house. We're going over his locker and computer with a fine-tooth comb, as well," he said. "As for you, Prophet, you need to recuperate. You wouldn't want to cause a hike in our workman's comp premium, would you?"

Sam ignored the attempt at humor. "We still don't know how Bud gained access to inside information at the Wonderworld subsidiaries. He may have had an accomplice."

"If the searches turn up anything that points to a conspirator, we'll act on it immediately," Max said.

Nora jumped in. "What's my status, Chief? I could take care of this."

"I'm trying to get you back in the field as fast as possible," he said. "Based on your statement and the witnesses', you did nothing wrong. But I have to run the facts by the D.A.'s office before we can reinstate you, and it won't be today."

"That means neither of us is out there working this case," Sam argued. "And you need at least one of us. No offense to Grant, but if Bud had an associate, he or she could be across the border before we figure it out." He slid off the gurney.

Instead of landing squarely on his feet, however, he swayed

and had to grab the table for support. Nora reached him before Max did, sliding her shoulder under Sam's arm to brace him.

She noted the swell of his rib cage as he caught his breath. Locking her arms around his waist, she held on. Although he remained upright, he couldn't help putting some weight on her.

Nora didn't mind. She liked being close to him. They still hadn't found a way to communicate in words all they'd been through emotionally, but their bodies conveyed a sympathy of their own.

The doctor came in, her expression harried. No doubt she'd been dealing with a crowd of gashed and bruised restaurant patrons. "Mr. Prophet?" She regarded the patient disapprovingly. "Please lie down. I strongly recommend that you stay overnight for observation."

He might have refused, except that he had to grip the table again. "Well…"

"The nurses will move you to a room," the doctor said. "With concussions, we don't like to take chances."

For once in his life, Sam backed down. He didn't look happy about it, but he could hardly demand to be released when he wasn't able to stand under his own power. Wearing a dour expression, he sank onto the examining table.

Nora released him regretfully. She missed the contact.

When a nurse asked the visitors to step outside, Max and Nora complied without an argument. Judging by Sam's scowl, he didn't want them around anyway.

"Unless your hands are too sore, I'd like you to file a report about what happened today," Max told Nora in the corridor.

She made a dismissive gesture. A few scrapes weren't going to sideline her. "You got it."

"And let me know if you need any help replacing whatever got blown up in your purse."

"Thanks, Chief."

Nora found a pay phone and put in a call to Sam's mother.

Angela calmed down as soon as she learned the injuries were treatable and promised that she and Mary would arrive shortly.

"I have to go back to work," Nora told her. "I ought to warn you that he's in a toxic mood."

"Enforced bed rest, eh?" inquired his mother. "He never did like that."

"Was he a difficult child?" she couldn't resist asking.

"As tough as they come," Angela said. "But you know what? Once he cheered up, he'd give me a big hug that more than compensated for it."

Nora hoped she could look forward to the same treatment.

At the office, she complied with Max's request. By the time she finished the report, the afternoon had vanished and her hands and neck were stinging like crazy.

SAM DOUBTED he would ever forget the moment when he'd heard the bomb explode behind the restaurant.

He'd been stretched on the pavement, his head throbbing but his heart satisfied because he'd saved the woman he was falling in love with. Yes, falling in love. He'd admitted that to himself on his frantic drive to the café, when he could think of nothing but finding a way to prevent tragedy.

Then the second bomb went off. For one black moment, he'd believed Nora must be dead. He knew she'd have put her life on the line to protect Barbara, and it didn't seem possible that she'd escaped again.

He'd done his best and it wasn't enough. He'd been blindsided, just as he had when the roof collapsed on his father.

Adrenaline and disbelief had powered him to his feet, despite the confining neck brace and the paramedics' protests. When he rounded the building and saw Nora prone on the pavement, he must have gone into shock. Even when she'd pushed herself to a sitting position and Sam caught her scraped hand to help her up, he'd experienced only a kind of numb relief.

He didn't know if he could bear to consider a future with a woman he might lose at any moment. Objectively, he knew that no relationship came with a guarantee, but most women didn't go around making themselves into targets as Nora had done today, and might very well do again.

Sam stirred uncomfortably on the hard hospital bed and winced at the chorus of complaints from his body. He'd refused pain medication because he didn't want his mind dulled. He intended to keep thinking about the case even if he couldn't act, because some hidden fact might leap out at him.

As a downside, he couldn't stop himself from mentally replaying the day's events. The image of Nora flat on the ground, her hair spreading around her like a bloodstain, was engraved on his soul.

He knew better than to believe she would change her ways for his sake, even if by some lucky chance she loved him back. He didn't know how to resolve this, how to make it work.

In the end, maybe it simply wasn't possible.

NORA ARRIVED at the police station early on Wednesday to meet with Grant in the detective bureau and go over the results of the searches. His team had turned up a wealth of incriminating material, including plastic explosives, disassembled cell phone battery packs and copies of documents from Speedman Company, Finder Electronics and Esmee Engines.

Bud's computers at work and at home had yielded an array of e-mails, including some that Nora had exchanged with Sam. Together with the mechanic's background as a demolitions expert in the military, the information painted an eerie portrait of a man stalking his prey with lethal determination.

Nora wished she could have been part of the search. It particularly galled her that the bomb squad had had to recover the explosives without her supervision. At the same time, she understood that being temporarily confined to desk duty protected both her and the department.

"We think someone on the inside must have helped him obtain some of these documents," Grant told her.

"Agreed," she said. "And we'd better find him or her fast."

"I can take care of it if you like," Grant said. "Any suggestions?"

"I'd better find out what Max wants us to do," Nora answered. "Sam will hit the roof if we proceed without him."

The detective regarded the piles of material grimly. "I'm happy to turn everything over to whoever the chief designates. It's not as if I don't have other things to work on." He headed back to his own office.

As it turned out, Max found Nora minutes later in the hallway. "The D.A. cleared you," he told her cheerily. "Back to work, Sergeant."

She grinned. "That's great news. How about my partner?"

"What, that grumpy old pain in the neck?" the police chief responded loudly. "I should think you'd be glad to get rid of him."

His tone clued Nora to turn around. Sure enough, there stood Sam, his body held stiffly and the side of his face an interesting shade of blue-black.

To Nora, he looked wonderful. Still, Max's presence and her own uncertainty held her greeting to a plain, "Good to see you."

"You too." Sam gave them each a nod. "I understand we've got an accomplice to track down. What do you say we start by reinterviewing Rose Chang?"

Nora refrained from teasing him about the fact that, unlike when they first began, he didn't propose they examine all the evidence before taking action. "That suits me."

"I'll let Grant know you're handling things from here," the chief said.

Nora paused long enough to check on Carl Garcola. He was improving steadily, his wife told her. "He said he's sorry your partner had to read his lips," she added with a chuckle.

"What he told Investigator Prophet saved my life," Nora answered. "Please thank him for me."

A short time later, she and Sam headed for Speedman. They took another car the fire department had assigned while a repair shop replaced the blown-out windows on Sam's sedan.

Nora would have preferred her intimate coupe. Still, she didn't want to drive any more than necessary until her hands healed.

At least they were alone together. "Do you want to talk?" she asked as he put the car in reverse.

"Only about the case." He headed away from the station.

"Sam!" She didn't try to hide her exasperation. "Don't shut me out!"

"We're on the job," he reminded her. "If you want to talk about private stuff, we can do it tonight."

"Fine." Nora's throat squeezed at the coldness of his manner. The fact that he hadn't even cracked a smile seemed to confirm her worst fears.

His behavior reminded her of the way he'd shut Elaine out. This time, however, Nora had a suspicion what might be bothering Sam, because of something his sister had said earlier. Maybe he'd rather give her up than accept the kind of risks she ran.

At Speedman, the guard called ahead, and then waved them through the gate. Nora drove around to the side and parked near Rose's office.

A secretary ushered them into the president's office. Ms. Chang, looking not at all surprised to see them, shook hands with Sam and Nora.

"I talked to Barbara on the phone a few minutes ago," she

said as she waved them into seats. "Her mother's taken a turn for the better, I'm happy to say."

"I'm glad to hear it." Nora made a mental note to send flowers.

Rose paced across the room. "I apologize for not answering your questions about the driver. If I had, you might have wrapped this up a lot sooner."

"True," Sam said.

"When I saw a picture of that man, Bud Patchett, in the newspaper this morning, it rang a bell," the president continued. "I've seen him around, although not recently."

Nora sat up straighter. "Around Speedman? What was he doing here?"

"Dating one of the secretaries," Rose replied. "Her name's Terri Simms and she works in the engineering department. She's horrified about what happened. I hope she's not going to face criminal charges."

"That depends on what she did," Nora said. "And on whether she's willing to cooperate."

"Of course." The president buzzed her assistant on the intercom. "Please ask Ms. Simms in engineering to join us." After clicking off, she added, "You're welcome to use my office to interview her."

"Under the circumstances," Sam said, "we'd prefer to take her to the station."

Sam hadn't checked with Nora, but she agreed. "She's a material witness to a series of murders and attempted murders," Nora explained. "This is going to take a while."

"Are you arresting her?" Rose asked, troubled.

"Not at this point." Sam couldn't promise any more than that.

Terri Simms turned out to be an attractive woman in her thirties with anxiety written all over her. She waived her right to an attorney. "I want to get this cleared up. I had no idea Bud intended to commit any crimes."

She rode back to the station with them and spent the next few hours filling in the missing blanks. With her permission, Sam set up a video camera to record the session.

She'd met Bud through his brother and dated him occasionally, Terri said. After Tim's death, he'd disappeared for a while.

Aware of his lawsuit against Speedman, she'd understood why he didn't want to see her. When he began calling after the case was thrown out, he'd lost his usual ebullience.

"I knew he must be depressed and I wanted to help," she said. "He asked for information about the chip, how it was developed and what went wrong. I thought getting answers might help resolve his grief."

"You gave him company documents?" Sam asked.

Tears glistened in her eyes. "Yes. I'm going to lose my job, I know, and I deserve to," Terri said. "All those people died partly because of me, but I didn't mean to hurt anyone."

Nora couldn't deny a twinge of sympathy for Terri Simms. She'd learned an expensive lesson about trusting the wrong person. On the other hand, if she hadn't violated her company's trust in her, she wouldn't be in this situation.

"What about the e-mails?" Nora asked. "How did he gain access to the computer system at Speedman?"

Terri blew her nose before continuing. "I guess he saw me input my password. He must have been watching the keystrokes. He offered to help fix my computer once when it kept screwing up, and maybe that helped him get access, too."

"Didn't you ever get suspicious?" Sam asked.

"Once." She swallowed hard. "He started raving about a conspiracy of silence. He said each of the people who approved the chip had personally struck a blow against Tim. I tried to calm him down. I said he didn't even know for sure that it hadn't been a surfing accident."

Nora listened intently. "How did he react?"

"He started shouting that Tim had called him right after the crash and complained about dizziness," Terri said. "Bud urged him to see a doctor but he shrugged it off."

"So Bud knew about his condition. Maybe he felt guilty that he didn't insist on getting help." Nora began to understand Bud's motivation better. "It must have devastated him when Tim went surfing and drowned, so he turned his rage on others."

"The people at Speedman swore under oath that Tim hadn't shown any signs of injury," Terri explained. "Bud said they lied. But I honestly don't think Tim told anyone except his brother."

"And Bud cracked." Sam shook his head. "I always thought he was stronger than that."

The secretary took a sip from what must be her third or fourth cup of tea that afternoon. "Ms. Chang said once that, in Asia, people consider bamboo strong, even though it looks fragile to us, because it can bend in a storm. Bud was too brittle. That's why he snapped." She sighed. "I feel so awful about the people who died. Thank you for saving Ms. Noot. And I hope Mr. Garcola's all right."

"He's getting better," Nora assured her.

Finally they released the witness. Although the D.A. would review the case, her full cooperation and obvious ignorance of Bud's intent should weigh in her favor.

Nora checked her watch. Five twenty-eight. Although massive amounts of paperwork remained to be processed, her cuts were starting to throb. Besides, no one expected them to wrap up such a complex case overnight.

She still wanted the promised talk with Sam, but before she could bring it up, he headed for the door. "I've got errands to run," he said. "How about dropping by my place around eight?"

"I'll see you there," she said.

With a casual wave, he strode out.

No welcoming dinner, no pretense of camaraderie. Well,

he wasn't going to escape that easily, Nora vowed. If Sam Prophet intended to break off with her tonight, she'd make yesterday's explosions look like child's play.

CHAPTER EIGHTEEN

DARKNESS HAD FALLEN by the time Nora pulled to the curb in front of Sam's stucco home. A cascade of white sparkles illuminated a small tree in the front, and Malibu lamps marked the curving walk.

She'd accused him of decorating the house so completely that he left no room for anyone else's taste. Tonight, however, she saw the place as a beautiful extension of his personality.

Sam had put a tremendous amount of work and love into this cheerful home, Nora reflected as she rang the doorbell. The events of the past few days had changed her perspective.

The memory of his protectiveness yesterday wrapped her in contentment. Not only had he saved her life, he'd become a real partner in every sense. Their lovemaking had not blended them into a single person—she was too independent for that to happen—but into a real team.

At least, she hoped so.

Hearing footsteps inside, Nora straightened. She knew she needed him. But she also needed to be herself, because otherwise, even the most charming refuge in the world could turn into a trap.

When Sam opened the door, his expression warmed at the sight of her. He'd changed into jeans and a denim shirt, open at the throat. The array of adhesive bandages on his neck contributed to his raffish air. His hair begged to be mussed, but Nora held herself in check.

The scent of cinnamon filled the air. "Cider?"

"I'm baking an apple pie. The frozen kind." Sam loomed in the doorway. "Hope you're hungry enough for dessert."

Fast-food fried chicken hadn't filled her *that* completely. "With ice cream?"

"Is vanilla okay?" he teased.

"Any kind of ice cream is fine. Are you going to let me in or are you going to stand there blocking the door all night?"

He gave no sign of moving. "I want to apologize first."

"For what?"

"The house is kind of littered. It's not up to my usual standards." Only a quirk at the corners of his mouth betrayed his deadpan expression.

"Who cares?" Nora couldn't wait to find out what the man was up to. "I'm the last person to worry about your housekeeping."

"See for yourself." He shifted aside.

When she entered the living room, Nora didn't notice anything amiss. The same tasteful furniture filled the elegant space and the same arrangement of pottery graced the mantel.

Then she noticed a piece of paper taped to a blank space on the wall. Approaching it, she read aloud, "This space reserved for...messy bookshelves?" To Sam, she said, "What's that all about?"

"Read on." He indicated the coffee table.

A lined sheet that lay atop it read, "Feel free to put your feet and mug here."

With growing amusement, Nora paced through the house. On the archway leading to the bedroom wing, a note declared, "These rooms subject to redecorating, when appropriate." Outside the bathroom, a message informed her, "Plenty of room for another toothbrush."

Could this possibly be what it appeared? She tried not to read too much into it. This might represent Sam's idea of a joke.

In the kitchen, after she got past the mouthwatering apple pie smell, she read an eye-level memo: "Feel free to rearrange the cabinets." On the patio slider, he'd pasted a note, "This garden subject to change by mutual consent."

Nora stood rooted to the spot, staring into a yard transformed into a fantasyland by an array of delicate lights. Tears pricked her eyes. Sam must have hurried home from work to write these notes for her. But what did they mean?

"What's going on?" she asked.

"Maybe I'd better explain." Sam's voice came from directly behind her.

Without turning around, she said, "That ought to help."

"Something Terri said today got through to me." His breath warmed her neck. "It was the part about bamboo being strong because it can yield."

A yearning filled Nora for things she hadn't dared hope for. But she couldn't answer until he made himself clear.

"I've always figured I was pretty darn strong," Sam went on. "Dad used to say Mom was the strongest member of the family, but I assumed he was exaggerating."

Puzzled, Nora went on listening.

"I didn't realize it took more guts for her to let him go, to accept his putting his life on the line, than it took for him to do it." He stood behind her, talking without touching. "It was harder because she didn't have any control over what happened. He got to make choices and she didn't. In the end, he lost his life, but she had to go on living without him, so maybe she lost even more than he did."

After seeing Sam lying crumpled on the pavement, Nora grasped what he meant. But she'd rather take that risk than give him up. The question was, did he feel that way about her?

"So I guess..." He gave a little cough before continuing. "I guess I'd better learn how to be strong like bamboo."

He stopped. She couldn't respond, maybe because she wanted so badly for him to mean what she hoped he meant.

Go on, she urged silently. And waited.

SAM WONDERED if he'd gone about this the wrong way. The notes had seemed like a good idea and he'd just shared the flash of insight he'd gained today, yet Nora still stood with her back turned.

In the glass, he made out the oval of her face but nothing of her expression. What was she thinking? What was a guy supposed to say?

There ought to be an instruction manual to tell men how to move a relationship to the next phase. Unfortunately, he didn't have such a guide, so he had to work this out for himself.

"Since Dad died, I've been trying to make sure I'd never lose anyone like that again," Sam conceded. "But security's an illusion. It finally hit me that you have to live in the moment, to take what life gives you, or you miss the best parts."

"Which best parts?" In the glass, he saw Nora brush aside a hank of hair that had fallen across her forehead.

"The parts where you knock the sheets off the bed and eat ice cream for breakfast and laugh over stupid jokes that nobody else understands." In the absence of feedback, he struggled onward. "What I'm trying to say is that, for me, getting close to someone is the biggest risk of all. You can't manipulate the odds into your favor. You have to go with it. And that's what I want to do, if you do, too."

When Nora remained silent, he wondered if he'd said too much. Maybe she didn't share his feelings. Maybe, for her, this had been a short-term, on-the-job romance that wasn't going anywhere.

"Sam Prophet," she said softly, turning to face him. "That was beautiful."

"It was?" To him, his words had sounded awkward.

"You took a big risk," she said. "You trusted me enough to tell me what you're feeling."

"Actually, it's more than that." Sam decided he might as well go all the way. "I'm asking you to move in with me, if you'd like to."

"You're sure I wouldn't drive you crazy?" Nora asked.

"You might, but you're worth it." He hurried on. "I want to trip over your clothes on the floor and grumble about the dishes in the sink and get a hernia squeezing into your ridiculous little car where we practically have sex every time you shift gears. And I want to wake up every morning holding you in my arms."

Uh-oh. She had tears on her lashes. Maybe he'd blown it.

"I had kind of a funny experience yesterday," Nora said.

Sam had no idea where she was going with this but he hoped she'd hurry, because he could hardly breathe.

"It used to make me mad when people worried about me, because it felt like they were trying to hold me down." Her blue eyes shone as she gazed at him. "When I saw you lying there with the paramedics swarming over you, well, I've never been as scared for myself as I was for you."

"It could happen again," he warned.

"To either of us."

"Exactly."

They leaned forward instinctively until their foreheads touched, as if they could read each other's thoughts that way.

"So let's make the most of what we've got," Nora said.

"Sounds good to me."

For them, danger would always be an omnipresent shadow, he reflected, but he intended to cherish every moment life granted them. Starting now, he decided as he gathered her into a kiss.

SIX MONTHS LATER, they were married at the Church By the Sea with family, friends, and a large contingent of police and fire personnel in attendance. It wasn't easy preparing for the ceremony: Sam's insistence that they visit every jewelry store in town and compare rings on-line nearly drove Nora to distraction, while her half-serious suggestion that the two of them roller-skate down the aisle tempted him to propose an elopement.

But not only did they iron out their differences, they had fun doing it. And as Nora walked toward him on her father's arm, Sam reflected that he'd never seen a woman look so beautiful. When she stood beside him, he could scarcely hear the minister's words through his surge of joy.

He remembered watching her mahogany hair float in the sunshine as she drove up to the motel that first day they'd worked together. He'd believed there was no woman on earth less suited to him than Nora Keyes.

Sam Prophet had never been happier to be wrong.

CODE RED

Ordinary People. Extraordinary Circumstances.

If you've enjoyed getting to know the men and women of California's Courage Bay Emergency Services team, Harlequin Books invites you to return to Courage Bay!

Just collect six (6) proofs of purchase from the back of six (6) different CODE RED titles and receive four (4) free CODE RED books that are not currently available in retail outlets!

Just complete the order form and send it, along with six (6) proofs of purchase from six (6) different CODE RED titles, to: CODE RED, P.O. Box 9047, Buffalo, NY 14269-9047, or P.O. Box 613, Fort Erie, Ontario L2A 5X3. (Cost of $2.00 for shipping and handling applies.)

Name (PLEASE PRINT)

Address   Apt. #

City   State/Prov.   Zip/Postal Code

093 KKA DXH7

When you return six proofs of purchase, you will receive the following titles:

RIDING THE STORM by Julie Miller   TURBULENCE by Jessica Matthews
WASHED AWAY by Carol Marinelli   HARD RAIN by Darlene Scalera

To receive your free CODE RED books (retail value $19.96), complete the above form. Mail it to us with six proofs of purchase, one of which can be found in the right-hand corner of this page. Requests must be received no later than October 31, 2005. Your set of four CODE RED books costs you only $2.00 shipping and handling. N.Y. state residents must add applicable sales tax on shipping and handling charge. Please allow 6–8 weeks for receipt of order. Offer good in Canada and U.S. only. Offer good while quantities last.

When you respond to this offer, we will also send you *Inside Romance*, a free quarterly publication, highlighting upcoming releases and promotions from Harlequin and Silhouette Books.

☐ If you do not wish to receive this free publication, please check here.

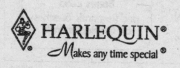

HARLEQUIN®
Makes any time special ®

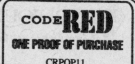

CODE RED
ONE PROOF OF PURCHASE

CRPOP11

SPOTLIGHT

*"Julie Elizabeth Leto always delivers
sizzling, snappy, edge stories!"*
—New York Times *bestselling author Carly Phillips*

USA TODAY bestselling author

Julie Elizabeth Leto

Making Waves

Celebrated erotica author Tessa Dalton
has a reputation for her insatiable
appetite for men—any man. But in
truth, her erotic stories are inspired
by personal fantasies...fantasies that
are suddenly fulfilled when she meets
journalist Colt Granger.

July

**HOT Bonus
Features!**

**Author Interview,
Bonus Read
and Romantic Beaches
off the Beaten Path**

HARLEQUIN®
Live the emotion™

www.eHarlequin.com

SPMW

COLLECTION

**The summer heat has arrived
with a sizzling new anthology...**

Velvet, Leather & Lace

USA TODAY BESTSELLING AUTHORS
SUZANNE FORSTER
DONNA KAUFFMAN
& NATIONAL BESTSELLING AUTHOR
JILL SHALVIS

Hot new catalog company
Velvet, Leather & Lace is
launching a revolution in
lingerie—and partners Jamie,
Samantha and Mia are coming
apart as fast as their wispy new
underwear! At this rate, they might
get caught with their panties
down. And the whole world
will be watching!

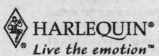
Live the emotion™

**Exclusive Extras,
including:**
Travel Tale,
The Art of Seduction,
Sneak Peek...
and more!

www.eHarlequin.com

SCVLL

If you enjoyed what you just read,
then we've got an offer you can't resist!

Take 2 bestselling novels FREE!
Plus get a FREE surprise gift!

Clip this page and mail it to MIRA®

IN U.S.A.
3010 Walden Ave.
P.O. Box 1867
Buffalo, N.Y. 14240-1867

IN CANADA
P.O. Box 609
Fort Erie, Ontario
L2A 5X3

YES! Please send me 2 free MIRA® novels and my free surprise gift. After receiving them, if I don't wish to receive anymore, I can return the shipping statement marked cancel. If I don't cancel, I will receive 4 brand-new novels every month, before they're available in stores! In the U.S.A., bill me at the bargain price of $4.99 plus 25¢ shipping and handling per book and applicable sales tax, if any*. In Canada, bill me at the bargain price of $5.49 plus 25¢ shipping and handling per book and applicable taxes**. That's the complete price and a savings of over 20% off the cover prices—what a great deal! I understand that accepting the 2 free books and gift places me under no obligation ever to buy any books. I can always return a shipment and cancel at any time. Even if I never buy another The Best of the Best™ book, the 2 free books and gift are mine to keep forever.

185 MDN DZ7J
385 MDN DZ7K

Name	(PLEASE PRINT)	
Address	Apt.#	
City	State/Prov.	Zip/Postal Code

*Not valid to current The Best of the Best™, Mira®,
suspense and romance subscribers.*

*Want to try two free books from another series?
Call 1-800-873-8635 or visit www.morefreebooks.com.*

* Terms and prices subject to change without notice. Sales tax applicable in N.Y.
** Canadian residents will be charged applicable provincial taxes and GST.
All orders subject to approval. Offer limited to one per household.
® and ™are registered trademarks owned and used by the trademark owner and or its licensee.

BOB04R   ©2004 Harlequin Enterprises Limited

SAGA

National bestselling author

KAY DAVID

brings readers a powerful new Guardians story.

NOT WITHOUT PROOF

When hired assassin Stratton Santana is framed by a dangerous drug cartel, he is forced to protect Jennifer Martinez, who is also a target—which means drawing her into his dark world of high-stakes murder and intrigue.

"Ms. David deftly weaves peril, passion and powerful characters together to create a page-turning romance."
—*Romantic Times*

July

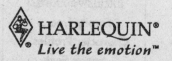

Live the emotion™

Exciting extras:

How To Pick the Perfect Diamond...
Recipes...
Map...
Travel Tales!

www.eHarlequin.com   SSNWP

SPOTLIGHT

A NEW 12-book continuity series starring the powerful and charismatic Fortune family!

THE
F RTUNES
OF TEXAS:
Reunion

Continuing in July with...

A Baby Changes Everything

by

MARIE FERRARELLA

After five years of commitment, Savannah Perez worried that her marriage to Cruz was doomed. She loved him, but his backbreaking devotion to their new ranch was ruining their relationship. Could Cruz show Savannah that she was everything to him...before it was too late?

The Fortunes of Texas: Reunion—
The power of family.

Exclusive Extras!
Family Tree...
Character Profiles...
Sneak Peek

Silhouette®
Where love comes alive™

Visit Silhouette Books at www.eHarlequin.com

FTRABCE